Praise for *Open House*

"Katie Sise has outdone herself with *Open House*, her latest ingenious addition to the world of domestic suspense. A sly, stirring whodunit with an ending that's nothing short of perfection. A must-read!"

—Mary Kubica, *New York Times* bestselling author of *The Other Mrs.*

Praise for *We Were Mothers*

"Sise offers an astute glimpse into tragic loss, the innermost lives of women, and the highs and lows and societal expectations of motherhood . . . This compelling character study will resonate."

—*Kirkus Reviews*

"Propulsive . . . compelling."

—*Booklist*

"Sise displays a sly sense of pacing; nearly every chapter unveils a new plot twist, keeping readers hooked. Fans of Liane Moriarty will eat this title up with a spoon."

—*Library Journal*

"Taut and suspenseful, *We Were Mothers* will keep readers on the edge of their seats until the very end."

—Bustle

"Katie Sise's *We Were Mothers* expertly snaps readers to attention with its grandiose opening . . . riming inner discourse and believable fiascos blend together producing fantastic scenes . . . Her observations and vulnerability carry the read."

—Associated Press

"If you can't resist a sharp, suspenseful novel, then *We Were Mothers* by Katie Sise deserves a spot on your reading list."

—POPSUGAR

"A close-knit community in a seemingly idyllic town is torn apart when a pretty college student goes missing and the first of many dark secrets is uncovered. *We Were Mothers* is a twisting tale of small-town complicity and deceit with some astute insights into marriage and motherhood. The escalating tension and the many surprises will keep readers urgently turning pages. An engrossing read!"

—Mary McCluskey, author of *Intrusion* and *The Long Deception*

OPEN HOUSE

ALSO BY KATIE SISE

We Were Mothers

OPEN HOUSE

A Novel

KATIE SISE

Little
a

Text copyright © 2020 by Katie Sise

Published by Little A, New York

www.apub.com

Amazon, the Amazon logo, and Little A are trademarks of Amazon.com, Inc., or its affiliates.

ISBN-13: 9781542092654 (hardcover)
ISBN-10: 1542092655 (hardcover)

ISBN-13: 9781542092678 (paperback)
ISBN-10: 1542092671 (paperback)

Cover design by Kimberly Glyder

Printed in the United States of America

First edition

For Brian, Luke, William, Isabel, and Eloise, always.

PROLOGUE

It was January, and the bucolic town of Waverly was covered with snow. Fires were lit; coffee was sipped; and the library at the University of Yarrow was filled with students. Most yearned to be somewhere else, their hearts pulsing with big ideas and plans for after graduation, or at least for Friday night. On the library's third floor, a junior named Oscar Mendez could no longer take the musty stacks, so he zipped his parka and headed outside in the late afternoon.

A few hours later, Oscar would tell the police that he had no idea where he was going when he left the library. He certainly never planned to descend into the gorge behind campus, but that's exactly what he did, snow crunching beneath his feet as he trekked down the frozen earth toward the vast, churning river. Besides a few brave hikers and runners, Yarrow students mostly avoided the woods and the cliffs overlooking the river because of Emma McCullough's disappearance a decade before. But Oscar didn't believe in ghosts. And it felt good to skid down the snowy trail, the incline so steep it made him feel alive and far enough away from the gleaming gothic architecture of the university. Oscar hated it at Yarrow, he really did; he hated the smug, self-satisfied professors and the preppy classmates mingling with the alternative ones, everyone a happy, bubbling mix on the surface. But what could he do? Transfer? He didn't have the energy. Quit? He was too smart for that.

The cathedral's clock tower chimed four times, warning Oscar that there wasn't long before darkness fell completely and obscured the path back to campus. He hurried farther upriver, turning around just once to take in the rocky cliffs that towered over the gorge. The cliffs were four stories tall on both sides of the river, and depending on where you were perched, it was either a straight drop into the water or onto a dirty beach made of mud and snow. The frozen ground was hard for Oscar to navigate, and he was careful not to get too close to the water's edge. A recent downpour had made the river even more furious, and Oscar watched the white-tipped current for a long time, wondering, as always, if he was going to be all right. The sun's final strips of light filtered through branches and illuminated a flash of silver near his feet. He bent to pick up a chunk of earth with a bracelet lodged inside.

For Emma, it read in scripted calligraphy, *my love.*

Oscar's sullen mood was suddenly forgotten, his mind sharpening. Could it have belonged to *her*—the elusive, mysterious Emma McCullough?

Probably not, he thought, but he pocketed it anyway, his heart thudding inside his chest as he retraced his footprints and climbed toward safer ground.

PART I

ONE

Haley

One week later

Haley McCullough stared down at Susie's dead body. She tapped her gloved fingertips against Susie's cold, white-blue skin—*tap, tap, tap, one, two, three.*

The tapping was a compulsion Haley had developed to cope with the waves of sadness and obsessive thoughts about her sister, Emma. Haley mostly tapped her right index finger against her left hand and counted. Sometimes she tapped objects that felt interesting to touch— the edges of a staple, or the scratchy fabric on the old armchair where she studied, or Susie even. If she was in public, she tried to conceal her compulsions. If she was alone, she closed her eyes and soaked up the sensation of the tapping.

Haley had been doing it for nearly ten years, ever since her older sister vanished at age twenty-one, and it worked, actually. Every time fury swelled inside her, the tapping calmed her body until she could function again. *Fury* was the most succinct word to describe it, but it wasn't only anger; it was a surge of regret, despair, and so many other things she didn't dare name, followed by a quickening of her heart and a thick swirl of blood in her ears. It was where her body went every time she thought of Emma.

That morning as Haley tapped Susie's shoulder—*tap, tap, tap, one, two, three*—her mind went to the clavicle and scapula that lay beneath, and she tried not to think about the things the young woman had done when she was alive, but she couldn't always help it. Had Susie used this shoulder to pitch a ball? Haley guessed the odds were that yes, at some point she had, so she imagined Susie's slight frame in a softball uniform, her skeleton of bones very much erect and alive, a sly smile playing on her lips as she considered her batter. Would she be wearing lipstick? *No, no.* Haley's mind quickly canceled that out. But her hair: it would be in a ponytail, most likely. Haley could see it now, trailing over the delicate curve of her spine.

Tap, tap, tap. Hello, Susie.

It wasn't Susie lying there dead that had Haley so worked up that she needed to tap; it was the phone call she'd received on her way to her Saturday-morning anatomy lab. *This has to be fake, this must be a prank,* she thought as Detective Hank Rappaport introduced himself. After assuring her there hadn't been any kind of emergency, he'd asked in a raspy voice, "Could you come down to the station later this afternoon, Ms. McCullough?"

"Of course," she'd told him, because that was the only appropriate response to a question like that. And ever since his call she'd only been able to think of Emma, her body like a live wire as she wondered why a detective was calling her in.

Susie's toes were painted, and she was pretty, too. Maybe it was wrong to notice her cadaver's looks, but Haley felt Susie was different. Special, even. And not just because of how much she reminded Haley of her disappeared sister, but because Susie and Haley were both in their midtwenties and each had small tattoos on their ankles. Haley sensed they'd be friends if Susie were alive, but maybe that was taking it too far. She was just so on edge lately. People had warned Haley medical school would do this to her. Every day after classes she raced down the University of Yarrow's halls, dying to get to a bathroom so she could scrub her hands, her dry, red fingers never feeling clean enough.

"Observe the aortic arch," their anatomy teacher, Dr. Brad Aarons, was saying, his voice echoing through the lab. (*Call me Brad,* he'd told them all at the start of the semester, and they did.) Twenty cadavers lay on stainless steel tables across the room, and the overhead lights were as bright as any operating room. They'd already sawed through the sternum and cracked open the rib cage, and now they were following the ascending aorta as it became the aortic arch and looped over the heart to become the descending aorta.

That first day in anatomy when Haley had been assigned to cadaver station number four, she gasped when she pulled the sheet from the body and saw the resemblance to Emma: perfectly pale skin, high cheekbones, long lashes, and a top lip with a deep cupid's bow. She'd glanced up at Brad and raised her hand as if to protest the match, but then lowered it, feeling utterly ridiculous. What would she even say? She renamed cadaver #347 *Susie* to humanize her, and as the first weeks of the semester wore on, there was this part of Haley—and she knew how damaged she was to even be thinking this way—that relished the similarities. She looked for her sister everywhere. Why not here, too?

"Identify each branch," Brad went on, changing the picture on the screen so that it showed a simulation of a gorgeous, pulsing heart. Haley loved the human body; she always had. She cut around the brachiocephalic artery, carefully moving aside tissue to expose its course, losing herself in the dissection. She didn't look up again until Brad said, "Eyes here for a moment," and changed the slide to an illustration of the heart, the veins and arteries curving in bright reds and blues.

Brad Aarons was a cardiothoracic surgeon at the end of his fellowship at Waverly Memorial Hospital. He was somewhere in his late thirties, and half the female students fawned over him, but Haley had no interest in that. He'd been teaching at the University of Yarrow ever since he graduated from its medical school, and Haley didn't know much else about him except that he was married to a woman named Priya, who'd once been a successful artist. "Note the way the brachiocephalic artery splits into the right subclavian artery and the right common carotid artery," Brad was saying. His messy red-blond hair was an inch too long and a shade lighter than the stubble blanketing his face, but even doctors could get away with a mussed look in a town like Waverly, because here they valued ideas, academia, and compost piles. Maybe it was because of the university hovering on the wooded outskirts, but Waverly didn't preoccupy itself with the kinds of things most wealthy New York City commuter towns did, and Haley wasn't sure whether that made it better or worse. Elitism was still elitism, even when you packaged it as being smart and noble.

As Haley moved on to the right subclavian artery, she thought about how much her sister would have hated this class. Emma would have barfed at least a dozen times by now. She probably wouldn't have even liked to know the cadavers existed on Yarrow's campus when she went to school here. But even though there wasn't a scientific bone in Emma's body and she never would have taken one of Brad's classes, Haley was sure Brad knew exactly who Emma was, and who *she* was, too: *the sister of the undergrad who went missing.* Everyone knew. Haley remembered the way Brad's eyebrows lifted when he read her name aloud the first day in class, and the way he'd taken off his black reading glasses to glance up and see her face, searching it for similarities. She knew he'd found the similarities when his eyes widened, and part of her enjoyed it. *Emma's sister:* if she was anything, it was that. Brad had tried to cover up the awkwardness by quickly resuming his roll call, barking out names, taking a few moments to get back on track. He'd been weird with her ever since, but that was nothing new. So many people were.

Emma went missing her junior year at Yarrow, when Haley was a sophomore at Waverly High School. There was no official explanation for her disappearance. The police had closed the case after investigating for months, interviewing everyone who was at the party that night in the woods with Emma, and sweeping the river—*Never a guarantee to find a body that way,* they kept reminding Haley and her parents. They never did find Emma's body, and they were convinced, just like most people in Waverly, that Emma had flung herself into the river from the cliffs behind Yarrow, where she'd last been seen.

But Haley knew in her bones that that was impossible. Emma had her dark side, but she wasn't suicidal. Haley believed Emma had been killed and that the police were too naive to figure it out, and once she realized her theories were falling on deaf ears in Waverly—including at the police department—she had to get out of there. She chose Stanford for college, far away from the dark and cold East Coast that had claimed her sister, and a plane flight from the parents who were trying so hard to keep it all together. At the airport Haley's parents warned her over and over to stay safe, but their warnings were hollow. Emma's disappearance made it too obvious that they didn't have control over anything.

It didn't take long for Haley to realize that California had been a mistake. She missed her parents and felt too removed from Waverly and where she'd lost Emma. Some magical-thinking part of her was certain she was the only one who could get to the bottom of her sister's disappearance, so after undergrad, Haley moved back east, to New York City, to be closer to her parents. That's where she met Dean, her fiancé, the only person besides her mother who'd ever believed her theories that her sister had been killed by someone else who was at the party that night. Her own father was convinced Emma might have just run away or been taken alive, and even Haley's friends at Stanford had nodded along when she got drunk enough to talk about Emma, clearly feeling very sorry for her, but also seeming not to believe her. *You're too close to see things clearly,* one of her roommates had said late one night, and Haley wondered if she just didn't have the right language. *Disappeared, missing, dead:* words Haley used interchangeably about what could have happened to her sister that night, the truth existing somewhere in the dark spaces between them.

Dean had supported Haley when she accepted an offer from Yarrow's medical school, and now here they were, back in Waverly where it had all started. Haley knew it was crazy. To want to live in the town she'd grown up in, where her parents still lived, and to walk the campus where they'd experienced their worst nightmare. To fall in love with Dean, who'd also attended Yarrow. But her grief was like a part of her body now, and she felt a visceral need to stay connected to her roots and her pain, and to her sister.

Haley looked down at the slim platinum ring she could just make out beneath her rubber gloves. An engagement. Dean had proposed a few months ago, and Haley knew something needed to change if she was supposed to start a new family. Because how could she move forward when the person she loved could be stuck, buried somewhere underground, her disappearance still a mystery?

TWO

Priya

Priya stared down at her phone to see Josie's text. **Need to talk.** She knew that she absolutely, positively shouldn't reply. She could practically hear Dr. Baker's voice telling her that it was time to *put the phone down . . . break the pattern . . . do something else . . .* but the phone was so warm and inviting in her hand, and she couldn't seem to keep herself from typing.

Please, stop contacting me, she wrote, but then she deleted it. She tried to breathe, to get the air all the way into her lungs like Dr. Baker had taught her to, but wouldn't Josie already know she'd started a text response because of those ellipses that phones displayed when the other person was replying?

Just breathe, Priya.

In, out, in, out . . .

Her cognitive behavioral therapy sessions with Dr. Baker were never far from her mind, all his tips and tricks for changing her anxious trains of thought, to *rewire neural pathways*, as Dr. Baker explained it all those years ago. Priya thought about the gift certificate for the sessions that her husband, Brad, had presented to her early one Christmas morning, and the way the smooth, embossed envelope had felt in her hand. Brad loved giving gifts, especially jewelry, but Priya thought the gift certificate was even better because it was what she really needed. She hadn't been right since Elliot was born. She loved him beyond measure, but she was so anxious, and the week before that Christmas, she'd had a very public panic attack in the parking lot outside Elliot's music class. She'd had to sit down and clutch her baby while she hung her head between her knees and tried to breathe, right there on the frozen pavement for all the other parents to see. When a well-meaning mother tried to pull Elliot from her arms, Priya lunged at her like a wild animal. After that morning it was even harder to make friends. And even now, nearly a decade later, Priya could never seem to stop the recurrent nightmare that someone would deem her an unfit mother and take away Elliot.

Leave me alone, Josie, please, Priya wrote in the text box, and then pressed send. Her fingers trembled against the phone as she tried even harder to recall the breathing techniques taught to her by Dr. Baker all those years ago. Priya was always trying harder. She knew how lucky she was to have someone as wonderful as Elliot, and though Brad wasn't perfect, at least he tried to help her. Those sessions were just one of the many examples of his devotion to making her better. In the early days of their marriage he'd seemed so hopeful that he could actually do it. Priya had always wondered if that was the hardest part of his career as a doctor: the frustration that he'd never be able to fix his own wife.

Please, the next text from Josie read, the phone buzzing in Priya's hand. Something's changed, and I need to explain.

Priya's mind drifted back to Brad. Was that even a real thing for him, his inability to make her okay? Or was she just worrying again, her anxiety always ready to rev like an engine and sweep her away?

Can you meet with me? asked Josie, and Priya reached into her bag for her medication, her heart pounding. Could it ever not be this way, with Priya terrified every time she heard her phone chime? Josie's texts only came through every six months or so. Once, a full two years went by without one, and Priya had felt safe for the first time in forever. She knew she could change her number, but what if that enraged Josie and made her do something unsavory with everything she knew?

Priya opened the yellow bottle and removed a pill with shaking fingers. She popped it onto her tongue and swigged it down with a gulp of tepid tap water. She couldn't help but wonder what it would be like to never, ever again hear from Josie Carmichael.

THREE

Haley

An hour after anatomy class ended, Haley sat inside her parked car with an indie rock station blaring. She stared at the new coffee shop on Main Street. All she wanted to do was head to the police station, but the appointment wasn't for another hour. Through the coffee shop's windows, she saw the profiles of her blond, beautiful real estate agents, Josie and Noah Carmichael. They were seated inside at a circular table.

You want this, Haley, don't you? You want a future with Dean in Waverly, so just go in, please, and try to act normal.

Josie was frowning at something Noah was saying, but then a man stopped at their table, and her expression changed. She tilted her chin and laughed as she stood to greet the person, maybe someone she once sold a home to. Noah stood, too, straightening to his full six feet, three or four inches, and extending a hand. He had a jawbone like an action figure.

It was 1:03, and Haley really needed to turn off her car and go inside, but she just couldn't yet. Facing them today felt insurmountable. Josie and Noah had been Emma's best friends back at Yarrow, and in the days after she disappeared, they seemed to have been her only friends, or at least the only ones who came forward with any information to try to help find her, turning over their phones immediately and leading the police to the journals Emma kept. Josie's brother, Chris, was on record saying something like *Anything could have happened to that girl*, as if disappearing were somehow Emma's fault, and the other students at Yarrow seemed to simultaneously obsess over Emma's disappearance while also distancing themselves from her. There were dozens of students at the party with Emma when she disappeared, but their statements to the police were unhelpful, mostly peppered with observations about how Emma was aloof, and how she and Josie were so insular that it was hard to get to know either of them. It niggled at the edges of Haley's mind, mostly because no one ever would have described Emma as aloof before college. She'd been incredibly well liked growing up in Waverly, voted homecoming queen her senior year of high school, which she mostly made fun of with self-effacing jokes, but still: it didn't make sense for her personality to have undergone such a transformation, and Haley had never been able to put her finger on what had caused it.

Anything could have happened to that girl.

It made Haley shudder. And now Noah and Josie were ten years older, married, and running a real estate business in town. Emma had loved them so much, which is why Haley tried to love them, too, but it was weird seeing them and being forced to interact. All Haley could do was picture Noah, Josie, and Emma ten years ago lounging on the quad at Yarrow, Emma and Josie wearing cut-off shorts and Noah in his lacrosse jersey. Dean had done his undergrad at Yarrow, too, and though he hadn't been friendly with Emma, Noah, or Josie during his years there, he was acquainted with them, and all these things put together meant it would be a snub not to use them as real estate agents. *It's a small town, Haley,* Dean had said when he dialed Noah and Josie's number, *let's not start off on the wrong foot.* Dean cared about things like that, about making a good impression.

Haley turned up the music even louder, letting her eyes settle on the coffee shop's blue neon sign: **MOSAIC**. She was pretty sure the owners were going for something swanky that looked different from all the other shops that lined the classic-looking Main Street, but it looked too futuristic, and it put a hard pit in her stomach, which made no sense when her future was supposed to look so bright, so safe. Just last night Haley and Dean had scrolled through wedding save-the-date cards and laughed about the pictures they could use to populate the blank spaces left for personalized photos. *Anyway, what's the point of these save-the-dates?* Haley had blurted when Dean opened up an option with cherry blossoms scattered along the borders. *If someone isn't close enough to know when we're planning the wedding, do we really care if they come?*

Dean had bristled, jiggling the computer mouse back and forth. But really, Haley had been thinking about Emma and feeling righteously pissed that her sister wouldn't be there when Dean's random, double-cheek-kissing aunts would. Still, maybe what she'd said had been too harsh. Dean had accused her of that before.

Haley loved Dean, she really did. He was the only man who'd ever truly understood her, definitely the only man who'd ever loved her in the way she wanted to be loved. She was still adjusting to being engaged at twenty-six when none of her friends from Stanford were, and when the guys she'd dated there were still binge drinking and pulling all-nighters at work. She'd never been the type of person who fantasized about a someday wedding; when she was little she never even sent her Barbies on dates, only to surgery, and when her mother found them all cut up, she got freaked out and threw them away.

Haley turned off the radio, exhaled. It was now or never. She opened the car door, got out, and slammed it shut. Everything sounded louder in this kind of cold.

Haley started toward the coffee shop and zipped her black bomber jacket higher. She was careful on the icy pavement, her mind flashing to her cadaver again. She could see Susie's still body lying on that table. Susie, like Emma, entered her mind uninvited all the time; Haley couldn't seem to stop either of them. Thinking about them—and about whatever peril they'd somehow gotten themselves into—kept her sharp.

There was a thin line of scar tissue that ran along Susie's forehead into her hairline, and Haley was always coming up with ways she could have gotten it. (A fall on black ice? A sibling who played too roughly?) In Haley's dreams—the ones she was pretty sure most people would call nightmares—Emma came often and always with new maladies that she needed Haley to fix. Sometimes when Haley was between sleep and wakefulness, Emma sat on the edge of her bed. *Sister,* she always said, followed by things like *help me . . . look closer . . . figure me out,* but Haley wasn't sure if Emma meant she was supposed to figure everything out *now,* or if she was talking about ten years ago. Of all the ways her sister haunted her, it was the images of how Emma could have died that Haley hated the most. She felt certain that her sister had fallen through the night sky: she could practically see it, hear it, and even smell the crisp winter air scented with evergreens. Sometimes—though she'd never admitted this to anyone—she felt Emma reverberating through her own body like the aftermath of a slap, like the ghost of her sister lived inside her and wanted the truth known.

Haley pressed her hands against the door to the café. The ice-cold glass felt like relief, and she shoved it forward and stepped inside. Smart-looking people chattered and unwrapped muffins from eco-friendly paper shells. An espresso machine hissed and made Haley startle. "Over here!" Josie called to her, pulling out a chair. Josie was glossy and beautiful, just like Emma used to be. Her blond hair rolled in waves over her shoulders, and her sparkling blue eyes were the color of pool water. Her skin was smooth and olive, a shade darker than most other blonds, and it made her look so healthy and alive, and like it was the middle of summer instead of freezing January. Haley sat quickly—it was a good way to avoid having to shake hands and get germs—and yanked off her knit cap. "Is this one mine?" she asked, gesturing to an untouched coffee on the table.

"All yours," Noah said. His light, thick hair was mussed from the wind. He, too, was rather good looking, and seeing them together was a little comical: they looked like they belonged in Hollywood, not inside an East Coast coffee shop discussing real estate. It had been like this when they were in college, too; the two of them were gorgeous and vibrant when most of the students looked tired and puffy. Even Emma had lavender half-moons beneath her eyes in those weeks before she disappeared. Josie had twice pointed that out to Haley back then, grow-ing agitated when she tried to tell Haley how worried she was about Emma, but Haley was still so young that she had no idea what to do with something like that. Why hadn't Josie told a real adult?

Noah smiled at Haley now, and she thought back to when she was only sixteen and meeting him for the first time in the student center and feeling immediately flushed and nervous the way you do when you're that age. Haley and her family lived only five miles from campus, so she often saw Emma, Josie, and Noah. Every time Emma and Josie would pull into the driveway to pick her up for coffee she'd go itchy with excitement, desperate to be out of her mother's sight and in the worn leather back seat of Josie's car. Josie would regale them with some story, usually about a guy and a hookup, which felt as scandalous a thing as Haley could imagine. She'd never seen a female friendship like theirs, and the thrill she felt to be included was unlike anything she'd ever felt before. It was like the three of them hovered on the precipice of something dangerous, like anything could happen at any moment, and whatever it was would be more exciting than the life Haley had known. And then Emma disappeared, and everything felt wrong, as though all the things they'd ever done together had led to tragedy.

A barista called out a drink order, and Haley tried to pull herself from her thoughts. She thanked Josie and Noah for the coffee and took a sip, forcing a smile as they watched her. She wanted to ask whether they'd had a recent phone call from Detective Rappaport, but she didn't usually bring up anything having to do with Emma. Josie and Noah had lost so much, too, when Emma disappeared, even if they dealt with it in different ways: Josie ditching her art degree and getting therapy and then her real estate license, and Noah taking a few drug-fueled years off in Australia, trying to party hard enough to forget everything that had happened, until his parents demanded he come back. Noah's dad had a major company in New York City that he'd always expected Noah to take over, and apparently Noah was a complete failure in his eyes for becoming a real estate agent. Josie said Noah's parents barely spoke to him now. Haley couldn't imagine ever letting go of a family member over something as unimportant as a career choice. But maybe people who did things like that didn't understand real loss.

Noah cleared his throat. "Ready to find your dream home?" he asked, and then he winked as though he were being ironic, like he didn't take this too seriously and neither should Haley. "You're gonna see so many beautiful properties this weekend," he went on, warm and casual, like a surfer talking about ocean waves.

"Noah's right," Josie said, and the sunny lilt in her voice made Haley realize Josie wasn't going to mention anything having to do with Emma or police stations. If Josie employed a tactic to cope with Emma's death, it seemed to be perfectionism, from her manners to the appropriateness of what she talked about. Haley watched as Josie reached into a butter-colored leather bag and retrieved a handful of brochures. All the fancier homes seemed to have them. "The first is a smart contemporary, set on two acres, but it might be too close to a main road for Dean's liking." Her voice was high and soft around the edges, and Haley considered the possibility that maybe Josie had just grown up, and this vanilla version of the person she'd been in college had nothing to do with Emma's death.

"Right, probably too close to the main road," Haley said, averting her eyes from the picture of the hulking gray-blue contemporary, and from Noah and Josie, too. She glanced around the coffee shop, at the stark white walls covered with an exhibit of oil paintings, mostly landscapes filled with black water and mossy lily pads. Astronomical prices were pinned on tags beneath each one.

"This one's right near town," Noah started, about to hand over a brochure for a house she recognized.

Haley shook her head to stop him. "That's the Lamberts' house," she said. Her eyes flickered to Josie, and she tried to discern if the name meant anything to her, but Josie's face was blank. "Emma dated their son, Frank, in high school."

There, she'd done it. She'd mentioned her sister by name. Color drained from Josie's face, and Noah's professional smile faded. They all stared at each other until Noah said, "I'm sorry, Haley," and carefully put the brochure back into Josie's bag. His smile came back, but it was gentle now, kind even. Haley swallowed over the hard lump in her throat. "It's okay," she said. "How could you have known?"

Noah was quiet. Josie sniffed, looking down at her hands. She shook her head, then raised her eyes to meet Haley's. "I'm sorry, too," she said. Noah's chair creaked as he shifted his weight, and the moment passed.

"Do you want to take a peek at this one?" Josie asked carefully, pushing a brochure across the tiny round table. Her real estate speak was softer than Noah's . . . *take a peek* . . . so completely nonthreatening, so devoid of what was really happening here, which was Haley choosing a life for herself and Dean: a house that might hold a family. It was paralyzing to think of the enormity of it. Did other people feel that way? Like one choice could set off a chain reaction that spiraled completely out of their control?

Noah nodded encouragingly at the brochure. "You'll see the kind of property Dean's looking for," he said.

"Four acres of land," Josie said. She unbelted her khaki trench, graceful as she slipped out of it and hung it on the back of her chair. "Hot in here," she said.

Haley felt their stares like a hand on her skin. She tucked her head and studied the cover photo showing a classic-looking colonial with green shutters. Her fingernails were covered in chipped silver polish, and she felt self-conscious about them as she unfolded the brochure to check out the photographs inside: a pristine white kitchen with a navy La Cornue stove and gleaming silver pots hanging above a marble island, a stone path leading beneath a trellis twined with greenery into a rose garden, and a glistening saltwater pool. Dean made enough money that they could afford the house, but could someone who wore Vans and chipped nail polish really live in a palace like this? Who was she kidding?

Haley shut the brochure. It wasn't the nail polish; it was Josie. Something about her gave Haley a temporary case of impostor syndrome.

"So what do you think?" Josie asked, her pale blue eyes roving the brochure. "It's very classic New England, right?"

"Classic New England," Haley repeated, the kind of thing someone would say who grew up in fancier circles than Josie did. *You don't need to pretend around me.*

Haley and Josie lost touch in the years after Emma's disappearance, but when she ran into Josie at a bar in Waverly a year ago, Josie had said that her career gave her *a new lease on life*, which made Haley wonder if she was trying to make a real estate joke. She'd told Haley how she and Noah had kept in touch while he was in Australia, and how Noah was the only man she'd ever truly loved, the only man who could really understand what she'd gone through because he'd gone through it, too. When Noah and Josie were together, you could sense it: the bond that connected them, a shared tragedy, a gaping hole where Emma should have been. Sometimes it made Haley uneasy, and she wondered if some part of her was jealous that she wasn't bonded like that with Dean yet.

Do you think I could have stopped Emma from doing it? Josie had asked that night at the bar, her words soaked with wine, and Haley felt the familiar anger surge within her. *She didn't kill herself,* she managed to say, and Josie's eyes had widened like she couldn't believe Haley could ever be so naive. Haley had changed the topic—there was only so much sadness people could handle in a conversation—and told Josie that she and Dean were considering a move back to Waverly. Josie instantly sobered and launched into real estate mode, seeming to forget that Haley had grown up in Waverly and didn't need to be sold on it.

Haley let go of a breath as the busyness of the café swirled around her. She knew she was being too quiet; she should seem more enthusiastic about the home with green shutters, and excited about the open house the next morning. "I think it's a lovely house," she said.

The corners of Josie's mouth lifted into a gentle smile. She seemed empathetic in that way, and Haley wondered if it was one of the things Emma had liked so much about her.

They all stared at each other. Josie crossed her slim legs, and her wool trousers lifted an inch to expose a red mark where the strap of her stilettos had rubbed against her skin. Haley wasn't sure what else she was supposed to say; she wasn't even sure why they had to meet in person when all these homes were online, but Josie had insisted.

"Hey," Josie said to the space above Haley's head, her voice suddenly strained.

Haley swiveled to see Josie's brother, Chris. They were stepsiblings, and even though they were unrelated by blood, they had the same piercing light blue eyes, which Haley had plenty of time to study because Chris always seemed to hold her gaze for a beat too long. He swiped a black lock of hair from his eyes and said, "What's up, Haley?"

Chris did admin at Josie and Noah's company, though you wouldn't know by looking at him. He was always dressed in flannel, and Josie and Noah always seemed a little embarrassed at the sight of him, though Haley couldn't figure out why. He was handsome enough to get away with wearing whatever he wanted.

"Nothing," Haley answered. "You?"

"Nothin'," he said. He ran his hand over a thick, short beard.

"Do you want to sit?" Haley asked, even though there wasn't a fourth chair. She made a halfhearted attempt to stand. She couldn't figure out if Chris had come into the coffee shop by chance, or if he'd come for a work-related reason.

"No, Haley, sit," Noah said, his voice too hard. He turned to Chris and asked, "Do you have the rest of the brochures?"

Chris shook his head.

Noah turned to Haley, barely able to conceal his irritation. "The house on Carrington is well priced, so we should act quickly tomorrow if you're interested after the open house," he said.

Haley sat back and watched as Josie glanced from Chris to Noah. Haley didn't mind strange family dynamics; she saw so much worse when she worked in the hospital.

Josie turned to Haley and forced a smile. "Tomorrow you'll see that the house is filled with unexpected details that make you look twice without being over the top," she said, "and if I know Dean like I think I do, he'll absolutely love it."

The comment surprised Haley. Josie didn't really know Dean that well.

Noah turned to Josie. "How many people are you expecting at the open house?" he asked.

Josie shrugged, quiet for a moment. A new song came on, filtering through the café with a low beat and indecipherable lyrics. "January is a slow month," she told Haley, not really answering Noah's question. "And plus there's the storm we're supposed to get, which will deter a lot of the New York City people, even if it never comes to pass."

Haley lifted the porcelain mug to her lips. Even the mugs were artwork for sale, these ones with handles carved into the shapes of fish and osprey. She took a big gulp, feeling the coffee warm her from the inside. She was sweating beneath her hoodie, but it was so deathly cold outside she welcomed it. She'd forgotten about the storm in the forecast. They were predicting a half foot of snow. Noah looked down at his phone, and Haley wondered if he was annoyed. Dean did that when he was irritated with her—he looked anywhere but at her, usually at his phone.

"I'm gonna grab a coffee," Chris announced. He turned and walked away from them, instantly lost in the swarm of patrons.

Josie's phone lit up. She snatched it off the table a little too quickly, her face flushing as she read the incoming text. She tossed it into her bag, and said, "I'm sorry to have to run, Haley. I've got a two o'clock appointment."

So do I, at the precinct, actually, Haley thought. "I'll see you at the open house tomorrow, then," she said.

"Can't wait," Josie said, standing. "Right at eleven? I want you to see it first."

Haley nodded, lifting her hand in a wave. "Thanks for the coffee," she said. She felt a little guilty that Josie and Noah usually treated, but they stood to make a lot of money in commission, and they probably didn't care too much about the five-dollar lattes. It wasn't like that with Haley and her friends. Most of them were still in their early twenties or midtwenties and could barely make rent. When she lived in the city, Haley had worked as a research assistant in a lab, but the money wasn't good enough to afford a New York City apartment and eat at the same time, so she'd supplemented it by bartending three shifts at a dive bar on the Lower East Side. And then Dean proposed, and soon after, he asked her to quit the bartending, telling her he could cover their rent so she could save for medical school. He said he couldn't sleep, always worrying something would happen to her in the middle of the night.

Josie wrapped a white scarf around her neck. "Say goodbye to Chris for me," she said. She belted her trench, and gave Haley one last apologetic smile before turning with a flash of flowing blond hair, her petite figure carving a path among the customers, then disappearing.

Haley turned to Noah. They hadn't really had that many one-on-one conversations. He was looking down at his phone, his eyes the tiniest bit sunken, making Haley wonder how hard he still partied. When he looked up, he said, "I'm sure you and Dean will be relieved to find a more permanent situation. Renting is never quite as satisfying as owning a home."

Haley didn't know what to say. She'd only ever rented. "The cottage you and Josie found us to rent is beautiful," she tried. "But Dean thinks it wouldn't be safe to raise a family so close to the rough water." It was one of the only things Dean had ever said about starting a family. He was adamant they could not live on that river, and of course, with Emma disappearing there, Haley agreed.

"He's probably right," Noah said. He looked away, scanning the customers, his eyes landing on Chris ordering at the counter. The girl behind the counter looked college-age, and she was blushing at whatever Chris was saying. When Chris tipped back his head and laughed, so did she. Noah frowned as he watched their interaction. "Anyway, those houses on the river are a fortune," he said.

Haley inhaled the scent of banana muffins wafting through the café. She needed to get to the precinct, but she didn't want to dash off the second after Josie had left because something about that felt awkward, and she'd been accused of being awkward before. She was trying to be less so, to be more of a *people person*, because bedside manner was important no matter what kind of doctor she ended up being. The doctors at the hospital always emphasized how important it was to be present with patients, to try to read everything that appeared on their faces, not just in what they said. And Haley was able to do that in the room with a patient, but too often in the classroom she was distracted, her mind wandering during lectures—a few of her professors had called her out on it. The grief was one thing, but the not knowing was what kept her mind constantly turning.

"The house with the green shutters, is it private?" Haley asked. "Not a lot of neighbors?"

"Very private," Noah said. "I don't think you'll even see the neighboring houses. It's surrounded by woods."

Haley nodded, hearing Dean's voice saying the words. *Privacy, Haley, we need a house with privacy.* As though they had something to hide.

FOUR

Priya

Sure. I'll meet. Where? When?

That was the text Priya had sent to Josie a few minutes ago, and now she was furiously scrubbing her kitchen, waiting for a reply. Her medication had kicked in, and she watched herself scrub the subway-tiled backsplash as though her hand were someone else's body part. Tears burned Priya's eyes and blurred her vision until the tiles smudged into each other, until she couldn't see them well enough to clean. She stumbled back, blinking, and then turned on the water as hot and fast as it would go, letting the white noise and scorching temperature dull her senses as she rinsed out the sponge. Elliot would be home any moment from the neighbors' house, and she needed to behave normally, not like someone being chased by skeletons a decade old. She put her soaking hands over her eyes and held them there until they turned cold and her breathing returned to normal.

Ten years ago, Josie Carmichael and Emma McCullough were Priya's art students at Yarrow. They were just girls then, really, and Josie always sat at the easel front and center. Sometimes Priya would look up from her own painting and catch Josie staring at her. It was uncomfortable even to remember it.

Priya wasn't sure how long she'd been standing at the sink. She'd been losing track of time ever since she started the new antianxiety medication Brad had prescribed, and it seemed to work in both directions: sometimes the minutes lengthened like taffy, and other times they sped up, scurrying together and vanishing before she could make sense of whatever she was supposed to be doing. She'd tried to tell Brad about the side effects at first, but he'd cut her off, asking, *Are you saying you're missing chunks of time? That's very serious, Priya.*

She'd shaken her head quickly and muttered a soft *no* because she wanted to stay on the meds, but now she wasn't so sure.

The front door opened, and Priya felt herself relax just a bit. She stood up straighter and swiped beneath her eyes to clear any rogue makeup stains. The thunk of Elliot kicking off his shoes was enough to make her exhale fully. Her son was back. Maybe everything could be okay.

"Elliot," she called, his name like candy in her mouth.

"Mama!" he called back, a word he only used when they were alone. In front of his father and his friends he said *Mom.*

"I'm in the kitchen," Priya said, and Elliot loped into the room with a smile tugging at his lips.

"I'm starving," he announced.

"Shocker," Priya said, smiling back. Elliot was reed thin just like her, but his appetite was endless. Priya held her breath and waited, suspended inside the moment when Elliot would either come close for a hug or keep a cool distance. She wanted to reach forward and pull him to her like she'd done when he was little, but he was ten now, and she respected his big-kid body. She didn't want to be the kind of mother who overtly needed his physical affection; she wanted to let him guide the terms of their relationship, which seemed to change every year, while staying the same in all the ways that mattered. He loved her, and it was all she needed.

Elliot stepped toward her as though he might hug her, but when he stopped short, the inches between them felt like a physical presence, like something Priya could wrap her hands around and squeeze the life out of. "So," she asked quickly, turning to open the fridge. She found the kefir smoothie she'd made earlier and passed it to him. She never directly asked Elliot about school, or how his day was, because that made him clam up. He was unlike his father, who loved talking about his day and seemed affronted when Priya didn't ask about it. In fact, Brad seemed to enjoy his life twice: once while living it, and then again when telling someone else all about it. But for Elliot, Priya kept her words to a minimum so he'd have room to talk.

"Thanks," Elliot said, taking a slug of the smoothie. His eyes were bright brown orbs rimmed with a black circle that made them look like a cat's eyes. His gorgeous, haphazard curls were courtesy of Brad. "Robby's helping me fix my science project," he said, an edge in his voice. Robby was a year older than Elliot, and he and his mother, Alex, were their only real friends on the street. The other neighbors mostly kept to themselves.

"Oh?" Priya asked, sensing he wanted to say more.

"Yeah," Elliot said. "Because it was a flunk this week in school."

"A flunk?" she asked. Her hands busied themselves by spinning her hair into a topknot.

"Yeah, you know, a flunk. It means like a failure."

"Hmmm," Priya said, nodding carefully. She always marveled at the way she could maintain eye contact with Elliot for so much longer than she could with anyone else. "How come?" she finally asked.

"Because the paper clip fell off the roof of the thing if I didn't hold the magnet exactly right. You'd think Dad being a doctor would mean I could at least have a science project that didn't suck," he said. He blinked at her like he was waiting for her to tell him to be respectful of his father or not say *suck*, but she really only did that kind of parenting in front of Brad. Elliot was a genuinely kind soul, and Priya had a feeling he was going to stay that way as long as no one got in the way, including her. And anyway, he was right: Brad had hurried through that science project with him, acting like it was a chore. Priya was never less in love with Brad than when he was a mediocre father. There had been a very low point in their marriage when she'd considered leaving him, but she knew if she did her son would change irrevocably. It was a few years ago, when Elliot was seven and sensitive as ever, and as she watched his heart unfurling to the world she knew better than to do something that would close it. Of course, Priya understood why women and men left each other, and there were things Brad could have done that would have made her leave, too. But not that silly checkout girl at the gym, the one with brown curly hair and curves in the places Priya felt sunken.

Priya's phone buzzed inside her pocket. Elliot was still standing there, drinking the smoothie. If she'd thought the text was from anyone other than Josie, she would have ignored it, but she didn't have many friends, and the ones she did have weren't the kind to text memes all day. She retrieved her phone from the pocket of her jeans, her chest tightening as she read Josie's words.

How about tomorrow morning at 11? I'm showing an open house at 35 Carrington Road. Come a few minutes before then, before anyone arrives, so we can talk in private? I'll be quick.

Priya started typing before she could think better of it. She vaguely thought of the nor'easter they were predicting, but she lived so close to Carrington Road—it would be fine.

I'll be there, she wrote, and pressed send.

FIVE

Haley

Haley's sneakers squeaked against the linoleum as she crossed the precinct's lobby, her fingers *tap-tap-tapping*. A compact man sat at a desk in front of a computer, and he didn't look up as she approached, which struck her as decidedly un-policeman-like. Weren't they supposed to be paying attention to every detail?

Haley cleared her throat. "Help you?" the man finally asked, looking up. His eyes crinkled at the corners in a way that made Haley like him.

"I'm here to see Detective Rappaport," she said, and she tried to smile, but she could feel her face messing it up. Why *was* she here? Had her father made some kind of disturbance again? Sometimes he came up with a new theory about Emma being still alive and out there somewhere, and when Haley and her mom couldn't calm him, he'd go to the police. The cops had never been anything but good to their family, despite not solving the crime, but part of that was because they didn't think there'd been one.

"Have a seat," the man said, gesturing to an orange plastic chair, the kind Haley hadn't seen in a waiting room since maybe the nineties at the pediatrician's office. She sat and watched him disappear through a door, presumably to get Rappaport. She sniffed a few times. She did that, too, when she was nervous. They were compulsions she could mostly control, meaning she didn't sniff or tap if she was meeting with a professor, or on a first date, or anything like that. She'd started doing the tapping in front of Dean six months or so into their relationship, but it didn't seem to bother him too much. When Emma disappeared and Haley's tapping compulsions started, her mom had tried to take her to a therapist, but Haley felt like she knew more than the woman (at least about herself), and it seemed silly trying to explain the OCD; at sixteen, Haley thought she'd read enough medical literature to know what she was doing. The obsessive thoughts about Emma and the tapping weren't exactly fun, but they weren't overtaking her life or anything, so what was the harm?

Haley glanced around the precinct's lobby. A fern wilted in the corner next to a banged-up water dispenser. The room was too hot, too quiet. Haley couldn't even imagine how different the life of a police officer was here than a half hour away in New York City. There had only been two major crimes in Waverly since Emma had disappeared: a robbery that went unsolved and a domestic dispute that ended with a shooting. It made Haley think about the different kind of life she had lived in New York City, which depressed her a little, so she tried to shake off the thought.

The door creaked, and Haley jolted upright. A well-built forty-something man emerged. He was wearing a worn ivory sweater and corduroy pants, and a neat part in his thick, nearly black hair. He looked more Dead Poets Society than detective. "Haley McCullough?" he asked, his voice even raspier than it had been on the phone.

Haley stood, smiling weakly. She had mentors at school: strong, indomitable female doctors who stood up and looked her in the eye when they spoke. She didn't understand how they did it.

"That's me," Haley said. She tried to use the sole of her Converse to push down her leggings from where they'd crept up over her ankles, but it was useless. The detective reached out a hand for her to shake. "Hank

Rappaport," he said. He was trying to make her comfortable by leaving off the *detective* part. She'd seen doctors do it when she shadowed them in the hospital; they'd enter a patient's room and say only their first and last names without the *doctor* prefix.

"Hello, Detective," she said, releasing his hand first.

"Follow me," he said, and she did. They traveled a long blue hallway to a door marked with Rappaport's name. Haley was feeling a little numb as he opened it, wanting whatever this was to be over. Then she saw her mother seated in one of the two chairs in front of a desk. "Mom?" she blurted.

"Hi, sweetheart," Liv said. When Emma and Haley were teenagers, they exclusively referred to their mom by her first name—not when speaking to her, but when they were in conversation together and referring to her. It had made them feel grown-up back then, and it had stuck; now it was just another way Emma had imprinted herself onto Haley's way of thinking and existing.

"What's going on?" Haley asked, glancing from her mom to Rappaport. She could feel blood swirling in her ears, her blood pressure ratcheting higher. *All natural responses to adrenaline. You know what's happening to you, Haley,* she told herself, and tried to breathe.

Liv stood. She was usually graceful, way more so than Haley, but her hip knocked into a pencil holder on Rappaport's desk, sending pens, pencils, and a mini stapler clanking across the wood. "I'm sorry," Liv said, righting the container and loading Rappaport's things while he assured her it wasn't a problem. Haley didn't try to help. Her throat felt so tight it was hard to breathe. Liv turned to watch her, her eyes on Haley just like always. No matter how terrible the hand Liv had been dealt, she was the one who took care of Haley, never the other way around.

"Please sit, ma'am," the detective said. Haley wasn't sure which one of them he was talking to, but they both sat.

Why are you here? What did he tell you?

The detective folded his long-limbed body into the chair and considered them with light brown eyes. Then he turned to Haley's mother and said, "We believe we've found new evidence in your daughter's disappearance."

Haley could feel her mother freeze beside her, but Haley's entire body woke up. They hadn't found any evidence before, not ever, and Haley wondered if this was the moment she'd been waiting for, the one that would irrevocably change Emma's story as they knew it. "Go on, tell us," Haley said, her tone harder than she'd meant it to be, but what was he waiting for? Permission? Her heart pounded as the detective opened the top drawer of his desk. He retrieved a sealed plastic bag with a silver bracelet and placed it between Haley and her mother, and he didn't need to tell them not to open it: they didn't even touch the plastic. They just stared.

"Do either of you recognize this bracelet?"

The right word was *bangle*. There was a clasp on the side that was open now, lengthening the perimeter by an inch so the wearer could easily slide it over a small wrist like Emma's. It was just thick enough to have tiny but readable script, but Haley didn't need to read it because she'd read it ten years ago when Emma showed it to her.

"It's Emma's," Haley said, and Liv's hand went to her mouth. Haley couldn't look directly at her. "It was a gift from someone. I don't know who because Emma was cryptic about it. And she was involved with a few different guys, so there are several possibilities for who might have given it to her." Liv shifted her weight, but Haley kept going, as though she were reading facts from a patient's chart. "Typically she mentioned guys she was seeing like they weren't a big deal, but she wasn't like that about whoever gave her this bracelet. She showed it off to me, but she put her finger over her lips when I asked who gave it to her. I remember that like yesterday, because I remember how young it made her look when she did it, like we were kids again." Emotion tightened Haley's chest, so she took in tiny breaths that didn't make it all the way into her lungs. It was one of her tricks for school, too, when she was so exhausted or jittery she felt tears coming. She preferred anything to tears—even the furious feeling.

"Emma was very free spirited," Liv said, her forehead creasing. Haley couldn't suppress her eye roll, and she knew the detective saw it.

"There was nothing wrong with Emma sleeping with or dating more than one guy at once," Haley snapped at her mom. "She was in *college*. You don't need to defend her."

Liv blanched, but Haley didn't apologize. It was one of the things that drove her crazy, the way people talked about Emma's behavior as though it were any different from everything everyone else was doing in college. "Haley . . ." Liv started, but Haley took her mom's hand and squeezed it. She turned back to Rappaport, and asked, "This bracelet, who found it?"

"It's not the *who* that matters here," the detective said, "it's the *where*." His voice was careful, but Haley knew it was an act; he'd determined how much he was planning to tell them long before they stepped inside his office. "As you know, Emma was last seen by numerous eyewitnesses at the party in the woods," he said, "but no one could place her anywhere after, so we had to consider the possibility that she left the party of her own volition and had an accident farther downriver, where it's a straight jump into the water. But the bracelet was found too far upriver, where the gorge has plenty of ground between the cliffs' edges and the water. Anyone who fell or jumped that far north would . . ." Rappaport's voice trailed off, and Haley willed herself not to shout at him to keep going. He cleared his throat. "Well," he started again, "it's a forty-five-foot drop from the cliff down to the dirt, and a body would have remained on the ground to be discovered. Which means if Emma was killed near the party, or if she fell or was pushed from those cliffs, someone went down into the gorge and disposed of her body so it wouldn't be found, whether by burying it, or, more likely, by putting her into the river."

"Mom," Haley said, and her hand found Liv's. It was freezing. Haley knew tears were next, so she asked Rappaport if he had a tissue.

He passed her an unopened package of the neon-colored kind of tissues kids take to school.

"I'm sorry to deliver this news," he said to Liv, and then he turned to Haley to say, "We plan to reopen the case, and though I wasn't the detective on Emma's case ten years ago, I want to formally apologize. I've seen several reports where you and your mother say you're certain Emma wouldn't have hurt herself." The detective cleared his throat, his face changing. "Emma's father," he said, "I haven't met Tim yet, but Detective Segal told me he's in a fragile state, understandably, and that he maintains his daughter might have run away." His brown eyes were gentle, and Haley was grateful for it. "This news will be devastating if it shatters a theory that might be protecting him, and it's why I invited only the two of you here, so that you could break the news to him however you think is best. But please let me know how I can help," he said. His face looked strained with awkwardness, but he was trying so hard Haley felt herself melt a little. Everything about Emma disappearing had been so indescribably hard, but it was the moments of unexpected kindness that always broke her. Her sister was gone, and even though Haley couldn't bring herself to use the word *dead,* she knew it was the truth somewhere deep inside, no matter what anyone else said when they tried to console her. And Rappaport was right: for the first few months after Emma disappeared, Haley's dad was absolutely sure Emma had simply run away. The years had eroded his confidence, but it always remained a possibility he held on to, something he fantasized about: the possibility that Emma was living a life far away in California, where she'd always wanted to go. It made Haley want to scream. Her parents could be overly protective, and Emma had been fighting with them (especially with her dad) before she disappeared, but they were good parents. How could her dad want to imagine a life where Emma hated him enough to run away?

"We'll break the news to Tim," Liv said, and then she let out a small sigh. "Could we have a minute?" she asked.

Rappaport looked surprised, but nodded and excused himself. The door shut, and Liv whipped around in her chair to face Haley. Her auburn hair was newly cut, and the tendrils that framed her face made her look younger than fifty-six. Her round brown eyes were red-rimmed from crying, but still smart as ever. "This is going to kill Dad," she said.

"It is," Haley managed, but then she stopped knowing what to say. Her dad's grief was too much. It was different when she was working with the doctors in the hospital and it was a patient's sadness. This was her family.

"Will you tell him with me?" Liv asked. She gripped the arm of the chair, her thin fingers going white. "Your dad will be more under control with you there. He won't want to scare you."

"Of course," Haley said.

Liv blinked a few times, looking like she was turning something over in her mind. "The detective didn't seem very surprised when you said the bracelet was Emma's," she eventually said. "Do you think Josie's the one who identified it first?"

Usually Liv never mentioned Josie by name, and whenever they ran into her, Liv barely spoke. Only once did she say anything about it, a muttered *It just isn't fair that she goes on living a life right in front of us, and Emma doesn't.*

"It had to be her, because who else?" Haley replied, tapping her thighs again. *One, two, three, four, five . . .*

She wasn't sure whether her mom didn't notice the tapping anymore or she just chose not to say anything. *Six, seven, eight, nine . . .*

The walls of Rappaport's office seemed to come closer. "I gotta get out of here," Haley said, thinking about how she couldn't wait to call Dean and tell him everything. "But I'll meet you tonight whenever you want to tell Dad."

Liv nodded slowly, and Haley let her head fall against her mom's chest, desperate for her comfort. Liv's arms were strong and warm, and Haley breathed in her familiar vanilla scent before pulling away and zipping her coat, preparing for the Waverly chill and the afternoon ahead.

SIX

Priya

That evening Brad shuffled his feet as he walked across the kitchen to greet Priya. It was a habit that irritated her, because he was only thirty-eight, a few years younger than she was, but the shuffling made him seem much older. He hadn't been athletic as a child or young adult, but right after Elliot was born he began working out so vigorously it gave his body the appearance of a lifetime spent as a well-muscled athlete. Only the shuffling gave him away.

"Hey," Priya said as she set out a steaming plate of stir-fry.

"Hi, sweetie," Brad said in return, and Priya forced herself to meet his eyes. Is this what other women did, the ones who knew their husbands had been unfaithful and decided to stay? She knew several women who stayed for financial reasons, but Priya had a modest amount set aside from her days selling her paintings, so it wasn't that. She stayed because Brad made her feel safe, or at least safer than she'd ever felt before. There was no way someone who'd never experienced an anxiety disorder could understand, but Priya didn't believe she could be okay all by herself without his care. It wasn't just that he medicated her—she could find a psychiatrist for that—it was the day-to-day monitoring of her behavior, her moods, and her fears. Who else would do that with such care? Priya was terrified of her own mental state, because what if she missed the subtle signs and then plunged into a downward spiral? What if she went off the deep end again with no one there to save her? What if that happened, and she lost Elliot?

Brad set down his bag, his green eyes searching hers as they always did, asking: *Are you all right today?*

It was a harder question to answer without Elliot here.

"How was teaching?" she asked, praying she could get through the whole evening without anything tipping him off that tomorrow she was going to meet Josie, whom he'd expressly asked her to stay away from.

"My day was terrific," he said, upbeat as usual after his anatomy lab. He loved being listened to, respected, and adored, and teaching gave him that.

"Great," Priya said as he hugged and kissed her. She knew she should press for details but couldn't come up with a good question. She uncurled from his hug and went to get water.

"The food smells delicious," Brad said, which was kind because they both knew it probably wouldn't taste that way. Priya had tried for years to get better at cooking; she couldn't stand being mediocre at something. She'd always chased the things she was wildly good at, mostly school and art, but there were so many regular-life things she sucked at, like organizing Elliot's closet or remembering to sign him up on time for Little League.

"Let me help you," Brad said, grabbing two napkins from the center stack and folding them. "Where's Elliot?"

"He's next door with Robby," Priya said, wondering what took him so long to notice. "I told him to be back by eight."

"Isn't that late?" Brad asked, and Priya was momentarily thrown. He usually let her make those kinds of decisions. *Not for a ten-year-old*, she wanted to say.

"Maybe," she said instead, not wanting an argument.

"We'll address it with him later," Brad said, looking satisfied for uttering something fatherly. Priya was sure he'd have been a better dad to a girl. He didn't get along that well with members of his own sex. There were always arguments at work he was telling her about, and they almost never involved a female colleague.

Priya sat at the table. If Elliot were here, it would be easier to fake being okay. She hated lying, and she knew omitting her meeting with Josie tomorrow counted as a big lie. Years ago, Josie had gotten in touch with Priya under the pretense of a new house on the market, prattling on about an appointment she'd made for Priya to view it, laughing over the irony that she'd once been Priya's art student, and saying something about how after graduating Yarrow she realized *you can't make a living off art, you need a real job!* Brad had wanted to move again, and Priya assumed Josie was the real estate agent he'd selected for them. She'd felt exasperated by the thought of another move, but she'd gone along with it, about to meet with Josie when Brad found out and exploded with rage. He'd told Priya that Josie was an agent trying to poach the sale from another agent, but Priya wasn't dumb enough to believe that that could ever justify his reaction, so she went to the meeting behind Brad's back.

"Let's eat," Brad said, sinking his large frame into a wicker chair. Priya had decorated the house a few summers ago with bright blues and yellows, and with colorful vases and wicker chairs that surrounded a farm table. Her décor choices struck her as ridiculous in the dead of winter.

Priya sipped her water. "How was your day?" she asked again, stupidly. She wanted to kick herself for repeating the question.

Brad raised his eyebrows, but said nothing about her misstep. He reached for his water glass. "How about you tell me about yours?" he asked instead.

"It was fine," Priya said, exhaling, grateful he was being easy on her. It was one of the things she loved about him: he didn't pick fights. Priya raised her fork above the chicken and vegetables. "Elliot mentioned the science project didn't go well at school this week," she said, spearing a pepper.

"Did he say what went wrong?" Brad asked. He gulped a swig of water and set his glass down too hard on the table.

"You should ask him," Priya said, dabbing at her mouth with a napkin.

Brad frowned, and Priya watched as he shoveled the stir-fry into his mouth. He didn't appear to enjoy it, but maybe he was just distracted about the failed science project. "We should go away," he said suddenly, chewing furiously. He took another sip of water, and locked eyes with her. "You, Elliot, and me. We should get away."

"Where would we go?" Priya asked.

Brad held her gaze until she looked down into her lap, embarrassed. Sometimes she felt so dumb in front of him. His mind worked faster than hers, even though it used to be the other way around. She knew part of the reason he'd fallen in love with her was her intelligence, but now her brain felt so clouded with worries, anxieties, and racing thoughts, and she couldn't seem to get it back on track.

"Anywhere," Brad finally said, not looking at her anymore. "Anywhere but here. Let's get out of Waverly for a bit. Maybe a fishing trip somewhere, the kind of thing we've always said we'd do, but we never have."

"It's January," Priya said, unsure of where he was going with this, unsure of what had brought it on.

"So we'll hop on a flight somewhere. Even better."

"Um, okay," Priya said. She supposed Elliot might like a vacation, and she certainly could use one.

"Great," Brad said. "I'll look into some options." His phone buzzed, and Priya watched as he nearly knocked over his water glass to conceal whatever message was on it. "It's the hospital. I'll have to call back. You don't mind?"

"Of course not," she said, forcing a smile at her husband.

SEVEN

Haley

That evening Haley sat on a stool inside her mother's immaculate kitchen, watching Liv carefully place an ice cube into the dirt of one of her potted orchids. Haley loved her parents' home with its wide doorways, exposed wooden beams, and stucco walls. It was the kind of house that was supposed to look lived in, and it used to, before Emma disappeared and Liv started maniacally organizing and cleaning each night. What Haley remembered most about the house from her childhood was the immense amount of artwork that always scattered the surfaces: kitchen countertops, side tables, even the backs of toilets next to scented candles they never lit. Emma's talent had been obvious from a young age—everyone remarked upon it—and it made Haley happy to be surrounded by her sister's art. She wasn't the type to get jealous, and besides, there was plenty of praise to go around, because that's how her parents were. And as Emma's artistic ability was escalating, so was Haley's academic ability. It had felt good to make her parents happy, and Haley wondered when the last time was that she'd done that.

"Where *is* he?" Liv asked, finally glancing up from her plants.

Haley sipped her coffee. "I don't know," she murmured. Bowling was the only activity her father still participated in outside the house, and he didn't carry a cell phone. He'd said he found the phone in his pocket unsettling, the fact that someone could call him with devastating news at any moment, and he looked at Liv and Haley as if they were insane whenever they urged him to carry one for safety purposes. *Nope,* he'd say, or, *no siree.* He didn't go so far as the grocery store anymore, or to the library, which he'd once loved, or to the town pool, even on the most sweltering days of summer. He hadn't made a new friend in the decade since Emma had been gone; he hadn't done anything at all, really, besides the bowling.

"I'm just so scared he's going to lose it," Liv said, gently touching the smooth leaves of one of her ferns.

"He's lost it before," Haley said. She set down her milky coffee. It was getting too cold. "We survived, so did he."

"You're very practical, you know," Liv said, and a small, sad smile worked at the corners of her mouth.

"I get it from you," Haley said. She cleared her throat. "We all would have fallen apart without you. You know that, right?"

Tears sprang to Liv's dark eyes. "Oh, stop it!" she said, but her voice was soft. "You'll make me cry, Haley, I mean it. No more of that kind of thing."

The doorbell rang. "Why would Dad ring the bell?" Haley asked, straightening.

"He probably forgot his keys again," Liv said. She smoothed the front of her striped top and made her way around the kitchen island. Haley waited, uncrossing and crossing her legs as her mom trekked through the foyer and opened the front door. Haley prepared herself to hear her dad's lumbering footsteps, to see his face fold when they started talking. But instead she heard her fiancé's voice.

"Dean?" Haley blurted when he entered the kitchen. "What are you doing here?" Her tone sounded more offended than she'd meant it to.

Dean's dark eyebrows shot up. "I'm here to say hello to my almost-wife?" His voice was questioning, like he couldn't imagine why she sounded so upset that he'd stopped by. "I saw your car in the driveway," he went on, clearly embarrassed that she'd spoken that way to him in front of Liv.

"I'm sorry," Haley said quickly. Cell service was spotty in Waverly, and Dean's phone had gone straight to voice mail when she called earlier after leaving the precinct. "I just thought I'd see you at home and explain everything and . . ." Why was she so awkward when she was caught off guard? "We got bad news today," she blurted, "and I've just been really concerned with how my dad is going to take it . . ." Her voice trailed off. She held her breath, determined not to be crying when her father arrived.

"What happened?" Dean asked, crossing the kitchen in two giant steps, his arms around her strong and sure. He sat down on the stool next to her, his hand going to her knee.

Haley exchanged a glance with her mom.

"He should stay," Liv said softly.

Haley nodded. Maybe it would be good for her dad to have Dean here, too, to deflect his pain somehow. She tilted her chin to take in Dean's brown eyes flecked with green. He was so tall she was always lifting her glance to see him, always arching onto her tiptoes to hug him. Even though it was Saturday, he was dressed in his work clothes because he'd had to meet for lunch with a client in Greenwich, and his perfectly tailored suit emphasized his shoulders. Ever since the first night they met while she was bartending, there had been something about Dean's presence. He settled Haley, and not many people did.

"They found a bracelet in the gorge behind Yarrow," Haley said, "right beneath the cliffs by where the party was that night." She watched the lines that crossed Dean's handsome face deepen. "It's Emma's," she said, "and it changes the way the police are thinking about the case. They always thought she wandered alone downriver where it's a straight jump into the water." Haley's hands went to her lap, and her fingers tapped a hard circle against her palm. "But the cliffs above where the bracelet was found drop four stories down to the dirt, where there's plenty of land before the water starts. If Emma fell there and died, or if she were pushed, a body would have remained on the ground. Which means if she was killed at the party or at the cliffs, the location of her bracelet shows that someone hid her body or put her in the river." Haley's voice broke, and the words echoed through the still kitchen, followed by a deathly silence. She thought of her sister, all alone, river water coursing over her body; she thought of her heartbroken father; and then she thought of the lifeless cadaver on that table in anatomy, and it was like every horrible thing she'd ever known was suffocating her. Her breathing started to go so fast she thought she would pass out. She looked down at the floor, focusing on her mom's bare feet against the tiles, and then she felt her mom's arms, plus Dean's, wrap tightly around her.

"Shhhh, it's over, honey," Liv was saying. "It's all over. No one's hurting her now."

Haley looked up to see her mother's calm face, wondering for the thousandth time how she was able to do this. Was it just because her father was such a mess, so paralyzed by his grief, that this was the only option left for her?

Dean kissed the top of Haley's head, and then the front door opened. "Hello," came her father's voice, a little wobbly. "Haley's here?" When had he started sounding like an old man? The clunk of his shoes came next, covering the floor with heavy footsteps.

"Tim? We're in the kitchen!" Liv called out, her voice quaking.

Haley's dad emerged, his wiry eyebrows shooting up just as Dean's had moments earlier. His striped Izod shirt was slightly askew, and there was a stain on his khakis. Haley felt Dean's hand squeeze her shoulder.

"Dad," Haley said softly. Her father looked at each of them carefully. He didn't speak. He crossed the kitchen and sat at the table. They watched as he situated himself in a chair and smoothed the wrinkles on his pant legs. Finally he looked up.

"What's going on?" he asked, his voice stronger than Haley had expected.

Liv took a long breath and told him about the found bracelet.

PART II

EIGHT

Emma

Ten years ago

Noah's kissing me in my dorm room, but all I can think about is what a mess I've made. I never even had a boyfriend in high school, and I didn't even lose my virginity until this year. Twenty-one is pretty late to lose your virginity, but I seem to be making up for lost time by sleeping with two different guys, and then stupidly going and kissing Josie's brother, Chris. I'm going to break things off with the other guy I've been sleeping with, because Noah's the one I really want, but trying to manage it has made me even more anxious than ever.

"Emma," Noah whispers. I kiss him back, trying to focus on him, because hooking up usually gives me a break from my sadness, but it's not working this time. I keep flashing back to the night I kissed Chris a few weeks ago. We were so drunk, and we just kissed, but if Josie finds out, she'll never speak to me again. The only other memory I have of that night isn't even my own; it's the video Josie showed me of all of us sitting around Noah's apartment, and I still shudder when I remember her expression as she shoved her phone at me. "Look at my brother," she said, and on the video you could see Chris's face as the camera panned across Noah's living room. You could see him watching me like he was waiting for something. He tipped his beer to take a swig, his eyes never leaving me. But you can tell on the video that I never saw him staring at me because I was too busy smiling up at Noah, who was telling some elaborate story.

"Look at how much Chris likes you," Josie said as she forced me to watch, her pupils made small by the glow of her phone. "It's so obvious. Remember what you promised me, Emma?"

I had no idea Josie was filming all of us that night, and it made me sick to watch that video. All our desires out on display.

Focus on Noah, Emma, please.

Noah's fingers trace patterns over my shoulders, my collarbone, my chest. He's the one I really want to be with, and I should be able to pay attention to him, but I can't control my thoughts lately—they go wherever they want, meandering along a dark path until I either get drunk or fall asleep. I feel the scrape of his stubble against my skin, and I think about how rough and warm he is compared to Josie. Whenever she and I get in bed to talk or watch movies, she's always freezing, always shoving her cold toes beneath the sheets and pretending she doesn't realize they're pressed up on me. It's weird how much more intimate hanging out and talking with Josie feels compared to hooking up with anyone, even Noah. He doesn't really know what to say to me, or how to listen to the things I try to tell him. Mostly he's just interested in the stuff he's telling me about himself or his family, like how his sister just had to drop out of Dartmouth because she couldn't cut it there. Noah said she embarrassed their family, which made Josie laugh and say, *Sounds like you and your family have no idea what the word* embarrassing *means.*

Noah pulls me closer, and I try to shake Josie from my mind, my closest friend, but she's in this room like a ghost, a figment of my imagination. Even when Noah starts whispering in my ear, I still can't pay attention, and it's the same way in my classes. Nothing I do lately seems enough; even my art sucks. Every time I go to paint something, it comes out wrong.

Noah. His hazel eyes are on me now, first locking onto my gaze, and then having their way all over my skin.

Did he start this? Or did I?

The thing about Noah is that he's just so good on paper. You take one look at him and you know he's the captain of some sports team (Lacrosse? Crew? Does it matter?); that he drinks protein shakes after lifting weights; that he's summered in Nantucket since his mother was pregnant; and that he thinks everything is all about him, but in an innocuous way that he'll hopefully grow out of just in time.

Josie sees it, too. "God, Emma, he grew up eating lobster at family picnics in Martha's Vineyard. He's nothing like us," she once said.

Right. Martha's Vineyard: not Nantucket, apparently. I have no idea what the difference is, and if I ever do, maybe it will mean that something has gone irrevocably awry.

But Noah's upbringing doesn't bother me, not even if mine is middle-class and boring in comparison. I like that he's so all-American without really knowing it. I think he actually considers himself something of a rebel, which used to make Josie and me laugh.

We don't laugh as much now. Noah, Josie, and I used to pal around together last year at Yarrow, but then this year I started hooking up with him, and Josie's been so annoyed at me every time I hang out with him, saying that he's stealing me away from her. And now there are these secrets piling up between us. I guess I used to think college would be a continuation of my formally safe teenage life, but it's not. I don't know if that's because of things I'm doing, or if this is just what college is like for everyone. I guess guys hook up with more than one person all the time, but my Catholic upbringing isn't dying easily. I'm nearly paralyzed with anxiety and shame, and I'm lying to everyone I care about—including my sister, whom I've never lied to before.

Noah pushes my camisole higher. "You want this, don't you, Emma?" he asks. I don't think he means to be cliché. I can sense the currents running beneath his skin, even if he can't express them in anything other than words that don't suit him.

His hands push down my pajama pants, and I can see him taking in the sight of my new lace underwear. Josie was the one who said I was too skinny for boy shorts, and on Sunday when we were bumming around the mall eating Annie's pretzels, she steered me into Victoria's Secret, and we found a pale pink thong on sale.

My fingertips trail a line across Noah's broad shoulders, but my eyes wander to the collage of my high school friends hanging above my desk, which actually really freaks me out, because none of my old friends would believe what I've been doing lately.

Josie's desk is lonely in comparison to mine. There's only one photo: Josie and her stepbrother, Chris, standing outside a stone church next to a nun who looks pissed off. Behind our desks, our shades are drawn to avoid imaginary creepers with telescopes in the dorm across the quad, and, maybe even more so, to stave off the four o'clock nightfall. We complain that the weather is *mind-numbing* and *sleepy* in conversations with our classmates, even if that isn't really the whole truth. Because here at college I'm always on the edge, and so is Josie: we're buzzing with something fear-inspiring and razor-sharp, and not even the frigid winter can take it away. We're too wired to sleep, really, except sometimes in the late afternoons when we're supposed to be studying. Josie tries to pass me Tylenol PMs and her prescription stuff, but I won't even smoke cigarettes or pot because that's how nervous I am about getting hooked on something, which drives Josie nuts. "Try being in college," she says every time she nearly convinces me to take something. But I'm terrified and only thinking about myself, about the threat of vast shame in it all: Emma McCullough, art scholarship student, gets nabbed for possession; loses scholarship.

Shudder.

When Noah and I finish hooking up, he checks his phone and says something about lacrosse practice. We climb down the ladder from my bunk, and Noah's yanking his warm-up pants over his boxers when the door swings open. "Hey," he says, seeing Josie before I do.

Josie stops in the doorway, her hand on the knob. Half of her light hair is tied back, and the rest falls in curls over her jacket. The cold has made her cheeks flush, and black mascara makes her blue eyes look even paler. Her face betrays nothing at first, but then her features crack into a smile. I can tell she wants to laugh at my half-dressed state.

"Hey," I say. College is so degrading.

"My class got out early," she says, and it comes out like an apology I don't really think she means.

Noah averts his eyes from her, which I'm pretty sure is because he knows how annoyed she gets now that he's over so much. The room suddenly feels far too small for the three of us, especially when Josie shuts the door behind her. She sets her satchel carefully on her prim white quilt. We bought that quilt together at Target when it went on clearance. Josie has the tightest budget of anyone I know at Yarrow, and she makes it work by buying only things that are perfect. *Less is more,* she always says, making me believe it.

I adjust the waist of my pajama pants as Noah makes small talk. Josie tosses her jacket onto the floor, which is the first sign that she's about to do something strange, because she never puts her clothes on the floor. She takes off her sweater next, and I can hear the break in Noah's stream of chatter. She's wearing a sheer lace bra, nothing else. She turns to us. "What were you saying?" she asks as if everything is normal, like she's just changing the way she would in front of one of the other girls from our dorm.

"Josie," I say, but she ignores me. For a second I think she's about to take off her jeans, but instead she opens a drawer and pulls out a tank top. She turns and looks at both of us before yanking it over her head.

Noah averts his eyes, but it's too late. He catches my glance and says, "I'm gonna go," and then he does, scramming from our room as fast as he can. I'm not stupid enough to think he doesn't want to see her naked. It's just that nothing could be worth the tension in here.

We stare at each other. "What are you *doing*?" I ask.

Josie shrugs. "What's the big deal?" she asks. She lies back against her bed, staring up at the cylindrical metal casing that keeps my top bunk from crashing down on her. "Why does he always take so long to leave?" she asks. She pats the quilt, clearly wanting me to sit beside her.

I give in and go to her. "Give him a break, Josie," I say, because she's always just shy of cruel to Noah.

"You think he deserves a cuddle?" she asks, her pink lips curving into a smile. "It must be why he likes you so much. You're so *nice*, Emma." She says it like an insult, and then shakes her head and sends shiny waves of hair over the pillow. "You're not in love with him, are you?" she asks, her blue eyes all over me.

"No," I say quickly, because I don't think I am, though maybe I could be with more time. Josie turns away. She moves to the window and opens our shades. The sky is the mottled inky color of a bruise, the kind of night that makes me want to press pause as dusk hurtles into darkness, the kind of night that makes me feel desperate. Sometimes I'm not ready for the evening hours with Josie, for whatever she has planned for us, especially when it involves her brother. Chris gets so drunk and picks fights, and it's embarrassing, really. I tried to say something to her once, but she shut me down before I could even finish my sentence.

"Noah's one of the good ones," Josie says as she stares out the window, and I think about how Noah's good in bed and good at life, but obviously I don't say that.

Outside, an oak tree is bare, with branches as thin as fingers. Josie cracks the window, and the branches point at us, accusing us of everything we already know is true. "Josie," I say, pulling the quilt over my legs as cold air rushes into our room. "Really?"

She smirks at me, and then everything switches, and we're okay. We're roommates, best friends, practically sisters. Noah could never come between us. And maybe Chris couldn't, either, especially if she knew it was just a mistake and would never happen again.

Josie comes back to the bed and sits. She pushes her slight body against the bedframe. She's olive-skinned, looking almost tan even in December, making my body appear ghostlier than ever.

My phone buzzes, and I see a text from my sister. "It's from Haley, I gotta get it," I say, reaching for my phone to open the text, but Josie gets it first and puts it in her lap.

"You and Noah are getting serious," she says.

"Um, I guess," I say. I'm not really sure about that, but I want it to be true.

"Are you sure that's a good idea?" she asks.

"What do you mean?" The bare skin on my arms feels cold and itchy, and I pull the blanket higher.

"I mean, you know, your art and stuff," Josie says. "What about our plan to live together in New York after school's done?"

"What does Noah have to do with that?" I ask. She shrugs, and I try to picture what it's going to be like when we graduate, when we make it to New York and live in an apartment together and try to get our paintings into shows. But lately when I try to imagine some great future for myself as an artist, I just can't do it. I try to conjure up the images: me walking the streets of New York City, meeting new people, and painting new things. But no matter how hard I try to fill in the spaces with everything I've always wanted, it all looks blank.

NINE

Haley

An hour after Haley and her mom delivered the news to her dad, Haley sat alone on the worn carpet in the Waverly public library and worried about how hard he'd taken it. She was sitting on the floor and leaning against the stacks of books, her butt asleep, when she got a text from Josie's brother.

Got something to drop off for you from Noah. You home?

Haley exhaled, not wanting to communicate with anyone right now. She pulled her knees tighter against her chest. I'm at the library, she texted back, thinking that would end the communication, but instead Chris shot back a reply.

I can be there in five. See you soon.

Haley sat up straighter against the shelves. Books pressed their spines into hers. I'm on the second floor, she texted back, and then tapped her fingertips against the scratchy carpet. She tried to breathe, inhaling the mustiness of the library she'd loved as a little girl. Her mind had been spinning ever since her meeting with Rappaport. She'd told

Dean she wanted to be alone, and when he blanched, she knew it was the wrong thing to say. Maybe she wasn't supposed to want to be alone so much, certainly not after what had happened at the police station and then with her father. She still saw her dad's body like a silhouette in her mind: slumped forward, shoulders heaving as he wept. She knew Dean wanted to be the person to comfort her, and she'd let him, listening as he told her over and over that this was the news she'd been waiting for, the news that confirmed what she knew about Emma's death to be true. But now she desperately needed to be alone, and to think.

Haley heard Chris before she saw him. It was a quiet library, and the sound of his work boots climbing the rickety stairs made her rise unsteadily. She leaned against a bookshelf, but the angle felt awkward, and as she straightened, Chris emerged and caught her standing there. If she appeared strange to him—waiting in the middle of a row of books, her arms crossed over her chest—he didn't let on. "Haley," he said. The carpet muted the sounds of his boots as he walked toward her. When he stopped, Haley was grateful for the few feet he kept between them.

"Are those for me?" she asked, glancing down at the brochures in his hand, surprised at how nervous she felt. But Chris didn't pass her the brochures. Instead, he brought a hand quickly over his mouth, as if he were brushing something off, and said, "I wanted to talk to you." He looked morbidly uncomfortable, and Haley waited for him to say something. They'd never been alone together.

"I got called in to the police station," he finally said, his blue eyes locked on hers, lashes blinking. "We all did, you know?"

"Josie and Noah, too?" Haley asked.

Chris nodded. Why hadn't Josie or Noah said anything to her? *"And?"* Haley asked, trying to keep the territorial snap out of her voice. She didn't want anyone else talking about her sister. Emma belonged to Haley and her parents, not to them.

"I was high that night at the party in the woods," Chris said, his words hushed.

"You and everyone else," Haley replied, more gently this time.

"I'm just trying to say that I don't remember much," Chris said. "I really liked your sister, but I always thought she, you know, I thought what everyone else thought."

Haley wanted to cover her ears with her hands like a child. Why was he here?

"The things she said to me this one night we got together . . ." Chris went on, and Haley's heart picked up speed.

"I didn't realize you'd ever been more than friends," she said.

"We weren't," Chris said quickly. "Trust me."

"I don't trust you," Haley said before she could think better of it, but Chris didn't seem to take it personally.

"I know what it's like to lose someone," he said, running his hand through his dark hair. "I think you know me and Josie lost our dad. Well, *my* dad, Josie's stepdad. And Josie lost her mom, too. My dad didn't treat Josie right after her mom died, because he never wanted her in the first place. He took stuff out on Josie, stuff that wasn't her fault."

"I'm sorry," Haley managed. Maybe he wasn't the enemy.

"Your sister was . . ." He started again, and when his voice trailed off, Haley waited. She'd learned how to listen in the hospital. You had to keep your mouth shut when you were with a patient; they couldn't tell you what you needed to know if you were blathering on with advice and medical knowledge. Chris's gaze went to the bookshelf, and Haley watched him scan the biographies. Finally he turned back to Haley and said, "That night we got together, your sister was so drunk, but the things she said were a little scary. I didn't take advantage of her or anything, with her being that drunk. That's not what I mean. I'm just telling you she was drunk so you understand she was telling me stuff she maybe wouldn't have otherwise, and it was bleak."

"Like what?" Haley asked, but Chris just shrugged, clearly agitated.

"I don't remember all the specifics," he said. "A lot of it was about how she couldn't paint the same way at Yarrow, how her head wasn't right. I remember she said she felt suffocated, but I didn't really understand by what."

Tears started somewhere behind Haley's eyes. "Why are you telling me this now?"

The brochures fluttered as Chris clenched and unclenched his fist. "I'm just trying to figure out what the cops have," he said, a twitch starting near his upper lip. "What they're getting at with all these crazy questions ten years later."

Haley didn't answer him. "What did you tell them?" she asked instead.

"Nothing new," Chris said. "I was at that party obviously, but so were a ton of kids. And everyone was messed up. Anything could have happened."

Anything could have happened to that girl. There it was again. But Chris didn't sound judgmental of Emma; he sounded like someone who understood that college was a fragile, precarious time. Blackout binge drinking, drugs, sex: Haley didn't understand how parents of college students could sleep at night.

"Look, Chris," Haley said. "I've never thought my sister killed herself. So you're talking to the wrong person if you're looking for reassurance that she wasn't killed by one of your friends at the party."

Chris's cheeks flushed. "It's not that," he said. "Those people weren't even my friends, except Josie and Emma, I mean."

Haley thought back to Chris at Yarrow with his mop of black hair and dingy clothes. After Josie's freshman year, Chris moved three hours east from their hometown to Waverly and worked in an auto body shop. He didn't seem to have anyone else in his life but Josie. The problem, of course, was how he clashed with all the college guys Emma and Josie were friends with. Their lofty, academic egos fed his insecurities like a shot of sugar.

"That night we hooked up, your sister told me how tired and anxious she'd been; she kept saying she just wanted to go to sleep," Chris said, breaking through Haley's thoughts. "And I already told the cops all of this back then when they questioned me, but on the night she disappeared in the woods, she told me she was scared. But not of someone specific. She said she was scared at how everything was about to change."

Haley felt the hair rise on the back of her neck. "Surely you couldn't have taken those words for some kind of goodbye," she said.

"In the moment I didn't," Chris said, his gaze still so far away, like he could still hear Emma telling him. "But in retrospect . . ."

"I'm sure it was easier for everyone, including you, to believe she did it to herself," Haley said. "The school, all her friends. But not my family."

"And maybe that's why you're so convinced she didn't," he said.

"Are we done?" Haley asked.

"I'm just saying, it's normal to want to protect yourself."

"I'm not normal," Haley said. "I've never been, even before my sister disappeared. And I'm not sure what you want me to say. That it's all in the past, and the cops are getting at nothing? I don't believe that, but I get why you might want to."

"What's that supposed to mean? Do the cops think I did something to her?"

"*Did* you do something to her?"

Chris's eyes flickered to the floor. "No. Though I suppose you have no reason to believe me."

"I don't," Haley said. "Murderers usually lie."

"You're cold," Chris said, his gaze darkening, angry now.

Haley shrugged. "Emma was the nice one," she said. "Should I take those?" she asked, pointing to the brochures he still held.

"Yeah, okay," Chris said, flustered. He passed them into her waiting hands, and she was thankful. It made it easier, really, to pretend their meeting hadn't been about something else entirely.

TEN

Emma

Ten years ago

I wake to darkness.

I can still feel the pressure of Chris's hands on me from the dream I just had, and I try hard to fully wake up. Sometimes after I get too drunk, the memories flood back with nebulous shapes and blurred edges, but after that night with Chris, there were no memories, only these dreams I keep having where he kisses me and tells me I should be with *him*, not Noah.

I feel pain in my temples like I'm hungover, even though I'm not. I pull the covers tighter around me, and Josie shifts in the bunk bed below mine. I can tell she's awake by the way she's breathing. The only time she and I can really sleep is during these early evening naps. We climb into bed when it's still light out, and then wake hours later from a syrupy sleep to a pitch-black sky. When I wake, I don't know where I am or how I got there, or if something terrible happened while I was unconscious. But the feeling melts away quickly enough that I forget and sleep again the next day. It's too easy to forget about the despair that follows something that feels so good in the moment.

"Sister?" Josie whispers. We started calling ourselves *sister* because Josie doesn't have a real one, and we like how it makes us feel when we say it, like we're tied by something greater than ordinary friendship.

"Yes, Sister?" I echo back. Of course, I'm careful not to call Josie that in front of Haley because she would probably take it as a diss.

I lean my head over the side of my bunk, and my long, inky hair drapes like a curtain. Moonlight splashes across Josie's pillow and silhouettes her like a halo. I'm pretty sure Josie lied back in August when we moved in together. Getting the top bunk sucks—everyone knows that—but Josie told me she fell out of the bed sometimes, which meant she really needed that bottom bunk to be hers. I'd shrugged and said, "Then let's debunk the beds," but instead of being easy—*sure, fine, swell idea*—Josie had said, "But then we won't have room for a sofa and a mini fridge."

So we did what she said. She's sort of the boss of us. I wish I could be stoic and matter-of-fact the way she is, but there are so many little decisions with their potential for big outcomes, and it's paralyzing, really: to think that any one choice could be the thing that does you in. You could die based on a whim, or some flippant choice you make, or careless thought said out loud to the wrong person. Last year I tried to be good and volunteer at a homeless shelter, but one of the homeless women followed me back to my dorm and started screaming nonsense stuff about Prada bags. (I wasn't carrying one or anything like that. I don't even own one, and even if I did, I would never be rude enough to carry it to a homeless shelter.) *You have to watch your back,* Josie said to me as the woman was carted off by campus security. Josie was the one who had the common sense to call them—she's an expert at taking care of unpleasantness.

Now she sits up so her eyes are even with my upside-down ones.

"You're not sleeping anymore, Sister," she says, and her blinking lashes are still so black with mascara I can make them out even in the moonlight. "So let's go out. Yes?"

"Let's go out," I echo back. Our bunk creaks as I kick off my sheets.

We're juniors, and about half of our class still lives on campus, but the other half moved off. Josie and I stayed on campus because we thought it would be a surprising move, and we liked to be surprising. Not that we really had that many friends asking us to live with them. We're a packaged duo, everyone knows that, and other girls mostly shy away from Josie because she's that beautiful and intimidating. Plus, staying on campus was cheaper, and we were broke.

"Noah's place?" I ask, descending the ladder, thinking once again about how Josie's never fallen out of her lower bunk.

"Do you have money?" she asks.

I turn on my desk lamp and dig in my top drawer. We probably won't need money tonight, but my mom taught me to carry an *emergency twenty dollars*, so I open my wallet and stuff a ten into my back pocket and another into Josie's sweaty hand. The only time she gets hot is when she sleeps. She also has nightmares and screams out stuff like *He's right there!*

I flip the switch, and light floods our room, illuminating my canvas propped against the door of our closet. I feel sick seeing it there, but I can't take my eyes off it: the small dog next to the immaculate hunting pony, which I thought was ironic, now looks flat and boring and too classic in the worst way.

"The shadows are all wrong," I say, my voice wavering.

"The light's terrible in here," Josie says. She knows I'm not talking about something the light in the room can fix, but she doesn't want me to get upset. *You're so emotional,* she's always saying, like it's a curse. Getting depressed seems to be a grave fault of mine, at least according to my mom and Josie. Last year my mother took me to a psychiatrist and said, "He'll know what to do with you," but he didn't. Or maybe I didn't say the right things. I wanted him to give me medication to stop everything that felt so very sad, but he recommended therapy first, and somehow the idea of that exhausted me so much I told my mom he said I was fine. She believed me.

The hunting pony stares back at us, too perfect for his own good.

Josie's a better artist than me. It's something I think she knows but would never speak of. Her work is textured and deconstructed. She tears materials to threads, and then reassembles them into color patterns birthed from her fingertips, making something no one else saw possible. Every professor we have drools over her except for Priya Khatri, our watercolor teacher, which is one of many reasons I like Priya's class the best. Josie's talent makes me jealous, but it also makes me love her even more, and not in the way anyone would think: I don't want her to be my girlfriend or something like that. I just want to be close to her.

"I need to shower," I say.

Josie makes a face like *Really?* but then she shrugs and goes to our sink. She turns the faucet on, and the sound of water fills our tiny room. I wait until she starts splashing her face, knowing her back will be turned long enough for me to dig in my bottom drawer and get what I need.

"Are you sure Noah's home?" Josie asks, her voice muffled in her hands. "Did you talk to him?"

I rifle inside the plastic bag. "They're having people over, not just us," I say, trying to sound casual.

"You think you're gonna get me into the woods, don't you?" Josie asks.

I whip around to face her. Noah and I had been talking about going to a party in the woods tonight because the temperature's finally in the forties and a bunch of his lacrosse friends are going. I didn't tell Josie that, because she's scared of the woods, and we thought we'd have a better chance of convincing her if we were all together at Noah's apartment and she was already drinking. The guys have food, drinks, and a tent packed in Noah's Jeep in case we decide to sleep there, and my job is making sure Josie wears her long puffer coat.

"Maybe," I say, trying not to smile. It's funny seeing something that makes Josie nervous, and it's so random: she grew up in the country, for God's sake. How is she so afraid of the outdoors?

She rolls her eyes. "You and Noah aren't as sneaky as you think you are," she says, but there's no menace in her voice because she's so sure she's right. When she turns back to the sink, I stuff the pregnancy test into my purse. There's a chance she asks why I'm bringing my bag into the bathroom, but she probably won't, and I need to do it tonight because I need to know if it's real; I need to know if that's why I've been feeling so off these past weeks, and I need to know before I see either of *them*. If it's real, if there's a baby in there, I know whose it is without a doubt, because my cycle is like clockwork, and obviously I know the days to avoid having sex.

I can't even imagine how upset my parents will be.

Josie turns from the sink and stares at me like she can read my thoughts. Water beads all over her face. "I'll go to the woods," she says. "I'll invite Chris. He knows those woods like the back of his hand." She says it a little too proudly, like it's an important feat, and then adds, "I'll feel safer with him there."

"Okay," I say, nervous. Does she know I kissed him? "It'll be a good night," I say, but it doesn't feel like the truth.

We stare at each other, and I force a smile. Then I turn and leave her standing alone at the sink. My legs are trembling as I head down the long hallway to the girls' room, and before I get there my phone buzzes with a text from Haley.

I'm downstairs. Come sign me in before I freeze.

I cut right to the elevator. As it descends to the lobby, I try to make my face normal, not like someone about to take her first pregnancy test. Haley knows me better than anyone, and it's uncanny the stuff she can intuit.

The elevator doors open to the lobby, and I see Haley standing near a crappy floral painting that belongs in a Florida hotel. "Hey!" I say as cheerily as I can. "Who signed you in?"

Haley nods toward a girl I don't recognize sitting at the check-in desk. The girl ignores us, her nose buried in a book. I turn back to Haley and smile at the sight of her in my dorm. Her black hair is cropped, and she wears an old army jacket of mine and combat boots. Her eyes flicker over me like always, seeing me. We throw our arms around each other because that's what we always do. "Here," she says when I finally pull away, thrusting a Ziploc bag full of sugar cookies into my hands.

"Thanks," I say, opening the bag, trying one. The smell of sugar fills the lobby air. "You could sell these," I say between bites. "They're amazing."

"I'm trying to get in touch with my nurturing side," Haley says.

I burst out laughing, but Haley's face falls so fast I realize she was being serious. "Sorry," I say. She's an oddball, but she's *my* oddball. "Seriously, they're delicious." She smiles at me, and I ask, "Do you think there's any way Mom lets you come tonight?"

"No way," she says. "You know that."

"I do," I say with a shrug. "But what if you . . ." My voice trails off.

"What if I snuck out again?" she finishes.

"Exactly," I say, swallowing the rest of my cookie. "I don't want to be alone tonight."

"You're not alone," Haley says. "It's a party."

I laugh. "You know what I mean," I say, but it sounds too hollow in the mostly empty lobby.

"I don't," she says, and I realize she really wants me to explain it. Haley's way smarter than me when it comes to academic stuff, but sometimes the day-to-day life stuff she doesn't get as quickly.

"Haven't you ever been with a bunch of people, and you still feel really lonely?" I ask.

"Yeah, all the time," Haley says.

"Well, that's what I mean."

She considers this. "I got it," she says. We stand there eating cookies together for a bit, not really needing to talk, just able to be with each other. For a while now I've wanted to tell Haley that I'm sleeping with Noah, but I want to wait until he's officially my boyfriend because she'll worry less.

"So see you tonight?" I ask. "Maybe?"

"Maybe," she says. We lock eyes, and all the years we have together fill in the spaces between our words. When we embrace again, she feels like home.

ELEVEN

Haley

Haley's head rested against Dean's chest. It was nearly seven, and they were back home in their bedroom in the 1950s bungalow Josie and Noah found them to rent. The walls of the house were mostly bare, and the rooms had minimal furnishings. It gave the bungalow a desolate feeling that wore on Haley, but the house was temporary, a placeholder, somewhere they could stay before their real life started. She snuggled closer to Dean. "And then Chris just passed me the brochures and left the library," she said, "which doesn't even make sense because we already have the list of places we're seeing this weekend."

"Maybe they're private listings," Dean said. They'd kicked aside the pillows and lay on the layers of winter blankets that dressed the bed.

"They're not," Haley said.

Dean shrugged. "He's a weird dude," he said. "And the three of them act like real estate is the most important thing. They're obsessed."

"So are we lately," Haley said. "And it's their job."

"I guess," Dean said. He was so warm beside her.

"Don't you think about our life in each of these houses?" she asked. "All the things we could be, all the things that could go wrong?"

"I don't think about it like that," Dean said, shifting his weight farther away from her.

"Why not?" Haley asked.

"Because it's not helpful," Dean said, like it was the simplest thing in the world.

They were quiet for a moment. "Chris came to find me in the library because he wanted to talk about Emma," Haley said. "I swear I didn't misinterpret things. It had nothing to do with the brochures." Dean rested his hand on her bare shoulder, and even though he wasn't saying anything, it was better with him there.

"I'm sorry, Haley," he finally said, and she melted into him. She was exhausted, but it was too early to sleep.

"Do you think my dad's going to be okay?" she asked softly.

"I do," Dean said. He slung one of his long legs over hers. It was pitch-black outside, no stars, and the only light in the room came from a desk lamp that cast eerie shadows over the cream walls and made the writing utensils look like weapons.

"He's so close to the edge," Haley said. "We all are, I think. But he seems the most likely to fall off it. It was like he lost Emma again tonight, in some way."

"And for you?" Dean asked.

Haley tilted her chin to see his features drawn. "I'm not sure," she said. "I'm not thinking straight. I keep thinking about Susie, actually."

"Who's Susie?"

"My cadaver at school, I've told you that," Haley said, trying to keep the snap out of her voice. "She looks like Emma, remember?"

Dean nodded, adjusted his body on the blankets. He would remember that part.

"I don't know how Susie died yet," Haley said. "But I'll likely find out over the next few months. And I keep thinking about bodies and evidence, and not just evidence that leads to someone dying, but even the evidence of how they've lived. It's all there in the body in some way, bad stuff like trauma, but happy scars, too—the cadaver next to mine has a cesarean scar. And ever since I started med school, I have these recurring thoughts about Emma's body, that if I could just see her again, I would know what happened to her." Dean was quiet. Haley swore she could hear rushing water, but it must have been a passing car or trick of the ear; they didn't live close enough to the river for it to be real. She propped herself onto her elbow. "Do you have any memories of my sister at Yarrow?" She'd only asked this question once or twice, because Dean and Emma weren't even acquaintances, let alone friends.

"I'm sorry, Haley," he said, a pained look on his face. "I really don't."

"You must have seen her from time to time," Haley said, her voice harder than she meant it to be.

"Sure, yeah," Dean said quickly, clearly trying to appease her, "around campus." His eyes cut away from hers like he didn't want to see her cry. At work Dean was so incredibly successful, so powerful, and part of that was his ability to sense and give his high-powered clients what they needed on a moment-to-moment basis. But he couldn't do that for Haley, and he knew it. At least not when it came to Emma.

"Well, what was she like?" Haley pressed.

"You knew what she was like better than anyone," Dean said, and Haley could tell he was trying not to sound exasperated.

"But how did she come off to other people?" she asked, unable to stop herself from trying. Just a morsel about Emma—that's all she needed.

Dean was quiet again for a moment. Then he said, "She just seemed artistic, I guess, something about her. The way she dressed, and how she carried herself."

He was right. Haley pressed her body closer to Dean, wanting to feel her skin and drown out her mind. Dean didn't say anything; he just squeezed with the exact amount of bear hug she craved. It was in moments like these that she understood how much she wanted him and all that entailed: a life lived together instead of an existence spent in limbo; a future instead of a past; and a quiet, peaceful respite from the ever-present thoughts of her gone sister.

TWELVE

Emma

Ten years ago

I'm in the bathroom stall—which smells like sugar cookies because I shoved Haley's care package in my bag—and my hands are shaking around the pregnancy stick. These are the kind of juxtapositions of college that make me so crazy. I'll do something like sleep with Noah, who isn't even technically my boyfriend, and then call my parents and have a totally normal conversation about something mundane, like the art project I have due. Or I'll drink too much and write an email to my grandpa, remembering some long-ago way he showed Haley and me kindness. Or like in this case, when I'm inhaling the homey smell of my sister's cookies while I take a pregnancy test. How messed up am I?

I already peed on the thing, and now I'm waiting for the words to pop up in the little window. It's taking forever. If I'm pregnant, the baby's definitely Noah's, because like I said, I know my cycle. I slept with someone else on the sixth day of my cycle, right after my period ended. I remember that, because I remember being worried that my period wasn't totally over, and I didn't want it to get on his sheets, because he was weird about stuff like that, which made no sense given his profession. Anyway, I didn't get my period on his sheets. And I almost broke things off that night, because stuff had been getting strained between us, but I didn't. Obviously I will now, even if this test says I'm not pregnant. Noah's the one I want—he's the one I've always wanted.

Obviously I wish Josie wasn't so annoyed by Noah and me getting serious, but she'll get over it. Plus she's seeing this other guy who's literally *tall, dark, and handsome*. He seems like more of a Goody Two-shoes than most guys she's attracted to, but I think in the end that would be good for her.

God. Why is this thing taking so long? I adjust my butt on the toilet seat. I guess I could pull up my pajama pants, but I'm not sure I can do that without jostling the pregnancy test around, and I think you're supposed to keep it level.

Creak goes the door to the girls' room, and I jump. Can someone see through the cracks in the stall doors? Is it Josie?

Footsteps pad across the tile, and my heart races. The sound of water whooshes in the shower stall. It can't be Josie—she would have said something; she would have tried to figure out if I was in here. Steam billows over the top of the shower toward my stall. Our shared bathroom areas are so small, and they get way too steamy if someone blasts the water on full heat. Now I'm sweating as I use my fingertip to wipe the window of the test, praying it won't steam over. But there isn't time for that to matter, not anymore, because the single word stares up at me, declaring my fate.

Pregnant.

My heart thuds like crazy against my chest. I knew it—or at least, I sort of did. I pull my pants up with shaking hands. I go to throw away the test in the tiny garbage can, but there's no trash in it yet, and everyone will see it. *Ugh.* I shove it in my pocket—I just need to get out of here. I push through the door to the bathroom and go looking for Josie.

THIRTEEN

Priya

Priya crossed the kitchen to unearth her phone from where she'd hidden it inside her handbag. There weren't any other messages from Josie, and as Priya locked the phone she thought of how funny it was that her husband, of all people, didn't have a password-protected phone, other than the one he used for work. Brad was careful in many ways, particularly with Priya, mostly treating her like a glass figurine that could go off kilter and shatter. But as careful as he was with Priya's moods, he wasn't particularly careful with his personal phone. It was where she'd seen the text from the woman he'd had an affair with three years ago. The woman had included a smiley-faced emoticon below her naked body, and it had taken Priya a while to realize who the woman actually was. She felt shocked all over again when she realized she knew her. The woman looked so different naked, and plus, Priya had felt so icky staring at the sexy photo that she kept having to look away. She'd finally poured herself a glass of wine to calm her nerves, as though she were settling in to watch a TV show instead of study photos of her husband's lover, but Elliot was in bed, and she had at least an hour alone to go through Brad's texts before he returned from the hospital. So, armed with a glass of rosé—which felt far too cheery for the circumstances, but it was all she had—she inspected the evidence. The woman had taken a photo of herself kneeling on bedsheets in that cliché pose of legs spread slightly apart, with a hand between them, and breasts caught in what seemed like midbounce. (Or maybe that was just what breasts that hadn't spent two years breastfeeding looked like. Were Priya's once that high?) The thing about the woman's pose was that it was the kind of thing you could only do early on in a relationship. Priya was pretty sure Brad would think she was insane if she did something like that.

Priya had studied the woman's face so carefully that night. It was heart-shaped and pale, with a glossy-lipped smile and subtle eye makeup, but it was absolutely the woman who worked the front desk at the local gym. The woman—*Tracy? Nancy?*—usually wore glasses and was always pleasant and not even a little conciliatory as she handed Priya a towel. Never once had her eyes telegraphed, *I'm so sorry I'm sleeping with your husband, but here's a fluffy towel!* Brad hadn't entered the woman as a contact into his phone, it was just a 914 number, and Priya had scrolled to see banal text messages that made her indescribably depressed.

Meet you at eight?

when do you get off work?

U teaching tonight?

And then she saw the one that made her cry. Did you tell her yet?

Was that truly how deep in he was with this woman, that they'd had some kind of discussion debating whether Brad should tell Priya?

That night, when Priya confronted him, he broke down. He said he'd made a terrible mistake, and that he'd never do it again, and that the woman was his only transgression since the mistake he made years ago. Priya feared she was being the most naive woman on planet Earth, but she believed him, and she decided to stay.

FOURTEEN

Emma

Ten years ago

I'm standing outside the door of town house 24B. I'm out of breath, because I practically sprinted here. At the last minute I decided not to tell Josie about the pregnancy and instead told her I just had to pick up art supplies I left in the studio and that I'd be right back so we could go to Noah's. I don't want her to find out about what I've been up to with this guy because I *really* don't want her telling Noah. It's part of the reason I'm coming here tonight to end it, so that nothing gets in the way of Noah and me. He'll take me so much more seriously if I end it in person instead of over text. He barely even carries a phone.

Town houses line the east side of Yarrow's campus, redbrick things with putty-colored frames on the windows. They're too new to be charming, but the people who live here—mostly professors and administrative staff—have tried their best, with flower boxes and old-fashioned bicycles leaning against iron railings. The teachers at Yarrow can be a little hipster and *above it all*, which is why I mention the old bicycles. Instead of buying shiny new ones, they ride along the sidewalks on the old dilapidated ones, sporting wan smiles and carting their books in the functional metal basket attached to the handlebars. It's a look, I guess. And it suits most of them.

But not Brad. I can tell he likes nice stuff by the way he decorated his town house. I've only been inside twice because obviously it's risky for us to be sleeping together, and I wouldn't want to get him in trouble, because he's not only superhot but also really sweet and decent, other than sleeping with a student, I guess . . . but it's not like I'm *his* student. And he's just a TA for a pre-med science class, which is barely even being a teacher. His real job is as a surgery resident at Waverly Memorial. Plus, he didn't even know I was a Yarrow student until we'd hung out a bunch of times. I didn't lie about it exactly; I just didn't mention it. We met at a coffeehouse and had lattes together, and it's all been mostly innocent. He said he thought I was really pretty and artsy, although I don't feel very pretty or artsy these days. He's a little intense, but not into drugs or anything weird, and at first he wasn't possessive about seeing me. I think that's what interested me when we started seeing each other, the lack of desperation, and the ease of it all. Plus I'd never been with an older guy, and there was something so exciting about that. I think he's in his late twenties or so, but I purposely haven't Google-stalked him because like I said, it was feeling so easy, and I didn't want to ruin it because being with him felt like a break from my other life with Josie and Noah. But lately Brad's been more desperate, more possessive.

I raise my hand and knock, thinking about the baby inside my stomach. How big is she? (I know she's a *she*—I just do.) She's got to be so tiny if I remember right from high school biology classes. What's Noah going to say tonight when I tell him? What are my parents going to say? What am I going to *do*?

The door swings open, and my mind trips over itself when I see the face in front of me. *What's my art teacher doing here?* Her black hair is usually tied into a high bun in watercolor class, but now it's long and loose and falling over her shoulders. Gone is her uniform of leggings and a paint-spattered tank, and in its place is a chenille robe, tied loosely over her protruding stomach.

"Priya?" I say, my heart pounding.

"Emma, hi," she says, an edge in her voice. Her hand goes to the swell of her stomach.

"Do you live here?" I ask. The town houses look identical, and it's dark out—is it possible I knocked on the wrong door? My neck cranes to check out the number again.

"My fiancé lives here, Emma," she answers, and the way she says my name sounds very different from the way she says it in class.

"Oh," I say, stalling, and then I start backing away from her, from *this*, inch by inch.

"Can I help you with something?" she asks, her eyes narrowing.

Lie to her. Think of something. Just tell her a lie!

But I can't. Something's wrong with me—I can't say anything at all. I back down the stairs, gripping on to the railing, scared I'm going to fall and hurt my tiny baby, which is probably not even possible at this stage of a pregnancy. And then I think about Priya's baby, who is apparently Brad's baby, and then I start thinking about how when these two babies grow up, they won't ever know that they were face-to-face like this one winter night, just a few feet apart when their mothers realized they were sleeping with the same man.

And then I throw up.

I'm still on the steps; I haven't even made it to the sidewalk yet. "Emma?" Priya says as I heave. "Are you all right?" I hear the door close behind her, and she comes toward me, but I don't want this—I don't want to make a scene; I don't want anyone else seeing us. I wipe my mouth and stumble down the steps. "Leave me alone," I hiss. I say it as meanly as I can so she won't come after me, and she doesn't.

I race over the sidewalk. I only turn around once to see Priya still standing on the steps in her robe, her hand on her stomach as though she can shield the baby—her future—from all of this. A streetlight sets her black hair aglow.

Finally the row of town houses ends, and I round the corner, collapsing against the redbrick wall. I catch my breath for a moment, and then I pull my phone from the pocket of my jeans. I fire off three texts to Brad, pressing the send key with shaking fingers.

Just went to your house and talked to your fiancé.

I know her. She's my teacher.

Stay away from me.

FIFTEEN

Priya

P riya was still in the kitchen fumbling inside her bag to find her
medication as Brad paced the creaking floorboards overhead. He'd
told her she could take up to four pills per day, but when she googled
the medication, the dosage seemed more aggressive than what WebMD
said to do.

Priya swallowed her fourth pill and went back to the table. She
sat, waiting for the blurry, numb feeling to come, staring at the empty
space across from her. Who had texted her husband to make him
hurry from the room? When her thoughts started to soften around
the edges, she drifted back to the texts she'd found ten years ago from
Emma.

Just went to your house and talked to your fiancé.

I know her. She's my teacher.

Stay away from me.

Priya had never stopped thinking about that night Emma showed
up on the steps of Brad's town house with their illicit relationship written all over her face; it was always right there on the fringe of Priya's

thoughts, where it belonged. Emma McCullough had haunted Priya for ten years now, and the girl would most likely haunt Priya until the day she died.

Brad's stir-fry sat unfinished on his plate, the soy sauce and chicken fat congealing. Priya could hear his muffled voice upstairs as she took a slow sip of her water and glanced out the french doors into her neighbor's yard. She wished she could catch sight of Elliot, but it was too cold for the neighborhood kids to be playing outside, and they did different things now on play dates, didn't they? Less outdoor play, more iPads and video games. When had that happened? Could they ever go back?

That night ten years ago, after Emma showed up, Priya didn't confront Brad right away. She'd wanted to talk to Emma once more, to get all the details before Brad could convince Emma not to tell her anything. But the following Monday morning, just as Priya was getting her classroom ready for nine a.m. watercolor class and trying to figure out what she was even going to say to Emma, a police detective knocked on the door. "Can I help you?" she'd asked, swinging it open. She was breathing heavily just from the trek across the classroom; she was due with Elliot any day.

"Have a minute?" the detective had asked, not waiting for an answer.

Priya had wiped paint from her cheek as she followed him across the studio, and he'd seemed almost relaxed as he studied the paintings clipped to easels. "You teach Emma McCullough?" he asked.

Priya's body had reacted before her brain. Adrenaline coursed through her, and blood rushed from her hands and feet into her midsection. Maybe it was her body's way of protecting the baby, but it left her with the odd sense of being dismembered, of floating through space as only a mother, a round pregnant ball without limbs to anchor it.

"Yes," she'd answered the detective, shifting her weight. "I do."

"Any of these hers?" he asked casually, studying the paintings as if they were at an exhibit together.

"This one," Priya said, gesturing to a watercolor of a cracked vase holding vibrant purple orchids. It wasn't Emma's best, but he wouldn't know that. Priya leaned against an easel, unsteady.

"Are you all right?" the detective had asked, his eyes traveling up and down her body, lingering on Elliot inside her.

"I'm fine," Priya had said. Sweat broke out along her hairline. "I'm just very pregnant."

"Please, sit down," the detective instructed, pulling out a chair. Priya did as he said, trying to focus as he spoke. "Emma went missing on Saturday night," he'd told her, his words even, "and now we're speaking with her teachers, trying to get a sense of if she was having any problems, any difficulties in school or with friends." The detective's eyes were on her face, and she prayed he couldn't see the way her chest was heaving as she tried to breathe. "We're trying to figure out if she had any reason to run away, or to hurt herself," he said, his words slowing, each one hitting her like a slap. Priya nodded as her heart raced on. Could Brad have done something to Emma? Scared her in some way, or worse? She didn't think so—she honestly didn't. Brad wasn't religious, but he was one of those people who believed life was sacred. It was what drove him to be a doctor, he'd once said, the idea of protecting God-given life. Surely he couldn't hurt a young girl? Or was Priya stupid to even think that? Did she know him well enough to know for sure? She was carrying his child: Could she really trust herself to think rationally about this?

After Priya lied to the detective and told him she knew nothing, she canceled class and raced home. Elliot's nursery was all set up for his arrival, and that's where she found Brad, sleeping in the rocking chair, still in his scrubs from the previous night when he'd assisted in an emergency surgery. Brad had turned on the sound machine, and a steady heartbeat filled the room. "Brad," Priya managed to say, and when he woke, he rubbed his eyes and grinned at her. She couldn't figure out why, until he asked, "Is it time? Is the baby coming?"

"No," Priya said as he got out of the rocking chair and strode toward her. Her heart was beating so fast she thought she might die right there and lose everything. She righted herself against the changing table. "A detective just came to my class, Brad. Asking about Emma McCullough."

Brad stopped dead. What he'd done was all over his face, and Priya knew she'd never need to ask if he'd slept with Emma.

She let go of the table. She felt a little steadier now. He'd cheated—she could deal with that; it wasn't a crime. But if he'd hurt Emma, she needed to know now, so she could end it. "Did you do something to her?" Priya asked, her words barely audible amid the pulse of the sound machine.

Brad shook his head. "No," he said. "No, no, I didn't. Priya? Sit." He gestured to the rocking chair, but Priya was sick of people telling her to sit down.

"No," she said. "I don't need to sit, I need you to tell me if you . . ." She bent forward, unable to finish her sentence. She tried to straighten up, but suddenly she wasn't feeling very well. Her stomach tightened like a fist, and she clutched her lower belly.

"Priya?" Brad asked.

She couldn't speak. Liquid trickled into her underwear and leggings. It wasn't a gush like in the movies, but it was unmistakable. It was time to have Elliot.

As they sped toward the hospital, Priya screamed through contractions, and when she had a break from those, she screamed at Brad. He admitted to sleeping with Emma—he didn't even try to lie. He apologized profusely, and swore up and down that he didn't hurt her, that he could never hurt her, or anyone. By the time they arrived at the hospital, Priya could barely walk. An orderly put her into a wheelchair and wheeled her into labor and delivery. The contractions were coming on faster now, and she and Brad spoke in hushed voices while nurses came in and out of the room. Tears streamed over Brad's face as he apologized, and Priya tried to face the reality that her fiancé had slept with a twenty-one-year-old girl who had disappeared and might be hurt. If she believed him, she needed to protect the father of her child, but if she didn't, she needed to turn him in, to protect someone else's child. This contradiction played through her mind on an endless loop, but then there was the urge to push, and suddenly she couldn't focus on anything other than this baby who wanted to be born. She looked up at her fiancé's pleading face hovering over hers, and she decided to believe him. She took his hand and started breathing and pushing, screaming and crying. Minutes later, Elliot emerged with cries of his own. Priya held her baby close, warm against her chest, and never spoke of Emma McCullough again.

SIXTEEN

Haley

Haley woke from her dreams drenched in sweat. Emma still filtered through her mind in the space between asleep and awake. *I'm waiting for you to find me,* Emma had said, dressed in the same white tank she'd been wearing the night Haley saw her in the lobby for the last time. *Figure me out, Haley. Please, look a little closer.*

"Dean!" Haley heard herself cry out. She turned toward him, but the sheets were empty. She swung her legs over the side of the bed and saw moonlight on the floor. The clock on their bedside table read just past midnight.

"Dean?" Haley called as she stepped across the wide wooden planks. A blue glow came from the bathroom, and she followed it. She swung open the door to see Dean sitting on the cold tiled floor, his back pressed against the bathtub. He was staring down at his phone, and when he looked up, his features were so furrowed she hardly recognized him.

"Haley," he said. He set down his phone with the screen side against the tiles, making them ghostly white. "You okay?" he asked, standing and coming toward her.

Haley rubbed her eyes, but she didn't feel tired anymore. She glanced down at Dean's phone. "I'm fine," she said as he wrapped his arms around her. "It was just a dream." She tried to let herself relax into his embrace, but she couldn't. "What were you doing in here?"

"Just work emails," Dean said. "I couldn't sleep." He pulled her tighter against his chest until she felt too hot and itchy against his Yarrow sweatshirt, until she couldn't breathe right. She pulled away, gasping. "Let's go back to bed," she said, trying to shake a feeling she couldn't quite name.

SEVENTEEN

Priya

The next morning snow fell heavily from a white sky. Priya drove along the interstate toward Josie's open house, gripping the wheel and arching forward. The wipers beat away the snow, and Priya tried to focus on the clean patch of road in front of her. It was 10:49, and she wanted to be there right when Josie had told her to be—just before eleven—so she could get this over with. Hopefully the snow wouldn't delay Josie's open house visitors, because Priya needed an easy out. *What a lovely home!* she imagined saying as she excused herself from Josie and any potential clients.

Priya drove past the Protestant church on Main Street with its spire shooting into the white winter sky, and then the yoga studio and the new coffee shop. Her nerves made her fingers shaky against the steering wheel. She had her medication ready if she needed it, but she was trying not to take it. She'd woken up this morning feeling not quite right, and she wondered again if maybe Brad had gotten the dosage wrong.

Priya had to admit, the open house was a good place to meet. If Brad ever found out, Priya could always say she saw the gorgeous colonial with green shutters online and wanted to see it for herself. Josie and Priya had met exactly three times over the past decade, and Brad had never caught her. The meetings always seemed to happen when the weather took a turn to frigid. (Emma had disappeared in the winter, so maybe it triggered something in Josie, something she wanted to try to make amends for.) During their meetings, Josie had said many condemning things about Brad, mostly involving the emails she'd found and deleted on Emma's computer back in college. Apparently when Emma disappeared, Josie's biggest concern was that Emma would be in trouble for sleeping with Brad because he was a teacher, and that she'd lose her scholarship, which is why she deleted all the emails between Brad and Emma before the cops could secure her laptop.

Priya could never exactly figure out Josie's motive for telling her these things. Was she trying to warn Priya, convinced that Brad had done it, or was she hanging it over Priya's head for some kind of blackmail to eventually be used against her and Brad?

Still, Priya went to the illicit meetings when Josie requested them. They seemed like a kind of therapy for Josie, the way she poured out her fears that Brad had done something to her roommate and that she should have stopped it. And Josie always seemed to take solace in the fact that Priya didn't actually believe her husband had hurt Emma. Josie listened intently as Priya went on about what a gentle person Brad was, and she always exhaled when Priya was done convincing her anew of Brad's innocence, as though Priya was absolving Josie, too, of having done anything wrong. Priya thought it must be what priests felt like, to absolve and console with that kind of power.

Something's changed, and I need to explain.

That's what Josie's text had said yesterday. But what could have possibly changed after all these years?

Priya turned right onto Carrington Road. She scanned for house numbers and tried to get her bearings, which was nearly impossible in the whiteout weather. A yellow farmhouse with black shutters and a red barn sat high on a hill, and Josie was pretty sure she could make out the number three on a stone pillar covered in snow. She hugged the right side of the road, careful not to veer onto a lawn. Carrington Road was much snowier than the interstate, and Priya's nerves spiked as she fishtailed once, then twice, failing to steady the car. She finally righted it, and pressed the accelerator to keep climbing the hill past two more houses. She tensed when the car skidded at the top, terrified the wheels wouldn't grip the slick pavement, imagining herself sliding back down the hill and into traffic. She glanced in her rearview mirror and saw a black Land Rover behind her. The person was driving too fast, coming too close. Priya had the childish urge to press her brakes and slow down even more. She despised people who drove carelessly in bad weather. Did they have nothing to lose?

Her foot was shaky against the accelerator. The car behind her was nearly at her bumper, and she could make out a dark-haired man and woman, the man driving and the woman gesticulating in the passenger seat. They were definitely arguing. Priya almost pulled over to let them pass, but she worried she'd get stuck on the side of the road, or that the people would crash into her car as they tried to swerve around her. "Back off!" she yelled, and even though she knew they couldn't hear her, the man seemed to notice how much he was tailgating her and suddenly slowed.

Priya let go of a breath. The Land Rover followed her down the slippery hill and around the next bend. Priya could barely see the road, but she made out three blue balloons tied to a mailbox, and thank goodness, because the snow had erased any sign of a house number. It had to be the open house. Priya pulled carefully into the driveway, but to her dismay, so did the Land Rover. Priya's heart raced as she followed the curve of the driveway. Why had Josie asked her to come only a few minutes before eleven? This was so foolish—Priya would never be able to talk to her alone now. She tried to breathe, tried to figure out what to do. The driveway was too narrow for her to turn the car around, even without the snow.

She kept going. The driveway was long and winding, and when the house came into view, Priya marveled at its classic beauty. She was so taken by the white house with green shutters that it took her a moment to realize that Josie's car wasn't the only one parked near the garage.

Priya's heart pounded as she studied the license plate of the Highlander.

Brad was here.

EIGHTEEN

Haley

T his is mortifying," Haley said as she and Dean went up the driveway toward the open house behind the Subaru he'd been tailgating. "This woman's going to think we're insane."

"Who cares?" Dean asked. It was so callous and unlike him that Haley's mouth dropped an inch. "Sorry," he muttered, navigating the snowy driveway. He pulled the car behind the woman's Subaru, boxing her in.

"Perfect," Haley said beneath her breath.

"What did you just say?" Dean asked.

Haley was so shaken from the fight they'd gotten into this morning over absolutely nothing, but she couldn't back down. "She can't even leave now, Dean," she said. "You've blocked her exit."

Dean grumbled something inaudible and backed up the car. The sound of snow and ice being crushed by tires filled Haley's ears. She hated winter.

"Sorry," Dean said again. "Okay? I'm sorry for the fight this morning; I'm sorry for tailgating the woman; I'm sorry about my parking job."

Haley nodded toward the woman. "She's the one you should apologize to," she said. Why couldn't she ever let anything go?

The top of the driveway was framed by a circle of evergreens, and Josie and Noah's SUV was parked in the driveway next to a Highlander, still running, beneath a basketball hoop. Haley tried to catch a glimpse of the woman in the Subaru, but all she could see was her black hair high in a bun. The woman was turned at an awkward angle, staring at the Highlander. Maybe the woman was thinking what Haley was, which was that there were more cars than she'd expected to see at an open house on a snowy January morning. Haley really wasn't looking forward to making small talk with other prospective buyers. She exhaled, turning away from the woman and taking in the house, a cream-colored colonial with shining green shutters, somehow both grand and understated. It was beautiful, exactly as Josie had promised.

Haley turned to Dean. His jaw was tight, and she could see his eyes roving the house. "It's gorgeous," Haley said, as close to an apology as she was willing to give him.

"It is," Dean said, and he turned to face her. The sky was darkening with the storm, and his five-o'clock shadow looked heavier than usual. She tried to smile at him, to let this morning go, but she was still so furious about the fight. She'd been prickly with him all morning—she'd woken up with such an awful feeling after her night dreaming of Emma, and she couldn't seem to shake it—but then Dean lost his patience and told her to snap out of her foul mood. She'd burst into tears, shouting at him that she should be allowed to be in a foul mood because of what she'd found out about Emma the day before at the precinct. Dean stormed out of the house, saying he had to get groceries before the snow got any worse, and he didn't come back until it was time to pick her up for the open house.

"Should we even be doing this?" Dean asked gently. The grand house was silhouetted behind him, the snow falling heavily, and the evergreen trees looming.

"What do you mean?" Haley asked, hating the insecurity in her voice. She knew what he meant: *Should we really be seeing a potential home right now, after how badly we fought?* She could still feel the hoarseness in her throat. "Are you saying we shouldn't be buying a house together?" A hot prick of tears started behind her eyes.

"No, Haley, that's not what I'm saying," Dean said gently. His hands were still wrapped over the steering wheel, like he wasn't ready to commit to leaving the car. Haley glanced toward the house, half expecting Josie to emerge at any moment through the front door. She turned back to Dean, about to say she was sorry, when she caught sight of the man exiting the Highlander. Reddish-blond hair poked out of a gray wool ski cap, and Haley saw the broad-shouldered body and the way his feet shuffled over the snow. "That's my anatomy professor," she said to Dean. "*God*, how *awkward*." She was aware of how young she sounded, like a teenager who'd spotted her teacher in the grocery store. She cleared her throat, hoping Dean hadn't noticed. There was a six-year age difference between them, and sometimes it felt like more. "Do you think he and his wife are looking at the house?" she asked, watching as Brad moved slowly over the snowy driveway toward the Subaru. Maybe the woman in the Subaru was his wife? Had they come separately?

Dean wasn't saying anything. He wasn't snapping out of this fight like he did others. "Dean?" Haley asked, and when he finally turned to her, his gaze was wild. "Are you all right?" she asked, studying his face. She was vaguely aware that Brad had stopped outside the Subaru. The woman had to be his wife, *Priya the artist,* as he'd described her in class.

Dean said he was fine and turned away, staring straight ahead through the swiping wipers. A tuft of his dark hair shot straight up, and Haley wondered why he hadn't showered today. He was usually so fastidious about his appearance. "We should go in now," he said, his voice hard. He turned off the ignition and opened the car door.

"Don't you want your coat?" Haley asked, but he was already standing in the snow.

Haley pulled on a snow hat and pushed open the car door. Cold air prickled her exposed skin, and she glanced nervously toward Brad. "Dr.

Aarons?" she called out, trying to sound respectful and friendly and not like a college kid calling out across the quad.

Brad lifted his eyes from the Subaru and did a double take when he saw her. "Haley, hi," he said. His eyes went from her to Dean, and then he straightened, looking unsure.

They were too far apart to make introductions, so Haley started toward the Subaru because she didn't know what else to do. She hated awkward social moments like this. "This is my fiancé, Dean," she said as they neared the car. The woman inside the Subaru still hadn't opened the door. Her wipers were off, and a thin layer of snow had obscured the windshield.

Brad left the side of the Subaru and came toward them. "Brad Aarons," he said, putting out a large hand for Dean to shake.

"Dean Walters," Dean said, and Haley imagined herself saying *Haley Walters* for the rest of her life, but it left a funny taste in her mouth. Maybe she wouldn't change her name after all.

"Freezing today," Dean said, his voice low and unfamiliar.

Brad nodded, and then he glanced over his shoulder at the Subaru, looking a little desperate.

The car door finally opened, and a petite woman emerged. She was fine-boned and beautiful, but she looked a little off, too. She wasn't dressed right for the snow, for starters, in her light jacket, jeans, and clogs, and her face was drawn and nervous. Haley tried to sound warm as she introduced herself, wishing she were one of those people who put others at ease.

"Hi," the woman said, raising a bare hand with long, skinny fingers. Her voice was nearly inaudible in the cold gusts of air, but Haley heard her say, "Priya."

So it was her. "I take anatomy with Brad," Haley said. Priya blinked, and Haley wanted to kick herself for referring to him so casually in front of his wife. "With Dr. Aarons," she added awkwardly, making it even worse.

"How nice," Priya said, and then she tried to shut the car door against the storm, but it wouldn't close all the way. She was the kind of thin that looked a little weak, and Haley found herself wishing Brad would just jump in and slam the door for her. The wind was picking up speed, whistling through the trees and making the branches sway.

Dean introduced himself to Priya, and then to Haley he said, "We should go in," but he didn't wait for her. He took off toward the house before she could say anything, and Haley felt paralyzed—it seemed like she should be friendly and wait for Brad and Priya, but Priya was still struggling with the car door, and every second Haley stood there waiting and watching her felt painful.

"I'll get it," Brad said, slamming the door with a thud, and the three of them followed Dean along the snowy walk. Josie must have attempted shoveling, because they could almost see the stones beneath. A branch cracked overhead, and Haley flinched. She glanced up to see it dangling over them, kept from falling by two other branches that cradled it in midair. She hurried to catch up with Dean. "Be careful," she said as he climbed the front steps.

"I got it," Dean snapped, but then he turned to help her. He reached out a strong, solid hand, and in that moment, he was hers again, her beloved fiancé, the person she loved and trusted above almost anyone else. Why was it that when they fought, she fantasized about leaving him? Was that normal?

Priya and Brad silently climbed the front steps behind them. Dean knocked on the door, and when there wasn't an answer, he rang the bell. Haley turned to exchange a sheepish look with Priya, who was tugging the sleeves of her denim jacket over her hands. She had to be freezing. Dean rang the bell again, and when there was still no answer, he turned the knob. The door opened easily into a wide foyer. Gleaming gray hardwood covered the floors, and an entry table covered with flower arrangements sat beneath a crystal chandelier. It was lovely, and Haley greedily, instinctively pushed inside past Dean, relieved to be out of the storm.

"Josie?" Dean called out. He followed Haley inside, with Priya and Brad on his heels. Brad slammed the door behind the four of them, and the house was eerily quiet without the sounds of the storm. It was also far too chilly, as though Josie had forgotten to turn on the heat. "Josie?" Dean called again. "Hello? Is anyone here?"

NINETEEN

Priya

Priya listened to the echo of the dark-haired man's voice as he called for Josie. *Dean*—that was his name. On any other day Priya would try to make small talk, but she was too focused on how fast her heart was racing, and the way Brad was trying to catch her gaze. She couldn't even bear to look at him—she couldn't piece together how or why he was here. He'd been waiting in his car when she arrived, so clearly he hadn't followed her. Had he seen her text exchange with Josie? Priya had memorized the location of the open house and deleted her texts, and she'd kept her phone on her all day yesterday and this morning, too, just to be safe. But she'd been so hazy with the medication, maybe she thought she'd deleted the texts but hadn't, or maybe there was some way to retrieve deleted messages?

"Hello!" Dean called out again. His wife (or had he said fiancée?), Haley, exchanged a sheepish glance with Brad.

Priya wished she could say something casual, but she couldn't come up with anything that would make sense. Should she pretend she was here at the open house with Brad to see the home as a potential purchase? She turned to watch Brad fidget with the zipper on his down jacket. He overheated so easily, and normally he tore his coat off as soon as he stepped inside any house, but this one was freezing.

On the entryway table was the typical sign-in sheet real estate agents use to record guests' attendance at open houses, and Priya moved toward it, trying to seem like everything about her being here was normal. "I'll sign us in," Priya said, still not looking at Brad.

"Maybe Josie's upstairs?" Haley suggested, her voice echoing through the high-ceilinged foyer. Priya turned to stare. Haley looked young, probably in her midtwenties, and with her cropped dark hair, leggings, and black bomber jacket, she seemed a shade too punk rock to be looking at such a classic suburban home.

Priya bent forward and wrote her name on Josie's sign-in sheet, smelling gardenias from the flower arrangement nestled inside a blue-and-white vase. *WELCOME!* Josie had written at the top. "She's definitely here," Priya said, pointing to what she figured had to be Josie's handwriting. No one said anything as Priya filled in her email. She felt the heat of her husband's stare against her back, and then turned and met his eyes. He didn't look as furious as she thought he would. He looked a little nervous, actually.

"Should we go upstairs?" Haley asked, staring at all of them. Priya glanced around and quickly assessed the home: new hardwood floors, top-of-the-line light fixtures, intricate millwork, and all of it complemented by tasteful furniture that looked straight out of a Lillian August showroom, though Priya imagined someone like Haley would decorate it quite differently if she moved in.

"Sure," Priya said. "Maybe she can't hear us down here." She followed Haley toward the staircase, but just then a whistling noise came from the back of the house, as though a window was open, and the storm was coming inside.

TWENTY

Haley

"Did you hear that?" Haley asked Dean, but he didn't respond. He turned on his heel and strode toward the sound.

"Josie!" Dean called, and Haley flinched at the intensity of his voice. The whistling noise came again, and Haley hurried to follow Dean, her pace lightning-quick to keep up with his long strides. Her boots were tracking snow through the house, she was sure of it, but the way Dean had called Josie's name made her feel an urgency that scared her. She rounded a corner into a massive marble kitchen and almost crashed into Dean, who stood still and stared at an open window. Brad's and Priya's footsteps sounded behind them. Priya was saying something beneath her breath, but Haley couldn't make it out. A glint of metal on the tiled floor caught her eye, and on closer inspection, she realized it was a knife coated with blood.

"Oh my God," Haley said, and Dean turned to take in the knife and froze. "Josie?" Haley screamed, twirling in a circle, her heart pounding. Where *was* she? "Are you here? Josie!" She knew how hysterical she sounded, and the rational part of her brain told her to calm down, but then she rounded the kitchen island and saw Josie lying facedown in a pool of blood. "No!" Haley cried, dropping to the floor. "Brad!" she screamed, and he was suddenly beside her, turning Josie onto her back. Josie's eyes were closed, her cheeks flushed. Bloody blond hair was matted to her face, but she didn't appear to have a head wound. Blood had seeped through her white sweater near her shoulder. Haley checked for a clear airway, and then lowered her ear to Josie's mouth to listen for breathing while Brad searched for a pulse. Priya was crying in the background, and Dean was frozen until Haley commanded, "Dean, call nine-one-one. Address is 35 Carrington." Haley watched the rise and fall of Josie's chest. "She's breathing," she said.

"She has a pulse," Brad said as Dean talked to the operator. Brad moved quickly to apply pressure to the wound near her clavicle.

Haley's fingers went to find Josie's pulse for herself. "Stay here, Josie, we've got you, you'll be all right," she said, unsure whether it was true.

PART III

TWENTY-ONE

Emma

Ten years ago

My phone buzzes, and I'm so sure it's Brad replying to my text about me seeing Priya that I nearly throw it against the pavement. But it's not him—it's my dad, writing to tell me that he's sorry for the things he said, and wondering if we can meet tonight and talk.

I sniff back tears. I used to be so sure that I was ready to leave my parents, and convinced that Yarrow was the ultimate freedom from them, even if I only moved a few miles away. But every time something goes wrong, I want them close the same way I used to as a kid.

OK, I text back, terrified my dad is going to kill me when I tell him I'm pregnant. When?

I'm still standing against the brick wall of the last town house on Brad's street. I peek around the corner just to make sure Priya's not coming after me, but the coast is clear. Maybe she's calling Brad now about my visit, accusing him of everything she must know is true. I slump down so I'm sitting against the cold pavement, my back resting against the bricks. When there were rumors that Yarrow had gotten Priya Khatri as a visiting artist, I already knew who she was and worshipped her accordingly. After making my case to the registrar that I absolutely, positively needed to be in her class—Josie did the same—I spent weeks scouring the internet and viewing her work and reading her reviews and criticism. But it's not like she was famous enough that there were paparazzi photos of her personal life online. When I started her class, I became even more enamored, and not just because Priya was so talented, but because she was also kind and exceedingly generous. She treated us like adults, and like our work was worth something.

But now *this*? Brad Aarons is Priya's fiancé? I'd watched Priya's stomach grow over the course of the semester, but I never asked her about the father of the baby, or about anything personal at all. And not because I have such great manners or boundaries, because I don't, but because I could sense she didn't want to talk about those things, maybe because they were so inessential to what we were doing together in her classroom.

It was Josie who used to go to Priya's office hours. She was completely obsessed with Priya, trying so hard to get Priya to like her.

We could walk the neighborhood like we used to, my dad replies.

I lean back, my puffy jacket swishing against the bricks. The fight my dad and I had feels so far away, like it can't even coexist in this new world I've found myself in. It was the worst we've ever had. I saw him in the parking lot of Key Food talking to this pretty woman in a way that felt slightly strange: nothing happened, but they were standing too close to each other. So I went all out and told him I knew he was having an affair, and he looked at me like I'd slapped him, and then he accused me of going completely insane. I'd never seen him so angry, and later that night when I was at my parents' house, I overheard my mom tell one of her friends that he was going off the deep end lately, which struck me as ironic. Maybe he's the one I get my instability from. I didn't tell my mom what I saw in the Key Food parking lot because I could have been wrong; it could have been nothing, and plus now I have bigger things to worry about. I have no idea what he'll say when I tell him I'm pregnant—I'm sure he'll be even angrier. But I have to tell him and my mom. Maybe tonight, just to get it over with.

I'll text you later, I respond to my father, and then I sit there for a minute or so, feeling like I don't even have the strength to stand. What if I just left? Isn't there somewhere I could go for a little while? Isn't that what girls who got pregnant used to do, especially Catholic ones?

The moon is full, emanating a yellow glow like it's bursting at the seams. The wind has picked up, and I rub the back of my neck, feeling stiff like I'm coming down with something, thinking about what a nightmare this is going to be for my family.

My phone buzzes, and I ignore it for a few more moments. I let my eyes glaze over as I stare at the moon. When I look down, I see two texts, both from Brad.

Where are you?

I'm coming to find you.

TWENTY-TWO

Priya

"We were here to see an open house," Brad whispered into Priya's ear as paramedics put Josie onto a stretcher and raced her out of the house. "Do you understand me? Josie invited us here, to see the house. Do you understand what I'm telling you, Priya? She might die, and if they believe we're here under any other circumstances . . ."

Moments later the police showed up, swarming the kitchen, barking into radios—*female, early thirties, assaulted, significant loss of blood, EMS responded to the scene.* They made calls to other police personnel and to forensics; they put on plastic gloves that made snapping sounds against their fingers; and they barricaded the kitchen with yellow tape. A stocky officer asked Dean, Haley, Priya, and Brad if they were all right, and then asked if they would *cooperate, please* by sitting in chairs and not speaking. Priya was shivering and trying to catch her breath, but all she could do was picture Josie all those years ago knocking on the door to the art studio, her hair askew and her face flushed from the cold, asking obscure art questions that didn't seem to have much to do with her own work.

"Someone should call Noah," Haley was saying to everyone, but none of the police personnel seemed to hear her. "Hello?" Haley tried again. She scanned the cops, and then her gaze fell on Priya. Priya's mind was working well enough to remember that Noah was Josie's husband, but it wasn't like she had his number.

"I don't know him," Priya said quickly, but her heart pounded as she realized her mistake: she should have pretended to know Noah. Though maybe Noah and Josie took on clients separately—maybe it was plausible she only would have met Josie. She didn't dare look at Brad. Was this really happening? Was she really at a crime scene, trying to figure out how not to implicate herself and her husband?

A cop knocked into a vase on the kitchen counter, catching it just before it shattered into a thousand pieces. "Should I just call him?" Haley asked Priya, but she didn't wait for Priya to answer before she started dialing. "Noah, this is Haley," she said into the phone, and it was clear from the way she prattled on that she'd gotten his voice mail. Priya's stomach dropped when she imagined Noah checking his messages. "There's been an accident," Haley said. "Someone hurt Josie, we just found her in the kitchen here at the open house on Carrington, and she was lying on the floor bleeding, and I believe they're taking her to Memorial Hospital, so if you get this message, just go there, please, and hopefully we can meet you soon."

Haley disconnected her call, and then a cop strode toward them. "I'd like to ask that you hand me your phones," the officer said. "We'd like to keep them while you're being questioned at the station." Priya's nerves flared, but she handed over her phone like everyone else, and then the cop asked them all to *please stand up,* and everyone obeyed except Dean, who couldn't seem to stand from his chair. His face was white, and he looked like he was about to pass out. Brad was studying him carefully, and Priya realized she hadn't seen her husband study anyone besides her in a very long time.

"The cars are here to take you to the station," the detective said, his voice neither hard nor gentle, just matter-of-fact. "You'll be driven separately, and interviewed there." When Dean still didn't get up, the officer asked, "Do you need some help?"

Dean shook his head and got to his feet. "Is she going to be all right?" he asked.

"We don't have that information, I'm sorry," the officer answered, and then he motioned to two policewomen and two policemen entering the kitchen. "Take them back to the station," he said.

TWENTY-THREE

Emma

Ten years ago

Please, Emma, says Brad's next text. Just talk to me.

I'm back in my dorm now, standing in the middle of the carpet. I have no idea where Josie is. The door was locked when I got here, and I opened it to find her gone.

What's there to say? I text Brad back, still standing awkwardly and unmoored like a guest in my own room. You know she's my watercolor professor, right?

He doesn't reply for a while, which means he either didn't know, or maybe he's with Priya right now, and she's screaming at him, or maybe he's just embarrassed and shameful and doesn't know what to say. And if it's the latter: *good.* Why should I be the only one who feels awful when he's the one with the fiancée?

I glance around our room. Josie's jacket is gone, which means she isn't just bouncing around the dorm. Gum wrappers litter her desk, and her laptop is open to her email. I've never felt the need to snoop on Josie, even though I know she's snooped in my email before. But now something pulls me like a magnet to her inbox. I stand there, zeroing in on an email from Chris's mom, who lives a few hours away upstate.

She's the one who raised Chris and Josie when they had no one left. Josie told me that when Chris's dad died, his mom tried to take only Chris back into her home, but Chris refused to go without Josie, so she took both. I recognize the woman's address because she's emailed me more than once wondering if everything's okay because Josie hasn't been in touch in weeks. Whenever I've brought that up to Josie, she just shrugs and acts like she forgot to call her and then assures me she will. *Weeks* seems like a pretty long time to go without talking to your family, but it's not her real mom, and Josie and Chris didn't exactly have a typical family life. Josie's dad abandoned her, and her mom eventually married Chris's dad. But then her mom died in a car accident when Josie was only six. Josie says Chris's dad was a rage-filled alcoholic who didn't want her in the first place, and hated her from the moment her mom died and he became stuck with her. And while Josie often tells me stories about growing up with Chris in a rural New York town she said could make you forget entirely about the city, she's only told me one about her stepdad and the day he died. It was more of a memory than a story, really, because she can't remember the beginning or the end—only the middle. It starts with her huddled on the floor, and then a slant of light spreads across the foyer, and she looks up to see Chris entering the house. It's Halloween, and Chris is dressed like a superhero, which strikes me as fitting because Chris is still Josie's hero, the one she truly loves, the only one she really lets in. In the memory, Chris's smile fades as he takes in the sight of his dad lying dead at the bottom of the stairs with a twelve-year-old Josie sitting beside him, patting his cheek and trying to wake him. Shards of glass from the dropped vodka bottle fan out like a halo and surround Josie and her stepdad. Josie said that sometimes her memories call her like a scab wanting to be picked, and that in this particular memory it was the halo of glass that concerned her the most. She couldn't figure out how she'd gotten inside it, sharing the epicenter with her stepfather, the glass like something in orbit swirling around them. She told me this when she was drunk and high, and the next day she pretended she never told me at all.

I stare at her computer, wondering if I can get away with scrolling through her inbox. I don't even know where she goes half the time, like right now, for example, but whenever she comes back (sometimes in the middle of the night) she won't tell me. She's either into heavier drugs than I give her credit for, or she's meeting up with her tall, dark, and handsome guy and sneaking into his dorm and staying the night there, or maybe something I can't even think of yet because it's so far outside the realm of what I could imagine. Josie's always saying I'm short on imagination for an artist. It's probably the meanest thing she's ever said to me.

I'm about to turn away from Josie's computer when I see another email a few lines down, this one from Noah. I can't help myself. My heart goes wild in my chest as I open it.

> What the hell, Josie? What does this even mean?
> Why are you emailing me something like this?

I scroll down to find an email from Josie, written today at 4:32 p.m.

> This has to stop. You know Emma really likes you.
> What are you doing to her, leading her on like this?
> It's cruel.

I step back like I've been slapped. Why would she write that?

I'm shaky at first, reading and rereading, but then I try to think clearly. Josie's always overprotective of me, but there's nothing Noah's said or done to lead me on that she's seen. No one even knows we're hooking up because Noah hardly ever touches me when we're in front of other people, even if the way he looks at me may as well be his hands all over my body. There was this night last month when Josie and I were drinking beer with Noah's roommates, but Noah wasn't because he had a test the next morning. Josie was watching the two of us like a hawk, like if she just stared hard enough, she could figure everything out. But then Chris got too drunk and said something rude to one of Noah's roommates, and Josie was distracted trying to defuse the ensuing argument, and in that moment I snuck away into the kitchen. Noah followed me. I tried to play it cool, scooping ice into my glass with my back turned to him. There was plenty of room for him to pass behind me. But he came right up behind me and put a hand on my hip as he passed. I turned toward him, only an inch between us, and then his fingers trailed a line right over my hip bone, which burns every time I think about it.

The door creaks opens, and I whirl around. Josie's standing there with an expression I can't read. I curse myself for not closing Noah's email. Josie's still wearing her coat, and the smell of the clove cigarette she just smoked wafts into our room.

"Are you reading my emails?" she asks, her voice strangely calm.

I swallow. "You've read mine," I say, trying to stand up a little taller.

"True," she says. She steps all the way inside and slams the door behind her. It feels too aggressive, and every inch of me tightens. We've never fought before, and I don't want this to be the first time, and maybe that's why, instead of asking about her email to Noah, I blurt, "I'm pregnant."

Josie's hands fly over her mouth. "What?" she says through her fingers.

I burst into tears. I still can't believe it's real. I start crying harder, feeling like I can't breathe. "I don't get it," Josie says, but I can't imagine what it is that she doesn't get. "Oh my God," she goes on, and there's a hint of fury in her voice. It sets me on edge. "Is it that *teacher's*?"

It takes me a minute to realize she's talking about Brad. I never told her about him, which means she gathered it from the emails she read, which is kind of impressive considering he and I mostly texted and barely ever emailed. "Who?" I ask, playing dumb, trying to stall.

"Who?" she echoes back, mimicking me.

I purse my lips and make myself stop crying. I don't want to be weak in front of her. I don't know whether to be mad at her for knowing all along about Brad and not saying anything, or for the snooping itself, but mostly I'm mad that she's not hugging me right now and trying to make me feel better.

She sees it on my face. That's the thing about Josie: she's eerily good at sensing what other people are thinking. "Come here," she says. She unzips her coat, revealing a camisole and bare skin. She tosses the coat onto her bed, and I can see the effort it takes for her to open her arms to me. But in that moment I'm just so relieved that I do what she says—I fold into her hug, my face in her hair. "Emma?" she asks softly. She smells like cigarettes and rosewater, and I start to relax a little.

"Yeah?" I answer against the soft skin of her shoulder.

"It's the teacher's baby, isn't it," she says, her voice almost cooing, like how you'd talk to a child. "Did he hurt you, Emma?"

"What?" I say, pulling back. "No—not at all. And it isn't even . . ."

Knock, knock, knock . . .

We both turn to face the pounding on the door. "Coming!" Josie says, and then she drops my embrace like a stone. She leaves me standing there all alone like I'm nothing to her, and then crosses the room and flings open the door. Noah's massive frame takes up nearly the whole doorway. He doesn't seem to see me at first; he looks at Josie, his features narrowing. Their email exchange curls through my mind like smoke.

"Emma here?" he asks pointedly, and then he looks past her, and his eyes find me.

"Noah," I say, and for the first time in a very long while, I have the fleeting sense that everything might turn out all right.

"Hey," he says, not breaking my gaze. He has workout clothes on, and he's still sweaty.

Josie's turned toward him, and I'm glad for that: I don't want to see the look on her face. She reaches both arms up to tighten her ponytail, and I watch as her taut back muscles contract and loosen.

"You guys ready?" she asks suddenly, and then she turns around to look at me, smiling like all is forgotten, but there's no way that's true. "The woods tonight, right?" she asks.

I swallow. "The woods tonight," I echo back, trying to ignore the sweep of cold over my skin, trying to focus on Noah, on his bright eyes holding mine.

TWENTY-FOUR

Haley

At the police station, Haley waited inside an empty interrogation room that smelled vaguely like tomato soup. She was still shaky, trying hard to distract herself with the details of the room: the bare cream walls with paint peeling in some spots and reinforced in others.

The door finally opened, and a fifty-something blond woman made her way inside. Her gaze was buried in a folder filled with paperwork.

"Haley McCullough?" she asked, still not glancing up.

"Yes," Haley said, taking in the woman's neatly pressed uniform.

"I'm Detective Peters," she said, and Haley immediately felt nervous. She had to remind herself she hadn't done anything wrong and neither had Dean. She thought of her fiancé in a similarly stark room, antsy without his phone to distract him.

The woman finally took her eyes off the paperwork and set them on Haley. She scanned Haley's face, clothes, and bloodstained hands, and Haley fought back the urge to cry. "Is Josie all right?" Haley asked, her voice trembling.

"She's alive from the last I heard," the woman said, sitting in the seat across from Haley. Her eyes were light blue and clear like Josie's, and Haley couldn't help but imagine Josie lying on the kitchen floor. "Any idea of anyone who would want to hurt her?" the detective asked.

Haley sat up straighter, determined to be helpful. "I don't know her as well as I used to," she said, "but I certainly don't know anyone who wanted to hurt her."

"As well as you used to?" the detective repeated.

"She and my sister were best friends during college," Haley said. "My sister is Emma McCullough, the student who disappeared from Yarrow."

Haley had only said it like that a few times in her life, and each time it made her want to retch. It was too factual, and as much as Haley loved facts, she preferred to talk about Emma in a more roundabout way, mostly in stories from growing up.

The police detective nodded, and Haley couldn't tell if she'd known about Emma before this moment or not. Maybe it didn't matter. "So you knew her well, years ago, as your sister's friend," she said, and Haley nodded. "And what is your relationship like with her now?"

Haley shifted in her seat, the metal chair creaking beneath her. "Josie's my real estate agent. My fiancé and I are looking for a house to buy, and she's been helping us for about a month." Haley swallowed. It felt so hot inside the room, and she needed water. "Well, I guess, longer than that, because she found us our current house to rent. But we've been actively looking at houses together during the past month."

The detective raised her eyebrows. "Funny," she said. "Josie and Noah sold my family and me our house, five or so years ago, when they'd just opened up their real estate business." She stopped talking, but held Haley's stare like she was waiting for her to respond to this tidbit.

"What a coincidence," Haley finally said, unsure of what else to say.

"There was a problem with the house, actually," the woman said, her eyes boring into Haley's, and again, she left an uncomfortable silence between them, as if she were waiting for Haley to respond.

"Oh?" Haley said.

"Oh," the detective repeated. "There was a terrible, and I truly mean *god-awful,* sewage smell that rose from the crawl space every time we did the laundry. My husband and I never understood how that didn't come up on inspection. Seems like a pretty big thing to miss, don't you think?" The detective shrugged. "Well, you know how it is. These things happen, I suppose."

Haley crossed and uncrossed her legs. She really needed water.

"Cost us tens of thousands of dollars to replace the septic tank, though," the detective added. Haley exhaled, and the woman finally dropped her eyes to her paperwork. "Crazy thing is, Noah's totally unreachable now," she said, perusing what looked like some kind of incident report. "And so is the only other employee at Carmichael Realty, a Mr. Chris Paxton."

"That's Josie's brother," Haley said. And then she immediately felt idiotic for telling the detective something she must have already known.

"Both of their phones are going straight to voice mail," the detective said. "Doesn't that seem strange? Real estate agents are almost always by their phones, almost like police detectives." She gave a chuckle that sent chills over Haley's skin. "But it appears Noah Carmichael and Chris Paxton have gone completely off the grid."

TWENTY-FIVE

Emma

Ten years ago

I sit in the back of Noah's Jeep with my legs crossed. The headlights illuminate the narrow patch of road ahead of us, and I watch as a small animal scurries out in front of the Jeep. Noah doesn't slow down. I gasp when he nearly hits the thing, and he laughs, and then so does Josie.

"You guys suck," I say playfully, but really my insides are turning. There's pressure on my bladder every time the road gets uneven, but it feels different from having to pee. I can't imagine the baby is big enough to make me feel like this, but maybe my body parts are moving around in weird ways?

I open my phone to see a text from my sister. I'm coming tonight, just text me where you are, ok?

Good. I need Haley tonight. I'll text her back when I don't feel so carsick. The Jeep gets so bumpy in the back seat, and Josie always says she has motion sickness and needs the front. "Can you guys roll the windows down?" I say, feeling way too queasy for a ride like this.

"It's freezing!" Josie says, laughing, but it's really just her way of saying no to me.

"I'm going to be sick, Josie," I say through gritted teeth, but Josie still doesn't roll down the window. Noah hits a pothole, and dirty water splatters the windshield. Finally he rolls down his window.

Josie turns and gives me a small, sad smile over her shoulder. Then she asks Noah, "Have you told Emma your big news?"

"I was going to tonight," Noah says, rounding a sharp corner.

I try to focus straight ahead through the windshield so I feel less sick, and my eyes settle on Noah's headlights scattering the gravel and flickering into the thick foliage. I try not to think about the creatures lying in wait, the coyotes and owls we all hear at night, and especially the black bear a handful of students have reportedly seen while running.

I want to ask Noah to turn back, but I don't. Instead, I ask, "What big news?" The engine growls as we pick up speed, and I can see Noah's wolfish grin in the rearview mirror.

"Australia," he says, looking utterly satisfied with himself. "I got into the semester abroad program for the fall."

No. A few weeks ago he told me he was applying, but I didn't pay much attention then because there wasn't a reason to, other than the fact that I would miss him while he was gone.

"Congratulations," I say, trying to do the math.

Josie beats me to it. "So that's what, in nine months or so?" she asks, and my stomach drops. How can she be so cavalier? I try to breathe. So she knows it's his, and the worst part is, she's right about the timing: If I'm doing the math right, this baby would be due in September, so how's Noah going to take it when I tell him there's a baby due during the course of his dreamy semester abroad?

"I guess, yeah," Noah answers Josie, his smile fading. He looks confused and annoyed, which is the way he gets when he senses we're talking about something more than just what we're saying out loud.

"Did you already put your deposit down?" Josie pushes.

Noah considers her. There's no way he'd guess what she's getting at. "Yeah," he says blandly. "I did."

"You're going to have so much fun, Noah," Josie says. "*Australia.* Wow. What a dream."

I slink farther down my seat, the leather cold against my skin. Noah doesn't say anything else. He just drives faster along the narrow road, plunging us deeper into the woods.

TWENTY-SIX

Priya

Priya clutched a Styrofoam cup full of coffee and nodded in response to one of Detective Salinas's questions. The police station's interview room was just big enough to fit a metal table and three chairs, and the empty chair made Priya worry that another cop would come in to join in the questioning. She was barely holding it together with just Salinas, and so far he only seemed to want a timeline of events.

"So, to review, you last spoke with Josie during the day yesterday afternoon, by phone?" he asked, his pencil poised in the air. The pencil and paper struck Priya as old-fashioned, but she loathed technology, so she appreciated it. There wasn't a phone or laptop in sight.

"No," Priya corrected, tapping her index finger against the table. "By text. I guess that's by phone. I'm just trying to be accurate, sorry."

"And what was the nature of your conversation?" Salinas asked, scrawling away on his paper in loopy cursive.

Priya cleared her throat. Another woman had been hurt, and Priya didn't want to lie. There had to be a way to tell the truth without implicating her family. "Josie and I have known each other for years," Priya started. "We're connected by the disappearance of Emma McCullough. Emma and Josie were my students at Yarrow; and as you maybe already know, Emma and Josie were best friends. I was close with both of them."

This was an exaggeration, but not a lie. Priya was only thirty-one when she was teaching Emma and Josie, and she related well to all her students. "And during the past few years Josie and I sometimes met up." It was obvious how interested Detective Salinas was in this part. Priya knew she needed to rein it back in. "Josie became a friend of mine as the years went by, even if we didn't get to talk that often. I told her that Brad and I were looking for a new home, and she offered to keep an eye out for us. She wanted me to meet her at the house on Carrington."

"Really?" Salinas asked, his round brown eyes steady. "A five-bedroom home for a family with one child?"

Priya's heart pounded. What a fool she'd been to think she was in control of this conversation. She imagined Brad in another exam room, telling the same story, and tried to steel herself. "People with one child like big houses, too, Detective," she said.

"Do they?" the detective asked. Priya willed her hands to stop trembling against the coffee cup, staring back but saying nothing.

"Let's move on," Detective Salinas finally said, glancing back to his loose-leaf papers. They seemed less quaint now and more incriminating. "What time did you and Josie arrange to meet?" he asked.

"She told me her open house started at eleven," Priya said. Also true.

"And did you drive straight from your house, or from elsewhere?"

"From my house," Priya said. She pulled her thick black hair over her shoulder and twisted it, a habit she'd had since she was a child. When her parents brought her to India at age ten, she saw her grandmother did the exact same thing, and it made her feel connected to something bigger, a line of blood that meant something more than what she could see.

"Did you stop off anywhere?" Salinas asked, which felt like the same question, but Priya answered anyway.

"No," she said, letting her hair fall loose again.

"And when you arrived at the open house, who else was there?"

"Dean and Haley," Priya said. It struck her that the way she said it sounded too familiar, like she'd known them before today. "Well, actually, they pulled in behind me. So Brad, Dean, Haley, and I were there the same time, I guess, and we all introduced ourselves."

"How nice," the detective said, putting a bad taste in Priya's mouth, making her feel increasingly like she'd done something very wrong. "And did you approach the house together, or separately?"

"Together," Priya said.

"How did you announce yourselves?" Salinas asked, and Priya paused at the odd phrasing.

"Um, well, Dean knocked on the door, and rang the doorbell once or twice. Is that what you mean?"

"Yes." He scrawled something across the paper, and then asked, "How long did you wait before entering the house?"

"Not long," Priya said. "It was freezing. At some point Dean just opened the door."

"So Dean was the first to enter the house?"

"He was," Priya said. "Or, maybe Haley was, actually? I don't remember. But Brad and I followed them both inside."

"How did Dean know the door was unlocked?"

"They usually are, at open houses," Priya said, trying not to sound snotty. But wasn't that obvious?

Salinas didn't seem offended. "Was the door ajar, or simply unlocked?" he asked.

"I think just unlocked. I definitely didn't see it open a crack or anything like that."

Salinas nodded. "And what happened next?"

"We called Josie's name a few times. Dean did, I think, and then Haley. Brad and I mostly followed their leads." Salinas looked at Priya like there was something wrong with that. "And I signed myself in," Priya said quickly, "because I saw that Josie had left a sign-in sheet for visitors. And Haley suggested that we go upstairs, but then there was a strange sound from the kitchen, so we all went back there, and that's when we saw Josie lying on the floor."

The door swung open, and Priya turned to see a thirty-something woman dressed in a traditional police uniform. The woman's gaze traveled all over Priya, and she didn't seem impressed with what she saw.

"Detective Harris," the woman introduced herself, "and I know who you are."

Priya's cheeks burned. Detective Harris was carrying a slim laptop, and she moved gracefully across the tiny room and sat next to Salinas, who grunted something indecipherable. Detective Harris opened her laptop, and she and Salinas stared at it for at least a full minute. Priya felt like crying, but she knew she couldn't, so she lifted her eyes to the spiderweb of cracks on the ceiling and counted the faint lines.

Finally Detective Harris spoke. "You arrived separately from your husband, if I have the vehicle registrations sorted correctly."

Priya met the woman's stare. "I did," she said.

"Why is that?" Detective Harris asked.

"Because I had plans after," Priya blurted, and then wanted to kick herself for mentioning something that Brad's statement would probably contradict.

"You had plans after the open house? In a storm like this?" Salinas asked, arching his eyebrows in mock incredulity. *"Really?"*

"Really," Priya repeated. She lifted her chin and tried to appear confident. "My neighbor is having troubles," she added, thinking about how Alex's husband had been laid off this week, and how that made it less of a lie, and in fact she'd planned to pick up Elliot and Robby at Alex's after the open house and bring them back to her own house for a day of play. That's what happened when two only-children lived next door to each other.

"So you were going to be a good friend," Salinas said. "That's kind of you."

Detective Harris smiled, but it was far from friendly, and it made the bags under her eyes pooch and crinkle. "I just interviewed your husband," she said flatly. "And he told me that you were in a fight, and that's why you drove separately. So which thing is true?"

"Both are," Priya lied. "We got in a fight, and I was going to my neighbor's after to pick up my son and his friend. I don't see what my marriage has to do with this."

Salinas nodded as though Priya were a child he felt terribly sorry for, and she tried to steel herself. They were wrong to think she and Brad had anything to do with this. She was sure of it.

TWENTY-SEVEN

Emma

Ten years ago

Just meet me. Talk to me.

I'm still slumped in the back of Noah's Jeep as I read Brad's latest text. We're parked now, and even though the sky is dark there's a full moon, plus a lone streetlight shedding a golden glow across the parking lot. It's not really a proper lot; it's more like a tennis court–sized gravel clearing in the woods that we're sharing along with a few other cars whose owners are probably already at the party. An aging wooden sign with a chalky yellow arrow marks the entrance to the trail that leads to the campsite. Josie unbuckles her seat belt and makes fun of Noah for needing to cheat off her test this week in their sociology class, saying that he's going the way of his Dartmouth-dropout sister, and I can tell she's pissed him off by the set of his jaw. But he pretends she hasn't gotten to him, telling her to *please shut up* because he's trying to write a text. Finally they both spill out of the car, and I stay in my seat for a bit longer, exhausted just thinking about trekking all the way there and setting up camp with Josie and Noah like one big happy threesome when we're not. And I'm nervous thinking about what Noah has planned for the tents: Are we all sharing one? Josie's email to Noah is really bothering me, and I know I need to ask her about it, but I also need to deal with Brad. The weird thing is that I *do* kind of want to see him, to have closure, and maybe also to get a break from this night with Josie and Noah. I unlock my phone and dash off a text:

Meet where? I write back, just to see what he'll say, and maybe just to keep it going, really. Maybe some part of me likes the drama; I can admit that, at least.

Not here, he sends back a moment later.

Obviously, I write back. How dumb does he think I am? I'm camping tonight, I write. Why don't you meet me here? I can find a spot where no one will see us.

Perfect, he writes back. Governor's Trail?

Yep, I text. There are only three real trails. The woods behind campus are only five or so square miles. I close my eyes and try to steady myself, but I feel even sicker from the sounds of Josie and Noah ribbing each other as they unpack the trunk. When I turn to look through the window, I see Josie sock Noah across the shoulder. It's childish, and I don't think Noah likes it. Josie is so incredibly beautiful, but he's just not under her spell like other guys are, and I think she knows it. I study him through the glass, the way he glances sideways at her, the way his smile looks forced, and the way he turns and buries his gaze in a red-and-white cooler. *He's all mine.*

It gives me a buzz of pleasure; it fortifies me. I push open the door and say, "Dibs on the fleecy one," because as juvenile as it sounds, I know that if I don't say it, Josie will claim the warmest sleeping bag, and I'm not going to shiver all night.

"They all have fleece lining," Josie snaps.

"You guys go ahead," I say to both of them.

Noah turns to look at me. "What are you talking about?" he asks.

"I'm meeting a friend on the trails."

"What friend?" Josie asks, making a face like I've said something absurd.

"A friend!" I say, laughing. They exchange a glance I can't read, and Noah shakes his head. "What?" I say testily. "Can't I have other friends?"

"Emma," Noah says, his voice sounding way too sure that he'll be able to convince me to stay with him. "I'd rather you not be in the woods by yourself. You don't really know the trails that well."

"I do, actually," I say. "I know them from when I was little and we used to come here."

"That's a nice memory," Noah says rudely, "but it's different at night."

I roll my eyes.

"Just tell your friend to meet us at the party," Noah goes on, stuffing a half-drunk grape Gatorade into his backpack. My heart starts beating faster. I really need to get rid of them.

"Maybe I just need a little break from you guys," I say, knowing it will work. I reach down to grab the black backpack I think is mine, but Josie leaps toward me and snatches it from my hands.

"Don't open that!" she says. And then, "That one's for Chris and me."

I look up, startled. "Um, okay, sorry," I say. The streetlight flickers, then makes a dull buzzing noise like it's about to die.

Her face is flushed. She breaks my stare and grabs a smaller bag. "This one's yours," she says, still not looking at me. "It's just waters and stuff."

I take the bag and wonder what she has in hers. Probably drugs, something harder than pot, or else she wouldn't be so weird about it.

Noah finally gives up on me. "Do you have your phone?" he asks, nudging his boot into the side of his pack, pushing it upright.

"I do," I say. "Do we definitely get service in the woods?"

Josie nods. Her blond hair is piled high on her head, and wispy tendrils frame her heart-shaped face. She always thinks she knows everything, but she's barely been in the woods this year. "Noah?" I ask, and he nods at me.

"We get service," he says. "But don't take too long to find us." He towers over me, and smiles. "The wolves come out at night," he says.

I roll my eyes. "Thanks," I say, making my voice sound a lot tougher than I feel right now.

I lift my hand in a wave, watching as they sling their backpacks onto their shoulders. Noah grabs the cooler and asks Josie, "Ready?" But she doesn't answer him. She just starts walking toward the woods, seeming as confident as she always does, even though I know deep down she's scared of where she's going. Sometimes I think it's that current of fear that keeps Josie moving forward toward something intangible, something she knows she wants but doesn't quite know how to get.

I pull out my phone. Meet me at Governor's Trail marker two, I text Brad.

I watch Josie's slim form and Noah's tall, broad back as they make their way into the woods and the cold night. I stare until they become swallowed by the darkness and disappear completely.

TWENTY-EIGHT

Haley

Haley let her eyes glaze over as she stared out the police car's windshield at the frigid white sky. An officer drove her toward Waverly Memorial Hospital, the audio from his radio buzzing in and out. Haley noted how much better the front seat of a police car felt than the back, and wondered if she'd been upgraded because the cops were now operating on the assumption that she hadn't done anything wrong. She tried to relax and close her eyes, but snapped them back open when images of bodies flooded her mind. She tried to blink the bodies away, to think of anything else. Her mind settled on Dean—on his pensive, handsome face and strong hands. She wanted his arms around her; she wanted the cops to release him to her so they could be a family again.

A *family.*

The cop slowed for a yellow light, and Haley thought about the word as they idled. She could admit to herself that it wasn't how she usually thought of Dean, but increasingly she found herself imagining what they could be to each other with time. She fantasized about holding a little boy between them who looked just like Dean, and she imagined the way she would love her child. She imagined all the ways Dean and the little boy would be her new family, and all the ways she would protect them from the fate that had befallen her old family.

The cop cleared his throat as he cruised toward the hospital. "Here we are," he said, and Haley wiped tears from her eyes as he pulled into the parking lot of Waverly Memorial. She just needed to make sure Josie was okay, and go from there. *One day at a time,* her mom was fond of saying. Haley had her laminated badge from med school in her bag, and she was pretty sure, with her credentials as a medical student whose college was affiliated with the hospital, that she'd be allowed in the room—unless they were forbidding visitors because of the investigation. It was worth a shot.

The officer pulled up to the front entrance and parked. Wipers slashed away the snow, and Haley fought the temptation to ask when he thought Dean might be released. "Thanks for the ride," she said instead.

She didn't look back as she stepped onto the curb, feeling thankful that no one she knew was standing outside the hospital to see her exit a police car. The last thing she wanted was to see any of the other med students with whom she'd made tentative friendships and have to explain any of this. Freezing air blasted her face, and wet snow landed on her nose as she hurried toward the revolving doors. Inside the hospital it felt so stifling that she tore off her scarf and jacket. She flashed her badge at the guard sitting behind the desk, and the mere action of that strengthened her. She was going to be a doctor. She didn't know which kind, or what it was all going to look like, but she knew she was going to help people. The thought of it kept her buoyed during every day of class and every night spent studying past midnight.

The security guard waved Haley past, and she sped through the hospital, breathing in the familiar stench of cleaning products. In the ICU, she didn't need to ask which room was Josie's; she headed toward the one with a uniformed cop posted outside the sliding door. She didn't recognize him from the station. "Hi, I'm one of Josie's friends," she said when she reached him, and then she held up her hospital badge. "And also . . ." Her voice trailed off, and she prayed the cop wouldn't look too close and see that she was only a student.

The officer rose from his chair. "You can go in," he said, glancing at the badge. Haley shoved open the door. Her breathing had quickened, and her cheeks felt warm, and she felt eternally grateful when the cop didn't follow her inside the room.

"Josie," Haley said in a whisper. Josie's blue eyes were open and blinking, her head slightly inclined.

"Hi," Josie croaked out.

Haley sat carefully on the edge of the bed.

Josie looked so thin beneath the bedsheets. "The cops have been here all day, asking me questions and freaking me out," she said, tears spilling over her cheeks. "I don't remember what happened, Haley. I just don't."

"That's normal," Haley said. "Do you want to talk about it? What you do remember?"

Josie shook her head gently like she was trying hard to piece things together. When she finally spoke, her speech was slow and filled with doubt. "I remember being at the open house setting up," she said, "and then Noah came to switch cars with me because of the snow. I remember that. And I remember talking with Chris because he came to help shovel the walkway, and I remember putting the flowers out in the foyer . . ."

Haley wanted to ask if Noah and Chris had been to the hospital yet—if the cops had even been able to get ahold of them. But she didn't know how to ask without upsetting Josie, and wouldn't they be here if the cops had gotten through?

"I don't even remember going into the kitchen," Josie said, "and that's where the cops said they . . . where they said you guys found me." She began to sob, losing her breath to the heaving of her chest, and Haley knew she'd made a mistake. She took Josie's hand, trying to calm her down. "Josie, shhhh," she said, "it's all right. Just try to relax. It'll help you get better faster, okay?" Josie kept crying, and after a few beats Haley put her arms around her as gently as she could. She hadn't hugged another woman besides her mom in a long time, and Josie's bones felt like they were made of nothing at all. "It's okay," Haley kept saying, even though everything felt far from it.

They sat together in silence as Josie caught her breath, the only sounds coming from the monitors beeping and the radiator humming. When a nurse entered the room, she took one look at Josie and her mascara-ridden cheeks and red-rimmed eyes, and then she turned to glare at Haley. "I hope you're not upsetting my patient," she said, making her way to the bed. "I've had just about enough of that today with the police and such." She spotted Haley's badge. "You're a student?"

Haley nodded, embarrassed. She prayed she wouldn't get in trouble for coming to the hospital for non-school purposes and using her badge. Josie shifted her weight, and a warning beep sounded from the pulse oximeter. The nurse lowered her gray-haired head, readjusted the oximeter on Josie's index finger, and then patted her shoulder. "Remember what I said," she warned Haley, and then she left the room.

Haley turned to catch Josie studying her, and it made her blush. The door opened again, and in came Detective Rappaport. "What are you doing here?" he asked Haley. There wasn't reproach in his voice, only what sounded like genuine concern for both of them.

"Visiting my friend," Haley said.

Rappaport was wearing plain clothes, just like yesterday in his office. He put his hands in the pockets of his corduroys. He nodded and looked around the room. "I'd like to talk to Josie now, alone," he said.

"I understand. I'll wait," Haley said.

"I'm asking you to leave, Haley," Rappaport said. "I'm prepared to wait here with Mrs. Carmichael for a few hours, if she'll let me stay." He exchanged a glance with Josie, his brown eyes gentle. "I think it's the safest option for her as of now, to have a police presence inside the room or just outside, as we've done since she's gotten here. And I'd like to be here in a professional capacity if—*when*—she remembers something about what happened today."

Josie looked away, and Haley watched her profile as she stared out the hospital window into the waning storm. "I think that's probably for the best, Haley," Josie murmured, her chin trembling.

Haley was quiet. She didn't want to leave, but she wasn't in charge of what happened inside this room. She was never in charge in the hospital, it seemed; there was always someone more senior.

"Your fiancé's been released," Rappaport said, offering that small kernel as he moved closer to Josie. Haley could feel the power shifting; Josie was his now.

Haley squeezed Josie's hand, but Josie didn't squeeze back. "Will you call me and tell me when I can come see you again?" Haley asked.

"We have Mrs. Carmichael's phone," Rappaport said before Josie could answer. "But I can arrange a call to you when she'd like a visitor."

Josie sniffed. She was still staring out the window, watching the snow.

Rappaport shot Haley a tepid smile. "And just as a reminder," he said. "You and Dean shouldn't leave town."

Josie let out a strangled laugh, and then she turned to Haley and said the oddest thing. "Whatever you do, Haley, please don't disappear."

TWENTY-NINE

Emma

Ten years ago

The night is getting colder. I've crept farther into the woods, already regretting that I didn't just meet Brad in the parking lot with the streetlight and the other cars. I've never been in the woods by myself—it was always my dad, Haley, and me when we hiked here—and now I feel foolish for always making fun of Josie for being scared.

I push through the brush, my mind flashing to Noah. I can see his deep hazel eyes and the sweep of golden stubble along his jaw. I can see his strong shoulders and the way his body looks without anything covering it. I start to calm down a little, but then, uninvited, I see Josie in my mind, too. I stop moving and squeeze my eyes shut. *Get out,* I try to say to the image of her in our room wearing only her bra, staring at Noah and me. My hands go to my cold cheeks and press hard against the skin, as if I can shake the memory free, and then I start to wonder if I've really lost it. I open my eyes and keep moving, picking up my pace. The evergreens along the trail seem to snake closer to my skin like a too-tight sweater. Pointy, jagged branches claw at my jacket, and I imagine painting this place when I finally get out of here. I can practically feel my fingers gripping a brush, and the way it will feel to drag it across the canvas with pine-green paint in its wake. I think about the first time Chris saw my paintings, and how, even with a real artist for a sister, he was rendered speechless. Maybe I just need to get out of my head and paint more and forget trying to make every canvas perfect. Or swim more. I used to do that in high school, but I wasn't good enough to make the team at Yarrow.

I blink. My eyes don't seem to be adjusting properly—there's a full moon, but every time the clouds get in the way it's too dark. I stumble over a rock and catch myself. Is this even the right way toward marker two? The clouds clear, and I press onward, hugging my arms over my chest, thinking about my dad and the weird text he just sent me. He wants to talk to me alone. We always talk as a family when we fight, but this whole thing started over me accusing him of having an affair. So the fact that he wants us to be alone probably means he's guilty.

A bird's cry cuts the night air. The twisting and turning of the path still feels so unfamiliar. I slow for a second to catch my breath, and that's when I hear the footsteps.

"Hello?" I call out. The sound of twigs and branches crunching is unmistakable. "Hello?" I say once more, but no one answers. Surely they're close enough to hear me—they should be saying something. I whip out my phone for the flashlight and see a missed call from my dad. With shaking fingers I tap his name on my phone and call him, thinking how much better I'll feel just to hear his voice, and plus then he can call the police if I get truly lost.

He doesn't answer. *Call me, Dad,* I whisper into the phone. *I don't want to worry you, but I'm in the woods, and I think maybe I'm lost . . . or . . . well, just call me, okay?*

Crack goes a branch, way too close. I freeze and contemplate hiding. But then fear overtakes me, and I start to run.

THIRTY

Haley

Haley sat on a pile of pillows inside her sister's old bedroom. She checked her phone again for a call or text from Dean, but there wasn't one.

The pillows were still stacked next to the bookshelf where Emma had arranged them after their parents said no to a beanbag chair that cost too much. Emma had liked lying on her stomach to read and draw, her body against the pillows and her sketchpad on the hard floor. Haley could still picture her that way, her dark wavy hair falling over her face, and the way she'd look up at Haley with big blue eyes filled with equal parts love and exasperation when Haley interrupted her work.

Haley snuggled farther into the pillows. She picked up one of her sister's old stuffed animals and held it against her chest like a child would. She couldn't bring herself to go back to her and Dean's house after the hospital visit with Josie. She had needed to go home first.

Home. Wasn't it a problem that she thought of her parents' house as her home instead of the one she shared with Dean? Was it just because that's where she felt Emma? Haley glanced around the room at all the familiar things: the knickknacks and chipped pottery Emma made in grade school, the toy horse with silky hair that stood midwhinny on her dresser. The bunk beds Haley had sometimes slept in had been replaced with a queen after Emma disappeared, which Haley thought was a huge waste of money when no visitors would ever sleep in Emma's room. Emma's posters still lined the pale yellow walls: mostly contemporary art peppered with a surrealist print and one of a femme fatale from a film noir. Her journals, sketchbooks, and art supplies filled the desk drawers. The cops had scrutinized every page of the journals before returning them to Haley's mom, declaring them *unhelpful to the case.* And they were, Haley knew that, but it didn't stop her from reading them every so often, or from flipping through the sketchbooks. The only person she'd ever shown them to was Dean. He'd pored over them, considering each one carefully, just as she'd hoped he would.

Haley remembered when Emma was in high school and their dad found a series of nude drawings she'd done. He'd lost his mind at their *inappropriateness* until Liv calmed him down, and Haley could still recall her mom's words when she'd overhead them from the top of the stairs: *There's nothing subversive about this, Tim; it's art.* He was so conservative, and Haley had sworn she'd never be like him, but sometimes when she looked at the naked drawings, she felt a little nauseous. Maybe it was just in hindsight, knowing that something terrible had happened to her sister, but when Haley looked over the male forms Emma had sketched, she couldn't help but feel as if Emma had intuited the darkness coming for her. The naked men she'd created were too leering, too subtly dominating over their female scene partners. The final drawing showed a man placing his large hands on a woman's shoulders, and the way Emma had drawn it made it impossible to tell if they were embracing or struggling. Haley felt a slice of fear every time she thought of whatever her sister was trying to work out.

Emma's journals were sunnier. There were entries about day-to-day minutiae, interactions with family and friends—*I can't believe today is the day T.J. and I met one year ago! It feels like we've been great friends forever. His art is amazing!*

Emma was only sixteen when she wrote those words, years younger than when she disappeared, but to Haley, it seemed like Emma went to

Yarrow and her bright persona took a plunge. Not that clothes meant anything to Haley back then—or now, even—but she couldn't help noticing the way Emma started wearing black T-shirts because that's what she thought true artists wore, and how it seemed like, after a few years as an art student, the dark T-shirts started seeping inward, clouding the sunny person she'd once been. Maybe the darkness from Emma's teenage sketches were inside her even back then when she lived with Haley and her parents, but the safety of living inside a family kept it at bay. Maybe it was percolating, waiting for the right people and place to bring it to the surface, and maybe that place was college.

The front door slammed downstairs. "Haley?" Liv called out, her footsteps already pounding the steps.

"I'm up here in Emma's room!" Haley called back. She held tighter to Emma's stuffed cat, her fingers finding the spot on its ear where Emma had kissed off all the hair.

Haley's mom flew into the room, followed closely by her dad. "What happened?" Liv asked. Her yoga-trained body collapsed onto the pillows with the ease of a teenager. Liv had the same almond-shaped eyes Emma did, and when she looked up from her spot on the pillows Haley saw her sister's blinking eyes and smooth, pale skin. She imagined the way Emma's mouth used to lift at the corners whenever she had a secret, and she always had a secret. "I'm sorry I texted you what I did," Haley said, trying to focus on the fine lines around her mother's mouth, trying to remind herself that Emma wasn't here, and that she was truly, irrevocably gone. "I just didn't know how else to explain it, and I wanted to see you."

Her dad's face was white. "This isn't about whatever happened in town today?" he surprised her by asking. "There are rumors swirling about an accident."

Haley straightened, feeling ridiculous that she was still holding Emma's stuffed cat, but not wanting to let it go. "It is," she said. "That's why I texted you that I was fine. But Dean and I went to that open house today. The house on Carrington Road that Josie was showing. And weirdly my anatomy teacher and his wife were there, too, and we all went into the kitchen and found Josie lying on the floor."

Liv covered her mouth. "Was she all right?" she asked.

"She'd been stabbed," Haley said, sucking in a breath at the sound of the word coming out of her mouth.

Her mom gasped. Her dad moved across the room and sat on Emma's bed. "Oh my God," he said. "Is she alive?" His eyes were sharp and more focused than Haley had seen them in a long time. She broke his stare and looked down at the blue throw rug between them. "I went to the hospital and saw her," she said, "and I didn't talk to the doctor, but I think she's going to be completely fine."

"Could she tell you who did it?" he asked, his voice so hard she barely recognized it.

"Tim, calm down," her mom said, putting a hand on Haley's shoulder. "She's upset enough."

Haley glanced up at her dad. His gaze was still so intense. "No," Haley said. "She doesn't remember."

Her dad seemed satisfied with this response, but then he made a fist and pounded it against the quilt. He shook his head slowly. "It has to be related," he said, his light eyes wild. "She was Emma's best friend. How many women do you think have violent crimes committed against them in this town? How can it be a coincidence?"

Haley turned to her mom. "I agree with Dad," she said carefully.

Liv's expression looked both scared and hopeful at the same time. "Do the police think so?" she asked.

"If they do, they didn't say anything to me," Haley said. "They questioned all of us—me, Dean, my professor Brad, and his wife, Priya—but at least to me, they didn't mention anything about how this could be connected to Emma."

"Did you say *Priya*?" Liv asked, sitting up a little straighter.

Haley nodded.

"Your sister had an art teacher named Priya at Yarrow."

My wife, the artist. How many times had Brad referred to her that way in class? "This woman is an artist," Haley blurted. "I don't know much about her, but I know that."

Her dad looked from Liv to Haley. "This is bigger than that stupid bracelet," he said. "This is something real. And Emma could still be out there."

Stop it, Haley thought, sinking farther into Emma's pillows. *Please, just stop saying that.*

"Oh, honey," Liv said carefully. "She's not, she's just not." But she didn't look at Haley's dad—she didn't comfort him. Haley wanted to pick up the slack, to make her dad feel better, but she couldn't. He infuriated her when he talked like this. "Don't you think we want to believe that, too, Dad?" Haley asked.

"Then why don't you, dammit?" he asked. He looked so out of place sitting there on the bed among Emma's stuffed animals. What had been the point of getting rid of Emma's old bed if they were going to keep the stuffed animals? It was insane. Maybe they all were insane, grasping at straws, believing they could ever make any of this hurt less.

Haley swiped at the tears running over her cheeks. No—*no.* She wouldn't be tricked. "Dad, please. Emma is dead," she said, and the air suddenly felt too hot and still with the forbidden word between them. "You have to know it," she went on, her voice softer now. "Please. It's so much harder to pretend she's not."

"Are you going to tell me what's harder, Haley?" he asked, his voice choked. "Are you really going to decide that for me? Can you? Can you know what I've done?"

Haley's mom put her hands over her face, and into her palms she said, "*Don't.* I beg you, Tim, please don't."

THIRTY-ONE

Emma

Ten years ago

I don't stop running through the woods until I hear my name, which might be the dumbest thing I've ever done. Don't the vast majority of murderers know their victims?

"Emma!"

There it is again, but I can't recognize the person because it sounds like he's trying to hush his voice. It has to be Brad—who else? Still, I edge my way off the trail into the brush. I stand there, not moving a muscle, and I try to tell myself I'm completely safe, but the only thing scarier than the dark trail is the even darker woods that surround it.

"Emma!" the voice calls again.

Something prickly brushes against my leg, and I pray it isn't alive. I let out a squeal. "Brad?" I call, hoping hard that it's him.

It is. He rounds the trail, and as he comes closer, I can see the grimace on his face. "Why are you running?" he asks. "What are you doing back there?"

"Hiding," I say, and then I start laughing way too loud, sounding completely insane. Another animal cries out—a coyote, I think.

"You said to meet you at marker two," Brad says, a little out of breath. He's not really in great shape.

"Sorry," I say, but now I'm suddenly feeling annoyed. "I got scared and ran away a little, okay? Things happen."

"Whatever," he says, but it sounds too young, like he's trying to talk in my language but can't. He's tired and lost, I realize as I look at him. Maybe we both are. It's quiet for a moment, and he steps a little closer. He reaches out to touch my waist, and I think about how close his hand is to the baby.

"I'm sorry I didn't tell you about my girlfriend," he says.

"Your fiancée," I correct him. "Priya is your fiancée."

"Yes. My *fiancée*. Sorry, I hate that word."

I shift my weight away from him, wondering if he can see the whites of my eyes rolling in the dark.

"Did you tell her?" he asks, his voice lower.

"That we've been sleeping together?" I want him to have to say it, but of course he doesn't. "I didn't tell her," I say. "But I'm guessing she figured it out. Haven't you talked to her?"

"Not yet," he says. "Look, I'm sorry." He runs a hand over his hair, and I can see how crystalline his eyes are, practically glowing in the dark. I think of how he was in bed, so sure of himself when we'd start taking off our clothes, like seducing me was part of an act. But then as the sex went on, he always lost himself in it. His hair would fall into his face, and he'd close his eyes like I wasn't even there. It made me feel hollow, like I wanted to slip away, to sink into the sheets and sleep. I didn't always feel that way, but it'd gotten way worse lately. Maybe I need to go back to that psychiatrist again. Or maybe I just need to break up with Brad.

Brad steps closer, and for a beat I think he's going to kiss me. "You're absolutely sure you didn't tell her?" he asks, almost coyly. It's so incredibly dark out here, but I can still make out a small gash above his eyebrow. I reach for it, but he grabs my wrist and stops my hand so quickly it makes me start.

"Ow! You're hurting me." His hand is still on my wrist, his grip too tight. "I didn't tell her," I say, just wanting him to let go of me. I'm relieved when my phone vibrates. I wrench my hand free and pull my phone from my pocket to see that it's my dad calling. All I can think about is how much I wish I were with my parents right now. "I have to take this."

"No you don't," Brad says.

"Now you're acting like my teacher, and I'm not into that," I say. "Maybe some of your other students are."

His face twists with what might be genuine hurt, but it's too hard to tell, the night is too black around us. "There aren't other students," he says as my phone keeps buzzing. "There's only you. And you're not my student."

"*Only me?* Really?" I ask, feigning surprise. "You mean only Priya and me?"

"You know what I mean," he says through a tight jaw.

I shrug, over this. "I'm pregnant," I blurt.

He blinks, considering me. "No," he says, slowly shaking his head. "No way."

"You're a doctor, so you understand how science works, right?" I ask, because I'm really getting sick of people and their disbelief today. Sex equals baby, even sometimes with a condom, and definitely without one, which was the incredibly stupid decision made by Noah and me.

"I also understand how birth control works," Brad says. "And we always used it—*I* always used it."

I should just say the baby is Noah's, but I have to admit that a part of me is enjoying the sweat that's breaking out on Brad's forehead, glistening in the moonlight now that the clouds have passed. He's always been slightly smug, like he knows so much more than me. It was an undercurrent in all our interactions, but it never bothered me enough to stop sleeping with him. But now I realize the power I hold over an older, almost-married man, and it makes me heady.

"Like I said, I'm pregnant," I say. My phone stops vibrating, and I put it back into my pocket, my hand bumping against the pregnancy test I stashed there, and then I do something I didn't plan to. I take out the test. I didn't bring it to show to anyone tonight; I just didn't want to leave it in my room where anyone could find it.

Brad grabs the test from my hand. He takes out his phone and uses the flashlight to read the word *pregnant*. His brow folds, and his face scares me. I'm about to tell him it isn't his when my dad calls again. "Listen," I say to Brad, wanting this to be over.

He looks up from the pregnancy test. "No," he says, shaking his head. "You listen to me, Emma." He goes to pocket my test, but I snatch it back.

"That's mine," I say, and he doesn't argue. He quickly moves toward me, his hands reaching for my neck. I try to back away, but he's too fast. I stumble, falling to the ground, and he does, too. He crashes on top of me, and the wind gets knocked out of my chest. *The baby's not yours*, I try to say, but I can't get my breath back to push out the words. Brad's hovering over me now, and I see fear glinting in his eyes as he stands and pulls me into the brush. I kick and scratch at him, still trying to catch my breath.

What have I done?

THIRTY-TWO

Haley

W hat have you done, Dad?" Haley asked. He was still sitting on Emma's bed, perched forward, his eyes filled with tears.

"You'll only hurt her," Liv said softly.

"Please don't talk about me like I'm not here," Haley said, inching away from her mom. She dropped Emma's stuffed cat and steeled herself. *"Dad?"* she asked again.

A shiver passed over him—Haley could see it in the way his shoulders and arms twitched. The physical grief Emma provoked in all of them was a beast. Liv hid it the best, crying every so often and then letting it pass. But Haley could tell that for her dad, the grief got trapped inside his body just like it did for her. He might not tap or perform the same OCD rituals, but Emma was there inside all of them.

Her dad finally spoke. "Emma called me on the night she disappeared," he started, his words slow at first. "She called me because she was scared. I could hear it in her voice when I finally listened to her voice mail."

"Okay, Tim, that's enough," Liv protested. "It's off your chest now."

He ignored her. "But do you know why I didn't pick up her call, Haley? Do you know why I declined a call from my Emma on the night she disappeared?" Haley suddenly wasn't sure she wanted to hear where this was going. Her dad stared hard like he actually wanted her to try to answer, and then he said, "I declined my daughter's call because I was with the woman I was having an affair with. I was cheating on your mother, and I was so wrapped up in it. And for the first time in maybe forever I didn't pick up the phone for one of my daughters." He shook his head like he still couldn't believe it, and Haley started crying. "The outcome for Emma could have been so different," he went on. "That's the truth—I've gone over it in my mind thousands of times—so don't try to talk me out of it. I've heard her voice mail a hundred times. She called me from the woods, from the last place she was ever seen, and she said twenty-six words, all of which sounded terrified. So don't tell me what I can believe and what I can't. There's a chance I could have stopped my daughter from disappearing, and believing she's still out there is the only way I know how to keep going. Do you understand me, Haley? This is the only way I can stay alive with what I've done. Because if she's out there, I need to be here for her to come home to."

Tears fell hot over Haley's cheeks. "Oh, Dad," she said. She knew him well enough to know what this must have done to him, carrying the weight of this terrible thing, the guilt of it all, thinking he could have stopped her—it must have nearly killed him. "I'm so sorry," she said. It all made so much sense, how small his world had gotten, how obsessed he was with the idea that Emma could still be alive, how stubborn he was whenever they tried to tell him she wasn't.

"You're sorry?" he asked, blinking.

"Of course I'm sorry," she said, and then she turned to her mother. "For you, too, Mom, that he did this to you, that he hurt you." She turned back to her father. "But, Dad, to know you've had this guilt, on top of everything else . . ." She was awash with empathy for him, no matter what terribly stupid thing he'd done, the tears falling even faster now. "Emma's not gone because of you," she said, making her voice as strong as she could. "I don't believe that. And *I* need you, too. What about staying alive because I'm here?" she asked, her voice a whisper.

Her dad ran a hand over his lined skin and looked out Emma's window into the snow. "You'd be okay without me," he finally said, and Liv started crying even harder, her eyes on Haley. "It's the truth," he said to both of them, "you know it is. I haven't been much of a father since Emma disappeared. And you're so strong, Haley."

"I'm not strong enough to lose you," Haley said. "I still need you."

Haley's dad sat back on the bed, sinking into the mattress. "I understand if you don't want to talk to me ever again because of what I've done to your mother and your sister."

"Never talk to you again?" Haley repeated. "Because of a mistake? Do you really think I'd give you up that easily, after everything we've all been through? I don't think what happened to Emma is your fault," she said again. "I just don't. And I never will. So don't even bother trying to convince me, and don't apologize."

"I cheated on your mom," he said. "Even if you don't blame me for Emma, you have every right to be furious at me for that."

Haley looked down at the pattern on Emma's rug, at the way the silky blue threads made spirals like those inside a seashell, and then said, "I'm furious about all of it, about everything that's happened. I don't think I've ever stopped being furious. And maybe if we were a different family, I would let this final detail tear us apart, but we're not a different family—we're us. And I can't pretend to understand marriage when I've never been married and can barely understand my own relationship. Your marriage is your business, really."

Liv stopped crying. Maybe she thought the news of his affair would destroy Haley in some way, but the truth was there wasn't anything else that could break Haley like her sister's disappearance had—at least nothing that she could imagine. "How did you find out?" Haley asked her mom. She wasn't sure why, but she needed to know.

"Apparently, your sister had seen them together," Liv said, her voice soft.

"And Emma told you?" Haley asked.

Liv shook her head. "She confronted Dad. And they were supposed to talk that night more about it . . ." Her mom's eyes cut to her dad, like she was worried she'd made a mistake, mentioned the wrong thing, but he picked up where she left off.

"Emma and I were texting. We were going to meet and talk more. I'd lost my cool earlier that week when she mentioned it to me; I regret that, but not nearly as much as I regret ignoring her call that night . . ."

He started to cry, and Liv put a hand on his knee, began rubbing circles. How many times had she been strong for him during the past decade? How did she do it?

"Mom," Haley said, squeezing Liv's other hand.

Liv let go of a breath and squeezed back. "Your dad told the police right away about the affair when Emma disappeared," she said, "because the woman was married, and God forbid it had something to do with Emma vanishing. But it didn't; the police looked into that thoroughly."

Haley swallowed, needing to ask her mother something, but afraid to. "And you didn't leave him?" she finally managed, as gently as she could. "I'm not judging you, I swear. I'm just wondering; I don't understand marriage yet, like I said, and . . ."

Her dad wiped his eyes and looked away, but Liv held Haley's glance. "Because we had to face something indescribably worse than an affair," she said, "and I knew the only way we could survive it was to face it together."

Haley tried to hold back more tears. Her parents exchanged a glance. "Is there something else? Anything you're not telling me?" Haley asked.

Her dad shook his head. "No," Liv said. "No other secrets."

"Good," Haley said, letting go of a shaky breath. "Then can we talk about what happened today, at the open house, if that's okay with you both?" she asked carefully. "Because I have a very strong feeling that the person who killed Emma was at the house on Carrington Road today. Which means if this crime gets solved, then maybe so does ours."

THIRTY-THREE

Priya

Priya drove straight home after the cops dropped her at the open house to retrieve her car. Where else was there to go?

There had been a time, years ago, when Priya would have gone to her studio on Yarrow's campus; she would have chosen to be surrounded by her work. But those paintings had all been sold or given away, and that studio didn't exist anymore. At least, not for her. The last thing she'd ever painted was a nude self-portrait with her belly at full capacity with Elliot, her face round and her ankles swollen. She'd never felt so beautiful and strange, and she wanted to capture that person who finally understood the meaning of the word *expecting*.

Now she sat on a wicker sofa and waited for Brad. It was almost five o'clock, and Elliot was next door with Robby. Alex had promised to keep him for dinner, and thank God, because there was no way Priya could have Elliot in the house when she confronted Brad.

Windows surrounded Priya on the porch. She looked out onto the snow that blanketed the lawn and weighed down the trees until the smaller branches looked like they would snap. The sun would set soon and leave her alone in the blackness with the man who may have killed Emma and hurt Josie. Was she supposed to try to protect herself from him? Was she a fool for not feeling terrified?

Priya kicked a quilt off her legs, wanting to feel the chill that matched her mood. She thought back to her and Brad's third night home from the hospital with Elliot, when Brad finally convinced her to rest between feedings. She'd lain there alone in her bed while Brad rocked Elliot down the hall, and though she tried to sleep, the adrenaline from birthing her precious creature was still coursing through her veins. After twenty minutes of tossing and turning, she'd tiptoed back down the hall to take over, but right as she was about to turn the knob, she heard Brad's muffled crying. She waited outside the door for a few moments just to be sure—Brad never, ever cried—and then she crept slowly into the dark room. "Brad?" she'd whispered.

"I'm here," he'd said.

She'd waited for her eyes to adjust. "What is it?" she'd asked, creeping over the carpet, not wanting to trip on a rogue nursing pillow or baby blanket. "What's wrong?"

"I'm so sorry," Brad said. "I'm so sorry for what I've done."

Priya's nerves had spiked. As she crept closer she could make out Elliot's tiny, still form against Brad's chest, and for a reckless moment she'd thought Brad had done something to her newborn. She was about to lunge forward when she heard Elliot let out a sleepy cry before nuzzling back into Brad's chest.

"What do you mean?" she'd asked him, her breathing still way too fast. Was he talking about the cheating? Or had he done something so much worse?

He'd never answered her, and she let it go, because she truly believed he didn't hurt Emma. But what if she was wrong back then? Could she be absolutely sure her husband didn't hurt anyone? Could anyone be that sure about another person?

The front door opened with a familiar screech of wood against the frame.

"Priya," Brad called out, his voice strangled. She braced herself for everything she was about to say, and for everything he might tell her.

THIRTY-FOUR

Haley

Haley pulled into the hospital's parking lot for the second time that day, this time in her own car. Rappaport had shooed her away, but the hospital—and Josie, with all her answers, whether or not she remembered them yet—drew Haley back like a magnet. She still hadn't heard from Dean, and as she parked and walked through a hazy mist of snow, she worried about why he hadn't called her back. He had to be freaked out; there was no way he'd ever seen anything like what he'd seen today on Carrington Road. Even for Haley, who worked on a cadaver and did rounds in the hospital where people lay struggling, what had happened this morning was too violent and scary to comprehend yet.

Haley flashed her badge again at the guard and headed to the elevator. In the ICU she strode toward Josie's room and saw the same police officer parked outside the door. There was no sign of Rappaport. The cop gave Haley a look like he wasn't thrilled to see her, but he still stood to slide open the door, and that's when Haley saw Noah, Chris, and—strangely—Dean. They were all staring down at Josie, their features drawn, and when they looked up to see Haley, Dean's face went white.

"What are you doing here?" Haley asked him, unable to hide her surprise.

Dean flinched, which was what he always did when she'd caught him doing something he shouldn't be doing. Not that she'd ever caught him doing anything terrible, but even little things: like if she walked in on him checking his phone when he'd told her he just needed to change clothes. She'd always thought it was sort of cute, but now it put a pit in her stomach. "I came to see Josie as soon as I could," he said, his voice all business, like Josie was a client or a coworker he was checking on, which was true in a way. It wasn't like Dean and Josie were close; it was Haley who'd developed a friendship with Josie. And that's why Haley was so surprised Dean would even feel comfortable enough to come here without her. "But why didn't you call me first?" she pressed. No one spoke, and the way Dean was looking at her made her realize how petty she was being to nag him with Josie lying there in a hospital bed. "Sorry," she muttered. She crossed the tiny room to stand next to Josie and put a hand on her forearm. She still looked like a wreck with her matted hair and deathly pale skin. "How are you feeling?" Haley asked softly.

"I'm okay," Josie managed.

Chris moved closer to Josie, and something about it struck Haley as too territorial. And then Noah said, "She's *not* okay, because today she was stabbed by some maniac."

Haley recoiled, unsure of why his anger seemed to be directed at her. "What's the latest from the doctor?" she asked. She'd grown adept at redirecting difficult family members in the hospital—recently one of the residents had commented on her ability to defuse tension, and the compliment had made her month.

No one spoke. Dean glanced at Noah like he should be the one to share any news, but he didn't, and in the silence Haley lost her ability to stay calm and rational. "So where were you guys today?" she blurted at Noah and Chris. "The cops said they couldn't find you."

"I was showing a client a home, and I didn't have service," Noah said, and before Chris could answer, Noah asked, "Are you accusing us of something?"

The room went still. Chris cleared his throat. Dean said, "I think we need to calm down and stick together."

"Stick together?" Haley repeated, incredulous. "What are you talking about?" She stared at Dean, trying to recalibrate.

Josie chewed at the edge of a fingernail, and Noah's sour expression faded. Chris wouldn't look at any of them. "Your professor Brad," Dean started, the slightest waver in his voice. "He was a teaching assistant ten years ago at Yarrow. Your sister was sleeping with him."

Haley felt blood drain from her face. Dean reached for her hand, but she didn't take it. "No way," she said, not because she couldn't believe it, but because something this big had never been uncovered during the course of the investigation. Emma had been sleeping with a *teacher* at the university?

"She was sneaking around with him," Dean went on. "And they were definitely in some kind of relationship when she disappeared."

"Are you absolutely sure?" Haley asked, holding on to the rail of Josie's bed like an anchor.

"We're sure," Dean said, exchanging a look with Josie. "Brad never came forward or told the cops, obviously. But you know his wife, Priya, who he was with at the open house today? She taught Emma and Josie art at school. Priya and Brad weren't married when Emma disappeared, but they were engaged."

"But how did you find this out?" Haley asked, her thoughts racing. "The police?"

Josie burst into tears. They fell over her cheeks, and she tried to sweep them away with shaking hands. "You're going to hate me, Haley, I'm so, so sorry," she said, crying even harder. She flinched as though the crying hurt her wound, and Haley wondered what kind of painkillers she was on—she seemed so lucid given what she'd gone through.

Chris and Noah moved closer to Josie, their synchronicity jarring to Haley. Chris got there first. He lowered himself onto the bed and put a hand on Josie's arm. "Please calm down, Josie," he said. "It was such a long time ago."

"Maybe for you it was," Haley spat, her cheeks burning. "Maybe you guys have all gotten over Emma's disappearance; good for you." Beeping monitors filled an awkward silence. What was *wrong* with all of them? She whirled around to glare at Dean. "I don't get it, Dean. *How did you find out about this?* Did you know something about it before today?"

Dean tried to take her hand. "Of course I didn't know anything about your sister and Brad," he said.

"I'm sorry I kept this from you," Josie was saying through tears as Chris held her arm, "and from the police, from everyone. I just honestly thought your sister killed herself, like everyone else thought. The last thing I wanted was for her reputation to be dragged down, too."

Haley's insides were twisting thinking of her sister and Brad, who must have been in his late twenties at the time. "Was Brad the one who gave her that bracelet?" she asked.

"Yeah," Josie said, like it was nothing, just another thing she knew about Emma that Haley didn't. Haley bit down hard on her lip, tasting blood. Chris was still staring at his hands, but Dean and Noah were watching Josie carefully. "Haley," Josie said, lifting her eyes, looking so indescribably sad when she said, "your sister was pregnant."

Haley's hands flew to cover her face, and then she couldn't stop herself from shrieking at Josie. "How could you not have gone to the police with this?" She leaned toward Josie, and then Chris lunged forward to restrain her, which infuriated her further because obviously she wasn't going to hurt Josie. "Stay away from me!" Haley hissed at Chris as he raised his hands to grab her arms.

"Get your hands off her," Dean said to Chris, his voice low.

Chris backed off, and Noah said, "Haley, listen, we all loved your sister, don't you see that?"

"And we were kids back then," Chris said, sounding so slick and sure of himself, like any of this was even close to excusable.

"So *what*?" Haley growled. "You're not kids now. You could have told the police any time during the past decade what you knew about my sister sleeping with a teacher *who was engaged,* and Emma being pregnant!"

Josie cried harder. Haley didn't care. "Tell me you didn't know anything about my sister being pregnant," Haley said to Dean.

"Not until a few minutes before you did," Dean said, calmer now. His gaze seemed surer, as though the ground was getting steadier.

"Your sister was my best friend," Josie said, but she sounded like she was trying to convince herself. She swiped at a piece of blond hair flecked with blood. "Why would I ever tell anyone her secrets?"

"Because they make her death seem suspicious," Haley said. "And you said *nothing.*"

Dean stood there, his face changing again. Haley was pretty sure she'd never seen him look like this, his expression so anguished and tortured.

"Josie's coming forward with it *now*, and it's better late than never," Chris said. Haley looked at Josie, at the way her normally olive skin looked yellow, her eyes bloodshot. *Keep it together, Haley.* "Do you think Brad or Priya killed my sister?" she asked Josie.

Josie nodded, and said, "I do, Haley. I think Brad did." Haley tried to swallow, but she felt like she was being choked. The hospital air was too hot, too thick.

"Brad and Priya aren't our clients," Chris said, his fingers working at a small tear on the arm of his flannel shirt. "We've never worked with them on a house."

"But couldn't they have been there to see an open house like anyone else?" Haley asked.

"It's a small town," Noah said, agitated as he moved a hand over his face. "We have no records of them ever coming to see one of our properties. It's too much of a coincidence."

"And who else could it be?" Josie asked, still crying. "Who would have attacked me if not Brad, or even Priya could have attacked me if she were trying to shut me up about what Brad did. I've talked to Priya over the past years about everything, and I've always really liked her, and I don't think she would ever try to hurt me, but I also feel like I don't know anything anymore. If Brad and Priya heard the cops were reopening the case—and people talk in this town—then they have all the motive in the world to shut me up. They both know that I know Brad was sleeping with Emma before she disappeared."

Dean's dark eyes were wide and hollow. Noah looked down into his hands. Haley stared at all three of them, and as her gaze settled on Chris, a chill passed over her skin. Something wasn't right.

"Do you have proof?" Haley asked.

"Proof?" Noah asked. "You don't believe her?"

"I believe her," Haley said. Her toes scrunched against the insides of her boots as she tried to ground herself. "But I also want the cops to."

"There's a pregnancy test," Josie said.

"And you have it?" Dean asked, barely able to mask how horrified he was.

"Where is it, Josie?" Haley asked. "We need to give it to the police."

"I already did," Josie said. "Well, I mean, I didn't exactly hand it over, but I told them where it was in our house. They searched our house today after everything that happened this morning. Noah says it looks like its own crime scene."

"But as far as the cops know, couldn't it just be your pregnancy test?" Dean asked.

"It'll have Emma's DNA all over it," Haley said. She swallowed hard, trying to stop her imagination from picturing her sister all alone, taking a pregnancy test and finding out she was pregnant. Why hadn't she told Haley what was happening to her? "Did she tell you back then, Josie?" Haley asked, trying to will herself not to cry again. "Or did you find the test after she disappeared?"

"She told me," Josie said, and jealousy flashed through Haley with such fury it was hard to hide it. Her fingertips tapped her legs in an erratic rhythm. She wanted to ask how Josie got hold of the test and why, but the whole thing felt so macabre. "How do you know the baby was Brad's?" she asked instead, the tapping growing so wild she knew the others saw it.

Noah averted his eyes from her. "I don't!" Josie said. "That's part of the reason I never turned in the pregnancy test, because the last thing I wanted was for her to be known as the girl who was pregnant and didn't even know who the father was, the girl who plunged to her death to escape it all." Josie sobbed harder, and Noah jumped in, saying, "That's enough, Haley. For God's sake, you're studying to become a doctor. I'm pretty sure this kind of stress isn't good for anyone in her condition."

"Then why don't *you* answer my question, Noah?" Haley snapped.

"I didn't kill your sister," Noah said, his words eerily calm, like he was explaining a math problem to a child, "and I didn't try to kill my wife today."

"You're still not answering her question, Noah," Dean said.

"What I'm asking you," Haley said, her voice a whisper, "is if the baby could have been yours."

Josie looked up at Noah, her eyes wide. "You don't have to do this," she said.

"I think he does," Dean said. He reached out his hand and took Haley's, and she steadied herself for whatever she was about to hear.

THIRTY-FIVE

Emma

Ten years ago

We stumble once more, and then Brad rolls off me and onto his back. His breathing is so heavy he's almost gasping. For a second I think he's having some kind of heart attack, but then I remind myself he's not really that old. "What is *wrong* with you?" I ask, still so unsure of what just happened, trying to digest the fact that someone I was sleeping with just tried to attack me. My lungs are still burning when I ask, "Were you trying to hurt me?"

He's just lying there with a hand over his chest. I can see the rise and fall of his parka, the zipper sticking straight up in the air. "No," he finally says. "Obviously not."

"Obviously not?" I glare at him. "You just pushed me down."

"I was trying to get the pregnancy test back. I panicked, okay? Rational thought dictates that you could just take another one." He turns onto his side with a muffled sound, and it occurs to me that maybe he hurt himself when we fell. I sit a little closer. Branches scratch at my arms, and tiny rocks and twigs poke my butt. "The baby isn't yours," I say, trying to get remotely comfortable in the brush.

He looks at me with bewilderment all over his face, and then pulls himself up to sit. We're both sitting cross-legged like two campers at a campsite about to roast marshmallows and tell ghost stories. "Then why did you act like it was?" he asks.

My heart is still pulsing in my ears from the struggle, my blood too hot as it swirls through me. "I don't know," I say, suddenly filled with so much shame. I run my fingers over a smattering of stones between us, wanting to feel anything other than this feeling. "Probably because I wanted to hurt you back."

When Brad reaches forward, I see dirt on his hands, and maybe blood, but it's too dark to be sure. He almost touches me, but he must think better of it because his hand freezes. "I didn't mean to hurt you," he says.

"You have a fiancée—a pregnant one, no less—and you slept with me anyway," I say.

He shakes his head, and a strand of strawberry-blond hair falls in front of his eyes. "I'm messed up," he says.

"We're all messed up," I say, starting to stand, because the ground beneath us is too cold, and I need to leave this place, to find Noah and Josie. Even seeing Chris right now would be a welcome relief. My legs are aching as I straighten up, and I think about Noah and wonder if I love him. I've never loved anyone before except my family members. College would be easier if I'd ever had a serious boyfriend, but my parents were so strict about me dating. Maybe I'm doing it all wrong.

"Are you going to keep the baby?" Brad asks, rising, too.

It's weird that he doesn't ask me whose it is, but the undergrad boys are probably all same to him. "I think so," I say. And then, when I add, "I hope so," I'm struck with the saddest, most lonely feeling. I think of Chris and Josie, and how they were all alone until they ended up in the same family, and I think of how they would protect each other over anyone else.

Family. The truth is that this baby is my family—and it's maybe the only truth I know for sure, the only one that matters. I swallow down tears and manage to say, "I need to go, Brad. I need to find my friends."

"Goodbye, Emma," he says.

"Goodbye," I say. We don't touch, not even to embrace. I turn and walk carefully back to the trail.

THIRTY-SIX

Priya

"What the hell was *that*?" Brad asked when he bounded onto the porch.

Priya didn't answer, and a moment later Brad collapsed onto the chair across from her and let his head fall into his hands. "Did you tell the detectives about our history with Emma and Josie?" he asked before raising his eyes to look at her. "Did they ask you?"

"Our history with Emma?" Priya repeated, curling her hand around the arm of the wicker sofa, pressing hard against it with her fingertips and bitten nails.

"Yes, *our history with Emma*," Brad said. "Emma as your student—Emma as my lover."

Priya's jaw dropped. "Your lover," she said, tasting the word and all the things it meant. Shadows fell across the porch's floor, mostly in the shape of foliage, and Priya's eyes landed on her cold-weather plants, the catmint and prickly wintergreen boxwoods.

"Stop repeating my words, Priya," Brad said. "This is serious."

"I'm aware of how serious this is," Priya hissed, inhaling the smell of mint. Elliot could be back any minute, and where would that leave them? "I'm also aware that the mess you made all those years ago still haunts us now. So before you start questioning me, I'd just like to ask you, once and for all: *How much* of a mess did you make back then?"

Brad blinked. "What are you talking about?" he asked. The collar of his oxford shirt was stained with something that looked like coffee. Had he really been relaxed enough back at the precinct to accept the cops' offers of coffee?

"Did you kill Emma?" she asked, the words like marbles dropping on a hard floor.

Disbelief contorted Brad's face. Priya waited. The plants seemed to take on dark, ominous shapes, as though they were threatening to outgrow their pots and twine around her ankles, keeping her trapped and tethered to this place.

"I can't believe you just asked me that," Brad finally said into the chilled air between them. "Didn't you believe me years ago when I told you I didn't?"

Priya's body felt on fire with nerves, her hands making fists against her legs. Brad stood too slowly. A candle flickered on the side table next to him, glistening amid a squat stack of coffee table books. "Do you really think I could hurt Emma?" he asked, seeming so genuinely offended that she was taken aback. "Priya," he said, stepping closer to her. "Is that what you've always thought?"

"No," she said, shaking her head. "But after today . . ."

"You think I stabbed Josie? You think I killed a girl ten years ago, and that for some reason, today, I tried to kill her former roommate? You think I'm a serial killer, is that right?" He was coming closer, his gait unsteady, unfamiliar.

Priya bit her lower lip. It sounded ridiculous when he said it like that. "People do unimaginable things," she said, stalling. "Maybe Emma was going to out you to your bosses at Yarrow. You would've had your career ruined."

"I'm a doctor; my job is to *protect* people!" Brad said, still so incredulous. "You think I would kill someone to protect my career? I took an oath! Don't you think that means anything to me?"

Priya's legs felt numb against the wicker sofa's flowered cushion. She sat there frozen, unsure of what to say. Finally she asked, "Why were you there today at the open house?"

"Because Josie invited me there," Brad said, blowing out an angry breath. "She told me she needed to talk to me, that it was urgent she tell me something." He studied her, still standing there, his gaze unrelenting as always, missing nothing. "Don't you know me better than to think I could ever try to kill someone?"

Did she know him better than that? She thought she did, but everything felt too confusing and blurred after this morning. "I was scared!" Priya blurted. "Okay? Can't you understand that after what happened today?"

Brad shook his head and sat down beside her. "You were scared," he said slowly. "Of course. You're always scared." He sounded so tired, and Priya felt embarrassed by the truth of what he'd said. "I don't know if I can go on like this, Priya, with your fear coloring everything we do, everything we are."

Priya started crying. How had all of this gotten so turned around? "I'm sorry," she said, "but it's not like you've been a saint, Brad."

"I know that, and I'm sorry, too," he said, and then he took her hand. "And just so you know, Emma wasn't going to out me to anyone," he said. "Obviously I should have told you this a long time ago, but she was breaking things off with me. Really, Priya. That night when she came to our town house? She was trying to call things off. She was pregnant, but it wasn't mine."

Priya's stomach lurched. "Oh, God," she said, her eyes burning with tears. "That just makes the whole thing sadder, which I didn't even think was possible. And how can you know for sure it wasn't yours?"

"Because we used protection. And because she was sort of play-acting like it was mine at first, but when I called her bluff, she admitted it was someone else's. I have no idea whose it was, which is why I didn't go to the police after she disappeared. I swear to God I would have gone to the cops if she'd told me. But I didn't even ask her whose it was; I was just so relieved it wasn't mine."

Priya pulled her knees to her chest. "You still should have told the cops she was pregnant."

"And you probably should have told them she was sleeping with me, but you didn't."

Priya flinched. It was true, of course.

"We all do things we're ashamed of," Brad said, his voice hard. "We all stay quiet when we shouldn't. But, Priya, listen to me. What would it have mattered if you or I came forward? I didn't do it. And that night when I watched her walk away, it was over. I didn't want her anymore, I wanted *you*. You might not believe me, but it's true."

The funny thing was, Priya did believe him. He'd returned to her that night with devotion all over his face and in every ounce of his body. "Maybe you were done with Emma, but you've been unfaithful since," she said. "I know that."

"Only once," he said, "and it was a huge mistake. And I put an end to it."

"It's still too many times, Brad. Something about us isn't right if you can't stay faithful. And it's not fair what I do to you, either, my anxiety, holding on to you because I'm too scared of falling apart without you."

Brad shook his head. "I don't keep you together," he said. "You do that."

Priya smiled weakly. "So do the meds you prescribe me."

"You could find a psychiatrist for that," he said. "Or get another therapist, better than the ones you've had."

"Someone else should be prescribing, not you, shouldn't they?" Priya asked carefully. She knew she was treading on dangerous ground—his career, his ego.

"I'm not doing anything wrong," Brad said, shaking his head. "I'm just trying to help you."

"I know that," Priya said, "I do. But I think maybe, the dose, isn't it a little aggressive?" His eyes went wider. "I googled it," she said, "that's all, and it seemed—"

"There's an acceptable range of dosage, Priya," Brad said.

"Oh, okay," Priya said, unsure how to respond.

Brad's face was sad and unfamiliar when he said, "It just seems in this conversation you've accused me of murdering someone, stabbing someone else, and poisoning you with medication."

"No, of course not," Priya said. "I know you would never hurt me. I just thought perhaps . . ."

"That I was overmedicating you," he finished.

"Yes," she said.

He pressed his lips tightly together. "It's a higher dosage than normal," he said, "but not out of the range of what's sometimes prescribed. And I told you I was starting you on the highest dose; we talked about that. Priya, it's not been easy, seeing you have these spells of anxiety, knowing you're caring for our son alone, and knowing you could have another panic attack at any minute, while you were driving him somewhere, even, and what if . . ."

"I've always taken good care of Elliot," Priya said. "I've always kept him safe and loved."

"I know that. God, do I know that. You're the most incredible mother I've ever known."

Priya blinked. He'd never said it like that. They were quiet, staring at each other, until Priya said slowly, "I'm going to get a new therapist, and a new doctor."

"There's a psychiatrist I know from work . . ." Brad started, but Priya held up her hand. "I'll find my own," she said.

Brad nodded, and then a knock pounded on the front door. Priya assumed it was Elliot and rose quickly, the blue-and-white tiles blurring beneath her feet as she hurried down the hall and into the foyer. Brad followed her, and they opened the door to see Detective Rappaport and two uniformed officers standing behind him. He flashed his badge, which felt entirely unnecessary, and then said, "Dr. Aarons, you're under arrest for the attempted murder of Josie Carmichael."

Priya covered her mouth. She glanced at her husband, standing there in the doorway with his face white. "Let's make this easy," Rappaport said as he began to frisk Brad for weapons. "We wouldn't want to make a scene in front of your neighborhood, Dr. Aarons."

"We didn't do anything!" Priya blurted.

"Forensics found evidence that gives us probable cause," the detective said, the words piercing the cold air like a slingshot.

"I'm going with the police," Brad said slowly, reasonably, and then he nodded toward their neighbor's house, and that's when Priya saw something so much worse than Rappaport and his all-powerful badge: her son was trudging through the neighbor's front yard toward hers.

"No," she said beneath her breath. *Please, turn back, Elliot, go back inside.*

Elliot was wearing Brad's oversized snow boots. Priya had shooed him out of the house so fast he couldn't find his own. He looked ridiculous in them, and he could barely walk through the snow without stumbling. What had she been thinking?

"Call our lawyer," Brad was saying, but his words were too fuzzy inside her brain. Elliot was still so focused on the snow he hadn't looked up yet to see the officers on their front step. The lights on the cop car weren't flashing, and nothing out of the ordinary seemed to have caught his eye yet.

"Priya? Do you hear me? Call our lawyer and send him to the station."

Their lawyer? Was Brad trying to sound tough in front of the detective? The only lawyer she ever considered *theirs* was Brad's brother. "Jack?" she asked, and he nodded. She swallowed, and the moment she turned back to Elliot, his eyes found hers. He stopped dead in his tracks. Snow crept halfway up his boots. She wanted to call to him, but she couldn't find her voice. Elliot's gaze went to his father on the front step with Rappaport and the other cops. His brown eyes went wide. He started to sprint through the snow toward them, but then he lost his footing.

"Elliot!" Priya called out as he fell facedown into the snow, and then she took off running toward him. Two neighbors across the way had opened their front doors. Neither came to help Priya. They just stood there, one with a phone pressed against her ear as she stared at the police car. The news of Brad's arrest would be all over Waverly within the hour, and Priya knew they deserved it.

Elliot pushed himself to his feet and started barreling toward her, and she toward him, both of them stumbling through the snow until they were in each other's arms.

"Mama?" he asked, a question in his voice she didn't know how to answer.

Priya held her son and watched as his father was handcuffed and escorted into the back of a police car.

THIRTY-SEVEN

Emma

Ten years ago

I text my sister where the party is so she can meet me, but then I lose my cell service deeper in the woods. The trees and foliage are thickening, and I'm cursing myself for hanging back and telling Noah and Josie to go ahead without me. I nearly stumble over a rock, catching my balance at the last second. I try to calm down, try to tell myself I'm overreacting, and that the woods *are* safe. I know this trail, and that it leads to a clearing as long as I keep following it. That's where Josie and Noah will have the tents set up, and I remind myself that as soon as I see those tony red-and-white coolers full of beer, I'll be in college again and everything will feel closer to normal.

I use the flashlight on my phone to illuminate the path, but my hands are shaking enough from fear and cold that the light scatters the dirt like a strobe. I sing a Bob Marley song my dad used to sing to Haley and me just to hear the sound of my own voice instead of the crushing brush and animal calls. I'm almost there.

Moments later I see a golden glow, and something like euphoria hits when I realize I've made it. I start to run, and the low beat from some song I don't recognize filtering through the trees gets louder as I push faster toward it. When I crash into the clearing I can't get over how many people are there. They must have taken the trails closer to campus to get to the party. There's a group of guys and a few girls I don't recognize, and then Noah's lacrosse teammates clustered together drinking beers. A girl who manages their team, who Josie doesn't like, hangs on the fringes of the lacrosse group like she isn't sure how close she should get. I can see her guitar resting against a large rock. She's got a pretty good singing voice, but that's not why Josie doesn't like her—it's not anything simple like jealousy. Josie doesn't like her because there's an air of desperation about her, and that's the one thing Josie won't stand for.

Chris is off to the side by himself nursing a beer, his eyes glinting with something I can't read, until I follow his gaze to Josie and Noah. The music pulses, and I feel sick when I see them together. Noah's sitting in a folding chair with Josie on his lap, laughing. Josie lifts her beautiful face and sees me over Noah's shoulder, and when she smiles it doesn't look right. I make my legs walk toward them, forcing myself to look less upset than I actually am.

"Hey," I say coolly, and Noah turns, guilt all over his face for whatever this is.

I try only looking at him instead of at Josie, attempting to somehow telegraph that I got freaked out in the woods and that I'm the one who needs him right now, not her. But Noah and I don't know each other well enough yet to communicate in glances. If anything, I'm sure it's Josie who can read my face, and it makes me so furious that my eyes well with tears. I don't want her to be the one holding all my truths in her hand like a fistful of candy.

"What's up?" Josie asks easily, almost kindly, but I don't answer her. I turn to Noah.

"Can we talk?" I ask him. To Josie, I want to say: *Can you please get off my soon-to-be boyfriend's lap?* but I restrain myself. I stand there and watch as Noah gets up quickly and practically dumps Josie off his lap into the dirt.

Noah's friends crank up the music, and one of the guys I barely know does a keg stand while the others cheer him on. As quickly as I've come, I want to get out of here. The woods suddenly seem too close, Noah's friends too childish and leering, and my supposed best friend too cruel and suffocating. I want to scream, but I can't: not here, not now.

"What's wrong?" Noah asks as he gets closer. His voice is full of something that feels genuine and worth trying for. I love Josie, and I never wanted a relationship with Noah to come between us, but maybe I was too naive to even think that could be possible. Maybe she's writing an email to Noah like the one she wrote today, not out of overprotectiveness for me, but because she likes him. Maybe she's been lying about being upset that he's stealing me away from her; maybe what she really means is that I'm the one doing the stealing. Maybe she didn't realize she wanted him like that until I wanted him, too.

"I need to talk to you alone," I say softly to Noah, and then I narrow my gaze on Josie, daring her to stand in my way. *He wants me, not you.*

Noah puts his hands in his pockets. "Okay," he says. "Want to walk toward the river?"

An image floods my mind: the choppy current of the river, unforgiving and unrelenting, the water black as night. It makes me shudder, but I want to be alone with him, and I want to be far away from this party.

"Emma," Josie protests, but I won't hear it.

"Sure," I say. "Let's go."

THIRTY-EIGHT

Priya

Priya held Elliot tightly against her and tried to stop shaking. Elliot was still skinny enough to fold up his limbs inside her embrace, and she held him curled in her arms like a baby as they sat together on a leather sofa in the TV room. She'd wrapped a raspberry-colored afghan around him, and now she rubbed circles over his bony back as he cried against her collarbone and begged her to explain what had just happened.

"A woman was hurt today at an open house we went to," she told him, trying to keep her voice as even as possible. "And because we were there, the police need to question us and make sure we didn't do it."

"But Dad would never hurt anyone," Elliot said, the words choked by his sobs.

"I know that," Priya said. *I know that now, at least.* She felt it in her bones that Brad had told her the truth today. For years she'd told herself she was absolutely sure he hadn't hurt Emma, but there was always the tiniest kernel of doubt. How had she allowed so many transgressions in her marriage, so many things she never thought she would tolerate? How foolish could she ever be to think a marriage built on lies could survive? For God's sake, Elliot was born two days after Emma disappeared. What kind of karma had she and Brad incurred, for standing by and never going to the police with what they knew?

"I'm scared," Elliot said, pulling back to look her in the eye. His T-shirt was stretched around the collar and damp from where snow had found its way beneath his scarf. His pale skin was so delicate, and Priya gently touched the spot where his pulse reminded her how alive they were, how vibrant.

"I know, Elliot. Me, too." Honesty was what she always tried to give him, but she couldn't remember another time when it had been this hard. "Dad didn't hurt that woman, so there's nothing we can do but wait until the police realize that, too, and let him go."

"But how will they realize that?" Elliot asked, too smart for his own good.

It's what Priya wanted to know, too. The only person who could exonerate her husband was Josie, which made her the very person Priya needed to get to.

"Sit tight for just a second, okay?" Priya asked Elliot. "How about I make you a mug of warm milk?"

Elliot looked unsure but nodded, so Priya carefully extracted him from her lap and set him down on the soft leather cushion, tucking the afghan around him. She crept into the kitchen and found her phone. She opened up her texts and typed a message to Josie.

> Will you see me if I come to the hospital? Brad was just arrested, Josie, but he wasn't the one who hurt you today. Which means the person who did is still out there.

THIRTY-NINE

Emma

Ten years ago

Noah and I sit together on the cold, hard dirt high above the river. Below us the water carves a winding course, and the melting snow has made the current faster than usual. I watch the white, frothy waves cut through the night, thinking about the slippery creatures beneath and what it would feel like to only ever hear the sound of rushing water.

"What are you thinking about?" Noah asks, his voice soft. He's been so quiet sitting next to me and breathing in the same night air. Our phones illuminate the night enough so that I can see his face, his gaze taking in the river. It's a straight drop down to the dirt from where we're sitting, maybe four stories or so. There are paths the runners take down to the water, but those are a ways away, in places where the decline is much more moderate. The cliff we're perched upon feels like a metaphor for the precipice Noah and I are hovering on, for what I'm about to tell him and how everything that comes after will be different. But maybe I'm just being dramatic. Maybe it's just rocks and dirt and nothing more.

"What are you thinking about?" I ask, turning the question around on him.

"I'm thinking about everything," Noah says, "and how messed up it's all gotten." His words are slurring a bit, and I stay quiet because I know the beer will make him give me a more honest answer. "The tension between you, me, and Josie isn't good," he finally says, and the words shoot through me like a warning. Noah's not good at picking up on moods and imperceptible shifts, and it makes me wonder if they've hooked up, if that's what he really means.

I swallow hard. Noah links his fingers through mine, and his touch brings tears to my eyes. I have the awful sense that something may need to break for a new thing to survive. I don't dare say it out loud because it feels too morbid, and I'm so full of life in this moment that I really don't want to put words to the sense of doom I get every time I think of Noah, Josie, and me: the impossible threesome.

We watch the river for a beat longer, and I think about what I really want to say. More than whether he hooked up with Josie, more than even the baby, is the question of him and me, and that's what I need to know first, before telling him everything else. The night air swirls around us, the smaller saplings swaying with the weight of it. I gather my courage, and then I ask it:

"Who do you want, Noah?"

My voice sounds thin in the wind, insubstantial. And when Noah doesn't answer right away, I feel that way, too. "Noah, please?" I ask. "Tell me the truth."

He turns and takes me in. "Don't you know?" he asks, his voice softer than I've ever heard it. I'm quiet, unable to speak, not wanting to be the one who says it. *"You,"* he says, and that single word has never meant something so big. "I want you, Emma, and only you."

The tears spill over my cheeks. Noah puts his hand against my face and tilts my chin so he can look at me. I smell beer and cold winter air, and then he leans closer like he's about to kiss me.

"Wait," I say, my breath coming faster. "There's something I need to tell you."

FORTY

Priya

C ome.

Josie had texted that single word, and now Priya was racing toward the hospital with her pulse pounding in her throat. As soon as she'd gotten the text, she called Brad's mother, who adored Elliot and was the only person Priya could leave him with under the circumstances. Priya had explained the situation briefly, and by some miracle Brad's mother didn't ask too many questions. *A case of mistaken identity,* she'd announced, as though this kind of thing happened all the time. Priya had settled Elliot by assuring him she'd be right back after a quick trip to the hospital to talk to the woman who'd mistakenly put the blame on his dad. She knew it was the only way to get his blessing for her to leave.

Priya pulled into the parking lot, the hospital looming tall against the cloudy night sky. She opened her car door and stepped into the cold, keeping her eyes on the pavement. Someone had plowed it, but a layer of ice had already formed, and she was careful not to fall. Streetlamps illuminated the slick black ground beneath her feet, and Priya didn't look up until she was at the curb. When she did, she saw Noah standing next to the hospital entrance.

"Noah," Priya said carefully. She took in his strong build and the way he'd stuffed his fists into his pockets like he was trying to punch his coat farther over his body. He was shivering, whether from the cold or trauma of the day Priya didn't know. She studied his perfect bone structure: high cheekbones, wide jaw, and deep-set hazel eyes. Could this man have tried to kill his wife today?

The night air was freezing, and Priya wanted to race into the warmth of the hospital, but with the way Noah was standing there, more imposing than any guard, she knew she couldn't.

"I know Josie asked you to come, but I can't let you see her," Noah finally said, breaking the silence. "You have to know that."

Priya felt steady and anchored to the snowy sidewalk in a way that surprised her. "I have every right to visit her," she said.

"Really? After what your husband did today?"

Something hot burned through Priya, something that felt an awful lot like rage. She'd never been comfortable with her own anger—it was far easier to stuff it down and deal with the resulting depression—but she felt it now, and she wondered if that meant there was still passion for her husband somewhere deep inside her. Or, more likely, was this all for Elliot, a burning desire to protect him from a father in prison?

"Brad didn't hurt Josie today," Priya said. "Josie was the one who invited him there. And I still don't understand why."

"Of course you don't," Noah said. And then he looked up to the sky like he needed to get his bearings. But his face was still furious when he returned it to Priya. "The cops found evidence in the gorge this week that makes Emma's death seem suspicious," he said, "and after Josie learned this, she arranged a meeting with you and Brad to tell you she was going to the police with what she knew about him and Emma sleeping together back at school, because for some reason, she feels a connection to you, or some messed-up version of loyalty to you for being there for her when Emma disappeared. Obviously her foolish idea for the meeting backfired, and your husband tried to shut her up permanently."

Priya recoiled. "Is this really what you think happened?" she asked slowly, turning all of it over in her mind.

"I do," he said, "and you'd be a fool not to."

Was she a fool? Why was she swinging so wildly between faith and disbelief? If only Brad hadn't broken her trust in other ways, maybe he'd be easier to defend.

"But what I can't figure out," Noah went on, "is if you were there when it happened. Did you see Brad attack Josie? Or, maybe *you* did it?"

Priya's mouth dropped open. "No, of course not!" she said. "Dean and Haley saw me arrive. I was driving a car length ahead of them."

"But maybe you circled back," Noah said. "How should I know what happened? The point is that Brad was there when the rest of you showed up."

Priya was shaking now. *You believe your husband, don't you, Priya?* came a small voice inside her. *Defend him.* "And what about you, Noah? Had you been to the house, too, this morning?"

A red flush crept up the exposed skin on Noah's neck. "I brought Josie my car because it handles the snow better, and I helped her set up. But I left before your husband arrived, and when I left, my wife was perfectly fine."

My wife.

There was something in his voice that turned Priya's stomach. *Possession, ownership:* the things about marriage she'd never been comfortable with. "Is that right?" she asked, her voice so dreamy it sounded out of place in the conversation. "But isn't it always the husband?" she asked. She remembered what Brad had said during their conversation tonight, and how relieved he was when it wasn't his baby. "Emma was pregnant, did you know Brad and I knew that?" she asked. "Maybe it was yours, for all we know."

Noah's features darkened, and she knew she had him. A rush of blood shot through her, and she felt practically elated at the turn of events. "The baby certainly wasn't Brad's," she went on.

She stood there so entirely certain of herself, right up until the moment Noah asked, "Then why is there a pregnancy test with your husband's DNA all over it?"

The edges of Priya's vision went black, and she tried to focus, tried to blink away the darkness.

"Maybe he was there with Emma when she took the test," Noah said slowly. "How supportive of him."

"He wasn't," Priya spat, but she had no idea.

"Or maybe Emma had it with her for some reason in the woods," Noah said, his gaze far away, like he was trying to picture it, to figure it all out. "That night Emma told me she was meeting someone on the trails, and maybe it was Brad, and maybe that's when he handled the test. How else would his blood get on it? The cops thought the tiny spot of blood was Emma's until they tested it, and imagine their surprise when they realized it was Brad's." Noah shook his head, staring hard at Priya. "Don't you see it, Priya? Your husband handled a dead girl's pregnancy test, a *student* he was sleeping with, no less, and then when my wife told him she was going to the cops with the evidence, he attacked her. And now he's going to pay for both crimes, which is exactly what he deserves."

FORTY-ONE

Emma

Ten years ago

Noah's eyes are piercing in the dark, two golden orbs surrounded by a bright white aura. The wind swirls around us, coming faster now that we're at the top of the cliff. A circle of rocks mark the ground between where we're sitting and where the cliff drops off, as though they're warning us how dangerously close we are. The cliff towers over the dirt below, and then it's twenty or so yards until the shore of the river. When my dad used to bring Haley and me to the woods above the gorge, he warned us never to get too close to the edges of the cliffs, but we were so little then. It's different now. Everything feels more perilous.

What I need to say to Noah comes slowly, crystallizing in my mind first, and then whooshing into my mouth with a weight of its own, something that bursts forth because I can hold it in no longer. "I'm pregnant," I say, my hands wringing themselves in my lap. "And the baby is yours."

Telling him feels like an exorcism. The whites of his eyes get bigger and bigger, but he says nothing. He stares, taking me in like he's seeing me for the first time. "We weren't careful," he says, and the evergreen trees behind us swish and carry away his words.

I wait until the air is still again, and then I say, "We weren't."

"I don't know what to say," he says, and for a second I think he's going to cry. I've never seen Noah cry. "I guess I'm surprised, even though I shouldn't be."

It's a relief to hear him say that, to accept what I've told him as the truth instead of questioning me like Josie and Brad did. "But I thought you were on the pill," he says.

"Why would you think that?" I ask. I draw my knees into my chest as though I can protect myself from the blame in his voice.

"Because we had sex without a condom," he says. "I just assumed you were on the pill to do something like that."

To do something like that.

Vulnerability washes over me. "This isn't only my fault," I say. "It's both of ours. You have to know that."

"I do know that," Noah says. An animal calls out behind us, and I shiver. Noah's voice isn't gentle enough when he asks, "But now what are you going to do about it?"

I look at Noah, and for the first time I see a child, a twenty-one-year-old who dreams of living in Australia for a semester, not an almost-adult who dreams of being with me exclusively forever and ever. "You think I should have an abortion?" I ask, trying on the word. It's the first time I've said it out loud about the baby.

"You just told me the news five seconds ago," Noah says, angry now. "I don't *think* anything yet."

Defiance rises in me. "I'll figure this out," I say. "I have my family." My words are so soft I'm not even sure Noah hears me. Branches rustle behind us, and Noah turns first. I follow his gaze, my eyes fuzzy in the dark but still able to see the streak of bright red parka that means Josie.

She crashes through the brush. Her eyes narrow on me, and then on Noah, like she's trying to figure out whether I told him the secret. The silence between the three of us is so weighty I want to scream. And maybe Josie can't stand it, either, because when she blurts out, "What are you guys doing?" her voice sounds uncharacteristically nervous.

"We're just talking, Josie," I say.

"Yeah," Noah says, running a hand over his jaw. "Just talking."

I know by the way he says it that he doesn't think I've told her I'm pregnant. Sometimes he's thick like that.

Josie considers us, and it feels so good to have the upper hand here, to be the only one that Noah thinks he wants, even if that might not be true. The forest towers above us, and I wonder how many love triangles these woods have seen, and if they're all basically the same, or if we're somehow special.

"So did you invite your *tall, dark, and handsome* boyfriend?" I ask Josie, because it's the question I would ask if I weren't always just a little afraid of her, and like I said, I'm high with my upper hand.

"He's not my boyfriend," Josie hisses. I can practically see her cheeks burning in the dark. Everything the three of us have been to each other weights the air between us, stifles us. "But yeah," she says. "I invited Dean. He's back at the campsite. Wanna come?"

FORTY-TWO

Haley

Haley and Dean were back at home, sitting across from each other at their makeshift kitchen table and avoiding each other's glance. It was an old-fashioned worktable, or at least a new table designed to look old-fashioned, the kind of thing hipsters purchased at design stores and put in Brooklyn apartments. Haley hated it. She rested her elbows on the thing, even though Dean abhorred elbows on tables. The things that bothered him felt so obscure and disjointed that Haley could never predict them. Was she about to spend her entire life trying to figure him out?

"I'm tired," Haley said, her head in her hands.

"That makes two of us," Dean said. He set down his mug of coffee, and Haley noticed a tremble in his fingers.

"Dean," Haley said, but he still didn't look up. "Are you okay?" she asked, softer now.

"I don't know what I am," he said. "Are you okay? I can't imagine what this must be like for you and your parents."

She glanced around the kitchen now, feeling helpless, not knowing what to say to him. In the hospital Noah had admitted that the baby could have been his, which surprised Haley but certainly didn't shock her. She could tell her sister had always had a crush on Noah.

Haley still needed to tell her parents about the pregnancy, but she'd put off calling them, wanting to know more answers before delivering a punch like that. "I just keep thinking about how devastated they'll be to know she was pregnant," she said to Dean now. "For them it'll be like losing two people instead of just one."

Dean nodded. Haley's eyes caught on a knife lying next to the sink, a sharp one Dean had used to slice tomatoes in his attempt to make her a sandwich. He was so fastidious about keeping the house clean, and it was the first time since she'd known him that he'd let dishes pile in the sink. The air smelled stale and unfamiliar as Haley went on. "I guess, well, first, I don't understand why Priya and Brad were both there at the open house," she said, trying to put words to the things that flooded her mind.

Dean shrugged. "Apparently Josie invited them there so she could tell them she was going to the police with what she knew, all these years later. She said she was a little scared of how they'd react, so she wanted to tell them somewhere quiet, but a place where people coming in and out would make it public enough."

"That makes no sense," Haley said. "Why would she even need to warn them?"

Dean's lips pursed. "Priya and Brad are the kind of teachers that cast spells over their students."

It wasn't like Dean to speak poetically. "What do you mean?" Haley asked.

"I think Brad and Priya were incredibly magnetic, especially for students who were twenty and impressionable. I'm sure Josie felt some kind of weird loyalty to them, and that's why she wanted to warn them she was going to the cops with the pregnancy test. And I absolutely don't think she thought Brad would try to kill her over it."

"Well, I suppose she was wrong," Haley said, her voice too callous.

Dean looked away, and Haley knew she'd been cruel. "That didn't come out the way I meant it," she said quickly.

Dean examined his fingernails. "I get that you're angry that Josie didn't tell the cops all of this ten years ago," he said.

"That's an understatement," Haley said, crossing her arms over her sweatshirt.

"She was only twenty-one back then," Dean retorted, and Haley opened her mouth to object, but he put up a hand to signal he wasn't finished. "Things twenty-something-year-olds do, they don't always make sense," he said. "Their brains aren't even developed all the way. And she got really hurt today. She almost died for coming forward like she planned to with that test."

Rage surged inside Haley, but she tried to quell it, tried to remind herself that Josie had loved Emma, too, and that she'd almost lost her life today. She tried to make her tone more palatable for Dean when she said, "Josie let Emma's death remain a mystery for so much longer than it might have otherwise."

"We still don't know who killed your sister," Dean said softly.

Haley swallowed. "I know that," she said. "I just . . . I wish Emma had told me she was pregnant. She didn't, obviously, but Josie could have told me at some point after Emma disappeared. I wish I'd known all this time, that the secret hadn't been hidden from my parents and me for ten years. It just feels like we should have known about the baby, talked about him or her, even in the past tense after Emma died. Maybe that sounds stupid."

"It doesn't," Dean said.

Haley cleared her throat. "I'm not a cop, but I've gotten to know Brad a little, from class. I don't think he's a psychopath. And that's what he'd have to be to murder my sister and then calmly go about teaching me in class. The first day of class, there was this uncomfortable beat when he called my name from the roster. He definitely glanced up, and then maybe looked at me a little funny. I assumed it was just because he was putting together that I was the infamous Emma McCullough's sister, but it also could have been the way you'd look at someone who was the sister of a person you knew intimately when you shouldn't have. But not someone that you'd murdered in cold blood—I just, that doesn't feel right to me. Wouldn't I have sensed something?"

Dean blinked at her, but then his eyes cut away. Did he think she was a fool for being so sure about something like this?

"Anyone at that party could have killed Emma," Haley said carefully. "But take my sister out of the equation for one second. What if Noah tried to kill Josie today for some reason we don't even know about?"

"Like what?" Dean asked.

"Anything," Haley said, her voice shrill now. "Whatever happens in people's marriages that we don't even understand, because we're not married yet. Look at my parents," she said. "Would you ever think my dad had been unfaithful?"

Dean's face blanched white. "Being unfaithful is different than physically hurting someone."

"Plenty of people do that in marriages, too."

"Haley," Dean said.

"Read the statistics," Haley spat back, remembering a particularly grim class at Yarrow on recognizing the signs of domestic violence.

"You're going a little dark, don't you think?"

"I don't, actually," Haley said.

"Do you think I could ever do something like that to you?"

"I think you're lying to me about something," Haley said, and as the words escaped her, she knew they were true. "And I want to know exactly what it is."

FORTY-THREE

Emma

Ten years ago

I should've just demanded more time alone with Noah, but I knew Josie would never go for it, and now as she and I follow him along the trail back to the campsite, my face burns with everything I just told him and how imperfectly it all went, and with shame, too, that I thought it would go another way. I hate them both right now, especially Josie for interrupting us. I want to kick the back of her hiking boots as she plods along; I want to yank the silky yellow strands of her ponytail; I want to hurt her somehow, like she's hurt me.

Of course, I don't. Because there's a difference between rage and acting on it, and I know the line. I wonder if Josie does, and what about Noah? Men are so unknowable to me, sometimes, with their quicker flares to anger. I think about my dad, whom I've barely ever seen yell except for when I accused him of having an affair. I hope so hard that I was wrong about what I saw. I need to talk to Haley about it, maybe tonight when she gets here. And I need to tell her how I've been sleeping with Noah, and about being pregnant, of course. Maybe I'll tell her everything tonight, and then we can tell my parents together tomorrow.

The trees tighten so we have to walk single file along the trail. I can barely see Noah anymore, and I hope he and Josie know where they're going.

What if I've trusted the wrong people all this time? How is anyone supposed to know who the good ones are? Maybe there's not even such a thing as *good*; maybe there are only shades of gray and circumstances and people reacting to them in myriad ways. Maybe no one should be surprised by anything anyone does. Maybe we're all just animals trying to survive.

I try to shake off the feeling, but it's too heavy, coiling around my neck and shoulders like a viper. Josie lets a branch snap back in my face, and I pray she doesn't turn and see the hot, angry tears that spring to my eyes. I want this night to be over. Tomorrow I'll go home and talk to my parents about the baby. They'll help me—they'll help *us*. I think about all the people in my situation who aren't lucky enough to have family that will support them, and it weighs me down even more, until I can barely make my feet follow Noah and Josie, until I just want to lie down and fall asleep beneath the stars.

The music jars me out of my mood.

A cheesy, poppy beat filters through the trees, and I exhale. We're almost there. I'm craving alcohol to numb me, but of course, I can't have it.

Noah pushes through the trees first, holding branches aside for us to pass into the clearing. I take in everything, the boys clustered around the keg, laughing, a few girls on the fringes, and then, of course: Dean.

He's tall and good looking in a classically handsome way, dark haired and well built. Brown eyes, I think, but I haven't really ever gotten close enough to know. He's standing by the keg, holding a plastic cup and talking to one of Noah's teammates. Dean doesn't strike me as the jock type, which means he probably really likes Josie if he agreed to come here tonight.

I turn to watch Josie, who appears a little annoyed to see him.

Meanwhile Noah slips quickly back into his element with his team-mates, smiling and laughing, and something happens in that moment as I watch him rejoin the party; in some way, I let him go. Or at least, the invisible thread that's tied me to him starts to fray. I'll be able to get myself back. And maybe at some point, I'll turn him over to Josie. Maybe in some way, if I'm right about how she's feeling, she needs him more than I do.

Josie.

She's changed her expression so that she's smiling now at Dean, but it's an act, of course. Still, she'd fool anyone other than me, certainly someone as unsuspecting as Dean.

Josie, my best friend—the person I thought was almost like a sister. But when I think of Haley and the fullness my heart feels at just the idea of her, I know that isn't true: Josie isn't my family; she isn't my blood.

I feel so calm all of a sudden, so peaceful. Even the woods don't feel as menacing as they once did.

One more night, I think to myself. *Just get through these hours and find a way to end the charade come tomorrow.*

Yes, I tell myself. *Tomorrow will be a new day.*

FORTY-FOUR

Haley

I *think you're lying to me about something, and I want to know exactly* *what it is."*

Had Haley really just said those words to her fiancé? Her heart pounded as she stared at him. She opened her mouth to say something else, but the doorbell rang. Dean's head jerked toward the sound of the bell. Haley put her palms on the table to steady herself, feeling like she was floating outside her body as she rose from the table to answer the door.

"Haley," Dean called after her, but she didn't look back. She raced across the living room, expecting to find her parents at the door. She braced herself before opening it. She tried to make her face look like she was okay, like today hadn't been too much to handle. But when she swung open the front door, it was Detective Rappaport on her front step. A lone overhead light lit his face, casting shadows and making half of his features look sunken.

"Good evening, Ms. McCullough," he said. "I need to bring Dean to the station again for more questioning. Is he here?"

Haley swallowed. "What's happened?" she asked.

"I think it's best if we question him first," Rappaport said, shifting his weight, "and then I debrief you."

Haley's blood felt hot, whooshing beneath her skin and into her ears until she could barely hear her own voice say, "This is my life, Detective. My sister; my fiancé. That's practically my whole world."

Rappaport looked past her. She turned to follow his gaze into the empty living room, hardly believing that Dean hadn't followed her to the door.

"Please," Haley said once more, and when Rappaport nodded, it felt genuine, like he could at least partly understand her situation.

"We found correspondence between your fiancé and Josie. They seemed to point to some kind of relationship; it seemed they were meeting in secret, without you or Noah knowing about it."

Haley thought she might be sick. She put a hand on the doorframe to steady herself.

"Nothing explicit," Rappaport said quickly, "please don't misunderstand me. But it's a hunch we have, given the emails between them."

Haley had always been the one to communicate with Josie. She didn't even copy Dean on the emails about houses, about their *floor plans, pool sites, new construction versus old-world charm* . . .

The lingo flooded her mind, the sheer pretense of it all so completely absurd. "Dean's in the kitchen," she said flatly, moving aside so Rappaport could take her fiancé away from this place, from this house that suddenly felt incredibly far from ever being a home. She heard Dean in the kitchen, protesting, but then Rappaport's voice rose, and Dean acquiesced. Rappaport emerged from the kitchen with Dean looking completely broken. Haley watched her fiancé, willing him to say something to her as he crossed the living room toward the outside world. When he finally paused and looked at her, his eyes held nothing reassuring, only sadness, and Haley watched as the man she loved left the warmth of their house for the cold, snowy night.

FORTY-FIVE

Emma

Ten years ago

What's most surprising about the party is how many people have shown up while I was at the cliff with Noah. There must be at least a hundred more kids here, and it's not just Noah's friends and teammates: there are bunches of people I recognize from campus but have never talked to before. That's how Yarrow is—too small to be anonymous, too big to know everyone. Kind of perfect in that way, I guess. I breathe in the night air tinged with smoke from the campfire, wanting to get lost in the swarm of kids drinking and laughing, wanting to shake free from Noah and Josie tonight, and maybe talk to someone I've never talked to before. It reminds me of the feeling I had when I got to Yarrow, when things were so new, when my life could have gone in any direction. I think back to the day I met Josie and Noah scooping bin candy in the student center, and how different everything would be now if we'd never met. I wonder if anyone can truly start over.

One of Noah's friends knocks into me, and I pitch forward. "Emma!" he says, slurring the syllables. "Sorry!" He offers me a hit from his joint, but I decline with a smile, and then I use the distraction to break free from Noah and Josie, plunging myself into the fray of warm bodies. Elbows poke my ribs, hips push me sideways. I move faster through the crowd, feeling a smile break on my face as the mob swallows me.

I've lost them.

A group of girls I'm pretty sure are on the soccer team talk and laugh, one of them gesticulating with her hands, looking vibrant as she holds her teammates' attention. There's a guy named Marcus I see by the keg, and I make my way toward him because he's always been nice, and plus he's talking to a girl I don't know, and I want a new friend, maybe—or at least a new face. But then I see Chris coming toward me, his eyes on me like he wants us to talk. I contemplate pretending I don't see him, but I don't want to blow him off and hurt his feelings. You can tell he's sensitive about stuff like that, about not fitting in with the kids at Yarrow. Josie said he dated some girl in our class for a little while, but then she dumped him as soon as she realized he worked in an auto body shop and never went to college.

"Hey," he says, his bare hands clutching a beer.

"Aren't you freezing?" I ask, because his long fingers are white around the beer, and he's only wearing a fleece.

"I'm good," he says. The corner of his mouth sags a bit like it always does when he's drunk. "Have you seen Josie?" he asks me.

I shrug. "I lost her," I say, like it was an accident. He stares at me, and my throat feels tight all of a sudden, like I might cry.

"You okay?" he asks. His eyes are so pale, just like Josie's, and in the dark night they glow, appearing almost otherworldly.

"I'm fine," I say, but he wraps his cold hand around my wrist. He's just like Josie—he picks up on the spaces between the words, on what I'm actually feeling, even if I don't say it.

"No, you're not," he says. I can't tell if he really cares about me, or if he's just hoping we'll hook up again sometime soon.

"You're right," I say. "I'm not really okay. I'm scared, actually, about how everything's about to change." I pull my arm away, and he starts asking me what I mean, but I just can't explain myself right now. "I'm sorry, Chris, I gotta get some air," I say, which is a crazy thing to say because we're already outside, but it strikes me then that this is how I sometimes feel with Chris and Josie, like I just need some fresh air, like the walls are closing in. I pivot and start walking, turning back once to see the flicker of anger and bewilderment in his eyes, his mouth open, right side still sagging, like he wants to call me back to him. I turn away and cut through the next group of kids. They're drunker, their warm beer-breath assaulting me, and I put my head down and barrel through them.

"Emma," I hear a low voice say.

A gust of cold air hits my face. It's Dean. He's standing alone, or at least alone amid a bunch of people, seeming not to be talking to any of them.

"Hi," I say, praying Josie isn't close enough to see him talking to me.

"Hi," he says back. I didn't even know he knew my name. His long lashes are blinking, and as I stare into his eyes, a jolt of adrenaline hits me, and I want to be away from him. "I need to go," I say, trying not to be too rude. "I need to get a beer," I lie, to soften the fact that he's the last person I want to be hanging out with right now.

"Can I talk to you?" he asks.

"Um," I say, stalling, because even just a conversation with someone Josie is hooking up with seems like a bad idea.

"Maybe somewhere private?"

"Sorry, no," I say, glancing over my shoulder to see if Josie's seeing this. But I don't see her and Noah anywhere. "I really can't, I need to . . ."

"Get a beer, right," Dean says, "you said so." There's an edge to his voice, but it's obvious he's trying to tamp it down when he says, "It'll only take a minute." He starts to inch away from the party. In the moonlight I can see how perfect his smile is. He looks so much older than most seniors, like he should be out in the world, not partying in the woods with plastic cups. "Come on," he says, and my feet start following him toward the trail. "Fine," I say, "but only just a minute. Because I really need to get back to my friends." Another lie—I can't seem to stop. I open my mouth to protest leaving the party, to ask if we can just stay here, but then he reaches back and surprises me by taking my hand.

"Only a minute," he promises.

FORTY-SIX

Priya

Priya lay in the dark with Elliot. He was on the cusp of sleep, his chest rising and falling a little more slowly. Brad's mom was still downstairs, and Priya could hear the clanking sounds of her loading the dishwasher. She stroked Elliot's hair and leaned in to gently kiss his temple.

The only light in Elliot's bedroom came from a plastic turtle that cast stars on the ceiling. Priya, Brad, and Elliot hadn't taken a vacation in ages, but a few years ago they did, and Priya had forgotten to pack the turtle. Elliot couldn't fall asleep without it, and Priya ended up sleeping in his bed the entire vacation, even though Brad had purposely booked a beach house with bedrooms on opposite sides of the kitchen so they could have some privacy. Elliot had needed her, and it felt so cozy and lovely to be snuggled up with him that Priya never tore herself away to go to her husband.

There were things she could have done differently over the years. She could have kept painting when she knew that was what her brain needed. Or at least, when she felt she couldn't pick up a brush, she could have done *something*. She'd shut that part of herself out, and then she shut Brad out, too. Did things like that make her complicit in all of this? Not in Brad's lies, but in the demise of her marriage?

No, no. Certainly, the woman at the gym from a few years ago had happened during a low point in their marriage. But Brad had cheated with Emma when Priya was vibrant, alive, and painting. She wasn't perfect— who was?—but she was herself then, a woman with a big, gaping hunger for life, art, and Brad. And he'd still cheated. She had to remember that.

Brad must have felt the shift in their relationship after Emma disappeared. Elliot had just arrived, and the stress of a newborn on any relationship was something to be reckoned with, let alone one that also bore the strain of infidelity and a missing girl. Could *any* couple recover from those things?

Elliot let out a wheezy sigh and turned away from Priya. He ran hot at night, and even in the dead of winter slept in a T-shirt and shorts. Her eyes rested on the slope of his skinny shoulder, and she imagined what things would be like if she left Brad and it was just Elliot and her alone.

When Priya and Brad first got together, more than sex even, they cuddled. Neither of them had ever said it out loud to each other, and Priya had never told anyone else, either, but it was true. They'd go see live music and sling their arms around each other the whole time; they'd go to an art show and never drop each other's hand; and they'd come home from wherever they were and collapse into bed and sometimes have sex but mostly just hold each other. They woke up every morning with limbs entwined. It went on that way for a year or so, and then Priya got pregnant with Elliot, and Brad proposed. But by the second half of the pregnancy Priya couldn't get comfortable sleeping with her burgeoning stomach. She tossed and turned, tried different pillows that were supposed to help, but as her stomach grew, she could barely stand to be touched while she slept, let alone held. She tolerated Brad's embrace while she was awake, or when they would lay in bed and watch movies on lazy weekends when he didn't have to work at the hospital. But sometimes, especially in the final few months, her stretched-out skin would start to crawl and itch, and she'd fling his arms off her as though he were a stranger.

And then, of course, Elliot came, and her embrace was for someone else entirely. Maybe some women tried to hide that fact when their babies were born, or at least tried to share. Priya didn't. Maybe it was because Brad had cheated with Emma, but Priya couldn't make herself be careful with his feelings after what he'd done to her. She soaked up her newborn, her arms and heart suddenly full again with love and purpose. And, of course, her anxiety skyrocketed, because how could she love Elliot the way she did and have him be in this world where he could get hurt? How did other women do this?

When Elliot was an older toddler, Priya knew it was time to put more of herself back into her marriage, but she couldn't seem to get it right. At music classes she heard the other mothers talk about date nights, but being intimate with Brad again felt like another world, one she wasn't sure she wanted to be part of. He tried, of course, and sometimes it worked; sometimes she followed him to the bedroom, and they slept together. But those times were few and far between. And then, when Elliot was no longer a toddler—and there was less of an excuse for the exhaustion Priya sometimes feigned—Brad cheated with the woman from the gym.

Priya closed her eyes, trying to forget. She listened to the sounds of Elliot's breathing and her mother-in-law cleaning up the kitchen, but her mind returned to Brad. If someone cheated in a marriage, did that mean there wasn't anything worth trying to save? It wasn't just the cheating—she knew they had other problems. But she thought there was something there still, and not just a shared love of Elliot, but something more—something good. She thought of Brad, held at the station for a crime she knew he didn't commit.

First things first. Priya slipped from Elliot's bed, careful not to wake him. She moved to his desk and scooped up her car keys as quietly as possible.

Downstairs, she peeked in on her wide-eyed mother-in-law. "I'll be right back," she said, already heading to the garage. "There's someone I need to see."

FORTY-SEVEN

Haley

Haley was in the study now, about to do the only thing she could think of. She turned on the desktop, and the seconds it took to buzz to life felt like hours. She tapped against the desk—*one, two, three, four, five, six, seven*—always an odd number. She glanced around the tiny room at the walls, which were bare except for the Yarrow diploma Dean had hung.

Next to Dean's desk was a porcelain jar full of ballpoint pens. The thing felt too sterile, making Haley think back to the homemade pencil holder she'd seen just yesterday on Rappaport's desk. She thought about the gaggle of kids the detective probably had, and then she wondered if she was about to lose everything she'd dreamed of having with Dean.

Haley exhaled. The backs of her legs were sweating against the ergonomic chair. Finally the computer found an internet connection, and Haley entered the same password she and Dean used for the joint banking account he'd set up for them to use for any wedding expenses. He'd put seventy-five thousand dollars into it, telling Haley he was a grown man who didn't feel comfortable with her parents throwing them a wedding. Haley had never seen an account with seventy-five thousand dollars in it. Hers always floated somewhere around three or four thousand dollars, depending on where she was with her student loan payments. When they got married—*if* they got married—Dean planned to pay all that off, which Haley had always reconciled in her mind by reminding herself she was studying to be a doctor, so obviously the money he spent would pay for itself eventually. How strange marriage was, with its debts and burdens, trade-offs and payoffs.

Haley shook her head, snapping herself back to the moment. She clicked the sign-in button and—*voilà!* She was in. Would a man hiding an affair really use the same password he'd given his future wife for a shared account?

Dean's inbox splayed out before her. She tried to scan for anything abnormal, but all she saw was run-of-the-mill emails from work, an alert about a J.Crew sale, and a group email chain Dean was on about a trip to Vail. She opened the Vail email and scanned the names copied, but it was just a group of four guys Dean kept in touch with from Yarrow.

Haley entered Josie's email address in the search box. There were several emails written to both Haley and Dean about houses. But then she found a chain farther down without a subject line, sent to Dean only, from last week.

From Josie.Carmichael@CarmichaelRealty.com
To Dean.Walters@gmail.com

Hey, Dean. Thanks for meeting with me today. I already feel so much better talking things through with you. Ghosts from the past still have so much power over me, but today I was able to let some of that go. Yours, Josie

Haley stiffened. She certainly wasn't aware of a time Dean had met with Josie alone. Why would he keep that from her?

From Dean.Walters@gmail.com
To Josie.Carmichael@CarmichaelRealty.com

Hi Josie. No problem. It was nice to meet. I'm
always here for you, I know you've been through
a lot.

Dean

From Josie.Carmichael@CarmichaelRealty.com
To Dean.Walters@gmail.com

I can't even tell you what that means to me. Thank
you! J

Dean hadn't replied to that one. But two days later, Josie emailed
him again.

From Josie.Carmichael@CarmichaelRealty.com
To Dean.Walters@gmail.com

Do you think we can meet again? There's something
I want to discuss with you. We can call it a working
lunch if we discuss some properties, too. Haha.

From Dean.Walters@gmail.com
To Josie.Carmichael@CarmichaelRealty.com

Should I have Haley come?

From Josie.Carmichael@CarmichaelRealty.com
To Dean.Walters@gmail.com

No, no. Sorry, shouldn't have made the real estate
joke. I'd like to meet alone.

From Dean.Walters@gmail.com
To Josie.Carmichael@CarmichaelRealty.com

Ok, where?

From Josie.Carmichael@CarmichaelRealty.com
To Dean.Walters@gmail.com

My house? Noah will be out tonight. Can you
come?

From Dean.Walters@gmail.com
To Josie.Carmichael@CarmichaelRealty.com

Yes but are you sure this is a good idea?

From Josie.Carmichael@CarmichaelRealty.com
To Dean.Walters@gmail.com

Maybe I'm being reckless, but please come. 8 pm.
xx J

There seemed to be no more emails between them, but maybe they'd switched over to text after this. Rappaport had said they'd found *correspondence* on Dean's phone, which could mean anything.

Haley spun the ergonomic chair around and stared out onto the lawn. A streetlamp glistened over the snow like a beacon.

Could this really be? Could Dean and Josie have been romantically involved? She didn't want to jump to conclusions from the emails, but the whole thing was so off. Dean meeting with Josie at her home and not telling Haley about it? What else could have been happening there besides an affair? And if that was it—if they'd cheated—what if Noah had found out? Haley's heart pounded. What if today's attack had nothing to do with her sister's disappearance? What if it was a jealous husband trying to kill his wife because of an affair?

Her stomach felt like a rock, and something dawned on her that scared her more than almost anything, which was that, in this possible scenario, she felt more disappointed by the possibility of losing the answers to her sister's disappearance than the prospect of her fiancé straying.

Haley put her hands over her eyes—she could worry about her cold feet later. She still felt sure she was missing something, and for the thousandth time she wished her sister were here to help her. Tears came, wetting her hands. "Can you hear me, Emma?" she asked, and the sound of her own voice in the empty room made her cry harder.

The doorbell rang.

Haley glanced up at the clock to see it was almost midnight. Dean wouldn't normally ring the bell, but he probably hadn't taken his keys when Rappaport took him to the station. She went to the front door and peered through the peephole. *Priya.* Haley's heart pounded, and she knew she probably shouldn't talk to Brad's wife, but curiosity propelled her. She yanked open the door. "Hi," she said, a blast of cold air hitting her face. And then, before she could think better of it, she said, "Come in," and Priya did.

Haley didn't look at her. She shut the door and moved into the living room, her bare feet hot and itchy on the carpet. "Do you want to sit?" Haley asked, gesturing to an uncomfortable-looking midcentury chair Dean had brought home from a tag sale.

Priya wasn't wearing a coat, only a knit sweater that she held together over her chest with skinny fingers. She had that same crazed, scared look in her eyes that she'd had at the open house. But she nodded, and after a beat or two she sat in the chair.

Haley sat on the sofa across from her. "There's a blanket behind you," she offered, and she watched as Priya unfolded the blanket and set it across her lap. It made her look older than she probably was, and so did the worry lines creased around her eyes.

"What do you know about my husband?" Priya asked.

Haley tightened. "Did you come here to interrogate me?"

"No, not at all," Priya said, shaking her head. "I'm sorry. I'll tell you everything you want to know about us. I was just wondering how much you already knew."

"I know you taught Emma," Haley said. "I know Brad was sleeping with her, and may have gotten her pregnant, though I'm not sure on that part. I know the cops are holding him now, and I know there's a pregnancy test with his DNA all over it. That's pretty much all I know."

Priya nodded. "Haley, first," she started, the worry lines growing deeper. "I'm so sorry about your sister. She was my student—like you said, you already knew that—and she was extremely talented, but I'm sure you knew that, too. She was also kind, and we were friendly, actually. I'm completely sure that she didn't know Brad was my fiancé, not only because I don't think she would have slept with him if she knew, but also because Brad and I kept our relationship private, mostly because we both taught classes, and we didn't want to ruffle anyone's feathers. Yarrow can be conservative in that way. We liked it there, actually, at Yarrow. We had good times together, particularly when I first got the job and traveled back and forth between Yarrow and New York to exhibit. Things went wrong, of course. Brad met your sister—I still don't know where, because we barely ever talked about it. I learned of their affair the night she disappeared. She came to our town house, and I could see it all over her face—the surprise at seeing me there, everything. It was awful."

Haley didn't want to interrupt—but the words came out anyway. "But why didn't you go to the police?"

"Because I honestly didn't think my husband did it. It was so wrong of me not to go to the cops, and I won't make excuses, but if I were trying to make you see it from my perspective, I would tell you that I delivered my son a day and a half later, and I was out of my mind with stress about the affair and what would happen to my newborn son and me if I told the police that Brad had been sleeping with not only a student, but one who had disappeared. Emma had her sad side, too, we all do, and I believed the rumors that she had hurt herself. I don't believe them now, not after what happened to Josie this morning, but I also don't believe my husband hurt her."

"I don't, either, actually," Haley said.

"You don't?" she asked, and Haley heard the incredulity in her voice.

"I don't," Haley said. "It's a hunch, and it goes against the obvious—a teacher sleeping with and possibly impregnating a student . . ."

Priya flinched. "All of it is so awful."

"It's awful that she's gone," Haley said. "The other things my sister did, the things people like to blame her for—I can hear it in their voices, that they blame her—is being promiscuous, by some definitions, and drinking that night, or so some reports say, and now, as we know, being pregnant . . . but those things don't mean she should have lost her life."

"Of course, you must know I agree," Priya said. She leaned forward, her legs adjusting themselves beneath the blanket.

"I don't know anything about you. I don't know you at all," Haley said. There was a bite in her words, but they were true.

Priya smoothed a wrinkle in the pillow closest to her. "So now what?"

"I don't know," Haley said. "I know you're here to absolve your husband, but I don't even know how to help you. I can tell you the cops found suspicious stuff between my fiancé and Josie, and some of that could mean they were involved in some way, and I imagine that's enough to get the spotlight off your husband for Josie's attack for the time being. But Brad still slept with Emma, and she was a student, and that's gonna come out, and you're going to have to deal with it."

"I know that," Priya said, her eyes welling. "Trust me, I know."

"Can you do me a favor?" Haley asked. She knew there were so many things she should be doing besides talking to this woman right now—like trying to get to the bottom of Dean's relationship with Josie, or trying to figure out what had happened today at the open house. But the chance so rarely arose, and now that it had . . .

"Can you tell me something about my sister?" Haley asked. "She was your student, an artist like you, and like you said—you were close. Can you tell me something I haven't heard yet?"

Priya wiped the tears from her face, sat up a little straighter. "Yes, of course I can. What would you like to know?"

"Everything," Haley said, and she pulled her knees closer to her chest, her entire being lifted as Priya started talking.

FORTY-EIGHT

Emma

Ten years ago

I follow Dean along the trail, wondering if this is how every horror movie starts, with a girl following a guy she doesn't know well enough into the woods. But of course, this isn't just some random guy: it's the guy Josie's been stringing along. Maybe a part of me gets some sick satisfaction by turning the tables, interfering somehow with a guy who likes her. Isn't that what she's trying to do to Noah and me?

In the silence, I swear I can feel something pulsing in the air between us, something that feels like frustration or anger, and I realize, sadly, that that's pretty much what Josie has made a lot of guys feel since we started at Yarrow. Josie loves being in control; she loves every eye being drawn to her when she enters a room and the way guys hang on her every movement and every word. She knows just how much attention to give someone until they feel special, chosen somehow. And then she snaps it away.

"So you and Josie are really close, right?" Dean asks when the branches start to thin out again. We're almost at the cliff's edge—I can hear the river. Dean's broad back blocks out some of the light, but I'm pretty sure we're about to see the full moon on the water.

"Yeah, we are," I say, pushing aside a branch. "I think we're almost there." I go on, and a beat later we emerge into the clearing. It's beautiful up here, the moon so incredibly bright.

Dean surprises me by plopping down onto one of the rocks. "Do you want to sit?" he asks.

I shake my head. He looks up at me with a pitiful look on his face, and I know it's there because he likes Josie a lot more than she likes him.

"I'm sorry to drag you out here," he says.

"It's fine," I say. I don't want to talk about Josie, but we don't have anything else to talk about, so I get right to it. "If you want to know if Josie likes you, I don't really know the answer to that. She talks about you and everything, but not specifics."

"I think she tried to break up with me today, actually."

"Really?" I ask. I don't know if he has his terminology right: Josie never made it sound like they were anything serious enough to require a breakup conversation. "I didn't really realize you were together," I say. "Um, sorry, I'm not trying to make it worse."

He waves me off, but I don't seem to have offended him. "You're probably right," he says. "That's not even why I wanted to talk. I wanted to talk to you because she told me she couldn't see me anymore because of you."

My pulse picks up. "Because of *me*? I never told her not to see you," I say, flustered. "I don't even know you."

"No, nothing like that," Dean says. "She told me she needed to spend time with you because you'd been drinking too much lately and doing drugs, and she was worried, and I just wanted to talk to you, because, well, I guess I got the idea she might be lying, and if that's the case, I need to just let her go. That's a crazy thing to lie about."

I shake my head, feeling sorry for him. "She's lying," I say. "I'm not an angel or anything, I drink a lot, probably too much, just like everybody else here. But I don't do drugs." I leave off the fact that Josie does.

Dean tips his head back, letting a breath escape.

"Don't bother being embarrassed," I say. "It's not just you. She's lied to me, too. A lot."

I decide to sit next to him. It's the least I can do. I know what it feels like to be on the other end of Josie's mistruths. It makes me think back to the email I found today on her computer, the one she wrote to Noah. "I actually don't know why she does half the stuff she does," I say. "I think it's just out of intense insecurity and past hurt, but it still sucks and seems to be escalating in terms of frequency. Or maybe I'm just starting to see it for what it is."

"She told me about how hard it was growing up," Dean says. "About her dad leaving and then her mom dying and having to live with her stepdad. She told me he was merciless."

My heart feels heavy in my chest. "I should go find her," I say.

"Let me first," Dean says, standing. "It's fine that she wants things to be over. It's probably for the best." He shrugs, considers me. "I'm going to say goodbye to her, let her know it's all good. And thank you, by the way, for clearing it all up. I might have kept pursuing her if I really thought she was just trying to help you out of a tough time. But I don't need someone who's lying to me about why they don't want to see me. Not to be cold or anything."

I smile up at him. "Good luck," I say, and I mean it.

"You coming with me?" he asks, but I shake my head.

"I think I'll just take a minute out here," I say. "It's peaceful."

He lifts his hand in a wave, and then turns to go. "Bye, Emma," he says, and he leaves me sitting there all alone.

FORTY-NINE

Haley

At sunrise Haley went to the precinct.

"Your fiancé is here voluntarily," Rappaport said when he met her at the front desk. "You know that, right?"

Haley wasn't sure why he was telling her that or the significance of it. She was too tired, her mind too taxed. Rappaport led her down the hall to a room a little bigger than the one she'd been interviewed in yesterday, and when he opened the door, Haley saw Dean sitting at a table, his head down. When he looked up, his eyes were sunken, the gray shadows beneath them darker than she'd ever seen them. "Dean," Haley said as she sat across from him, and everything that rushed through her felt nothing like she'd expected. She'd been so furious on the drive here, furious at him for carrying on with Josie in secret and lying to her, furious for something even bigger than Josie that she was sure he was keeping from her. But now, as she took in the sight of his face, she felt a wash of empathy and love she didn't know was in there. The things she'd been planning to say to him felt meaningless now that she was here.

"I'm so sorry, Haley," Dean said. "For all of this." His palms rested awkwardly on the table, his fingers splayed. Rappaport had left them alone, and Haley wondered briefly if there were cameras in the room, not that it would change anything she said. She wanted to hear the truth, both about what happened to her sister and what happened to Josie. And however Dean was involved in either of those things, well, she needed to know that, too.

"Tell me what you've done," Haley said, her voice a whisper.

Dean nodded. "I'll tell you everything, I promise, and I should have told you before, and the only reason I didn't was because I was terrified I would lose you, which I realize is what everyone who's ever told a lie has probably said."

Haley braced for the news of an affair, for the details of how and why he'd fallen for Josie, for whatever they'd done together. But when Dean opened his mouth, he said, "I was with your sister on the night she disappeared."

Haley's entire body went cold. "No," she said, shaking her head. "You weren't. You said you weren't at the party."

"I lied," Dean said, his skin paling. "I lied back then because I was a stupid, selfish idiot, and I didn't want to be in trouble for having been alone with her."

"Why?" Haley shrieked at him, her voice echoing through the interview room. "Why would you ever lie about her?"

"It was so stupid," Dean said. "And there's nothing I can say to you that will ever make it okay, and I obviously didn't hurt her, but I was alone with her that night, and I just didn't want anything to do with whatever tragic thing had happened to her, and I rationalized not going to the cops because I hadn't done anything wrong, and I didn't know anything that could help, either."

Haley put her head in her hands. The number of people who had kept things from the police, all in the name of believing they were innocent, or didn't want to get in trouble for something they didn't do . . .

"But then why did you lie to *me* all these years?" Haley asked.

"I lied to you when I met you because that night I came to find you at the bar I honestly just thought I'd see you once."

"What do you mean you came to find me?" Haley asked, her hands shaking. "You said you were there by chance, that your friend suggested the place."

"I lied about that, too, Haley. I'm so sorry. I swear those are the only two things I've ever lied to you about in our entire relationship, and I swear I will spend the rest of my life regretting it."

"I don't even understand what you're talking about," Haley said, her voice edging toward hysteria.

"I just wanted to check on you," Dean said, sweat beading his hairline. "Your sister's disappearance had always haunted me, and one of my buddies told me he'd run into *Emma McCullough's little sister bartending on the Lower East Side*, and I needed to see you for myself. I needed to see that you were okay, somehow. I never expected that we'd start dating, or that I'd fall in love with you and want to spend the rest of my life with you."

Haley's mind reeled. "You came to check on the sister of the girl you were alone with on the night she disappeared, a fact you hid from the police." The words were so morbid she could barely get them out. "Really, Dean? That's the real truth of how our life together started? That's so lovely, perhaps we should put that story on our save-the-date cards."

"I'm so sorry, Haley, I—"

"I'm going to be sick."

He reached across the table to take Haley's hand, but she withdrew it so fast he flinched. "Why were you alone with Emma?" she blurted, her voice like stones hurled across the room.

"Because I had a crush on Josie," Dean said, straightening.

"A *crush*?" Haley asked, barely able to believe her grown fiancé was using that word.

"Yes, a crush. Nothing more. I was in college, and I was still an idiot."

"You've already made that clear. *Why were you with Emma, alone, Dean?*"

"Because Josie had broken things off that day, but sort of in a weird way, like she didn't want to end it but didn't want to see me as much," he said, his words coming faster, seeming ruffled just like he always was when he needed her to understand something. "And she blamed it on Emma having drinking and drug problems. It sounded like a lie, and I wanted to talk to Emma and figure out if Josie was just trying to get rid of me."

"My sister didn't do drugs," Haley said. "The police thought maybe she was high that night because everyone else was, but I don't think so."

"I don't think so, either," Dean said, his voice softer, like maybe they'd found common ground.

Haley let out a cruel laugh. "So now you're an expert on my sister, after all these years of acting like you didn't know her. That's ironic."

Color came to Dean's cheeks. "I'm so sorry, Haley. Please know how sorry I am. Can't you forgive me for this? I was young and dumb, and I should have gone to the police and given a statement. I kept waiting for someone to pound on my door and take me to the precinct, but they never did. I guess no one saw us go off together, or maybe they were all so wasted they didn't remember."

"Lucky you," Haley said, furious tears on her face now. She tried to stand, to leave this place and never come back, but she felt frozen and unable to make her body cooperate.

"Haley, I swear to you I had nothing helpful to tell the police," Dean said. "I left that party the second I was done talking to her. I wasn't even there when she got hurt. She was completely fine when I left her sitting there by the cliff."

"*Sitting by the cliff,*" Haley repeated. "Where she might have fallen from, or more likely, where she might have gotten pushed from. You didn't bother telling the police what time you left my sister *sitting by the cliff?* Didn't you think that could have helped them figure out something—*anything?*"

"But back then everyone thought she jumped on purpose, and that's part of why I didn't think there was a reason to go to the police. If she'd hurt herself—"

"But what about all these years after, when you said you believed me that she'd been killed? Were you just lying?"

"No, I do believe you!" Dean said.

"Then why didn't you ever go to the police?" Haley demanded. "How could you have lied to me about her? Don't you understand, I loved her so much more than I love you!"

Dean's eyes went wide, blinking at her. Haley burst into tears at the truth of what she'd said. Dean stood slowly and pulled her up, to his chest. "I'm so sorry," he said. "What I did was wrong." She sobbed as he apologized over and over, stroked her hair, and held her tight. They stood there like that for ages, with Dean supporting nearly all her weight, until finally he lowered them both into one chair. He held her tucked in his lap, kissing her forehead. "I will spend my entire life making this up to you," Dean said softly.

"You won't be able to make this up to me," Haley said, wiping angry tears from her cheeks. "You shouldn't even try."

"I swear to you, with every bone in my body, I didn't think I could help your sister by going to the police, or I would have. And I should have told you a million times over, but I always chickened out. It ate at me all the time. It's part of the reason I agreed so quickly when you wanted to get out of the city. I just wanted to get some privacy and stop feeling like I was being watched all the time."

"And did it work?" she asked, knowing him well enough to know it wouldn't have.

"No, it didn't. I'm a coward for not telling you."

"You are," Haley agreed. Would she ever be able to get past this? Should she? "And don't you think it's a problem that you waited to talk to the cops until they dragged you into the station? Until *after* Josie was attacked? Why didn't you go to the cops right away, the second after I told you the bracelet had been found?"

Dean started to cry. Haley tried to feel empathy for him, but she couldn't. Was this seriously the same person she'd said yes to? The person she wanted to spend her life with, the person who always seemed to make the right choice? "Never mind," she finally said. "I can't hear you make an excuse, not about this, not about my sister."

"I'm so sorry," Dean said.

Haley sniffed, tapped, tried to get her bearings, tried to understand. "Tell me what this is all about with Josie," she said.

"The emails?" Dean asked, and Haley nodded. "The cops called her in to identify that bracelet a few days before they called in you and your mom," he said, "and I guess she went a little nuts about it. That's why I never told you about meeting with her, because she was starting to sound insane with her theories, and I didn't want to involve you in it. She wanted us to meet in private because she knew I'd taken that walk with Emma. She never told the cops that years ago, but she saw us go off together into the woods, and she wanted me to come forward, too, and say I saw Emma wearing the bracelet that night, just like she'd already told the police. She thought it would help the police pursue Brad if I backed her up. She said Brad gave it to Emma, and she had all these theories about the crime."

"That's what you were meeting with Josie about?"

"Yeah," Dean said. "It just seemed like she wanted to talk about it with someone who was there that night, someone who wasn't Noah. She said they were fighting and that Noah was a jealous type, so she didn't want him to know we were talking. After the night she said that, I didn't see her again alone, because I had such a bad feeling about the whole thing." He shook his head. "Josie kept talking about that bracelet, and obviously it was ten years ago, and I wasn't sure what the thing looked like, and I definitely didn't think I'd remember anything useful about it, which is what I told her. But then when I got here last night to the precinct and told the cops everything—that I was there on the night Emma disappeared, and that I took a walk alone with her—they showed me the bracelet. And the thing is I'm almost positive it wasn't Emma who was wearing it that night. And when I told the cops that, they didn't seem surprised at all."

"Who was wearing the bracelet?" Haley asked, her voice barely audible over the hum of a radiator. But then in came Rappaport, and the look on his face told Haley he'd been watching them, listening.

"I'd like to speak with Haley alone," he said.

FIFTY

Emma

Ten years ago

The moon is shrouded by clouds that make it hard to see where the cliff ends and the gorge begins. But it's so incredibly beautiful up here, and I'm not ready to go back to the party. My cell service is spotty, but suddenly it picks up a signal, and a barrage of texts and missed calls come through. The first text is from Haley.

> I'm trying my best to come tonight but of course mom is onto me, she knows something's up. Will keep you posted.

I put my phone away and close my eyes, thinking back on the times my dad took Haley and me to these woods when we were little. I try to get the buzz I usually feel when I think back on how happy my family used to make me, but then I hear branches crunch and shatter beneath someone's feet. At first I tell myself it's probably just kids from the party looking for a place to make out. But then whoever it is falls to the ground—or at least that's what it sounds like: a crash followed by deathly silence. And then the footsteps start up again.

I push myself upright so I'm ready to go, but it's too dark without the moonlight, and I'm nervous I won't be able to find the mouth of the trail. I fumble for my phone so I can use the flashlight, but then the clouds clear, and I can see again. I move closer to the sound of the footsteps so I'll be ready to pass the person and get onto the trail, but then there's a final *snap* and Josie appears.

Moonlight falls on her face. The tiny spots of blood on her cheek must be from the fall she just took, maybe from a wayward branch that caught her skin. I reach my hand forward to touch her face, but then think better of it and let my hand fall to my side. "Hey," I say gently, "what are you doing?"

Josie laughs. *"Me?"* she asks. "What am *I* doing? Emma, seriously? You've got some nerve, I'll give you that."

"What are you talking about?" I ask, and I feel like I can't inhale properly, like the oxygen is too thin up here.

"What were you doing out here with Dean?" she asks when I don't figure it out fast enough. "Did you think I wouldn't notice you sneaking away with him?" Her pupils are too wide. She's definitely on something.

"I didn't sneak away with him," I say. "He asked me to go for a walk." I know I should add *to talk about you*, but I'm suddenly so angry—she can't possibly think I want anything to do with Dean. I don't even know him.

"So do you just like the guys I want, is that it?" Josie asks.

I let out a disbelieving gasp. "Is that what you think?" I ask.

"It's what I *know*, Emma," she says, and her eyes are so angry they scare me. "We both liked Noah. Didn't you see that? He belonged to both of us, until you started fooling around with him, until you got pregnant by him." She starts to laugh, but it sounds too strange, like the deranged cackle of someone who's high. "Didn't you know I got with him, too?"

I swallow, a zing of pain coursing through me, but it doesn't surprise me, not after seeing them together tonight, the way her body was curled in his lap when I first got to the party. Something about it looked too familiar, the way two bodies fit together like a puzzle because they've done it before. "How many times?" I ask, because I need to know, I need to know how stupid I've been.

"Once, but why does that matter?" Josie asks. "The point is that he was both of ours, whether you want to admit that or not. But, not anymore, now I'm the one who's left out again, the one everyone wants to get rid of. Not good enough for you guys, I guess, right? Do you know what Noah just told me?" she asks, her words so hard and deliberate, as if she wants me to take every one like a punch. "He told me we can't *hook up* again," she goes on. "That's what he called it—*hooking up*, like we're still in eighth grade, like he can't call it what it really was, which was a *relationship*, whether he wants to admit that or not. You can't even deny that, can you, Emma?" Her shrill laugh is back, ripping through the night air.

"I don't know what was going on between you and Noah," I say, "and I don't even know if I . . ." I'm about to say *if I want him anymore*, but she freaks out and says, "What it *was*? Past tense? I was just with him, like, two weeks ago."

I let that sink in, the nitty-gritty timing of it, the fact that she hooked up with him right around the time I got pregnant, but it hurts less than I thought it would. "You just said he called it off," I say. "That's all I meant."

"Called it off!" she shrieks, incredulous. "Like it's a game!" The clouds shroud the moon again, and her face goes dark. She's really starting to freak me out, it's so black up here, and she's moving around frantically like she doesn't realize how close we are to the edge of the cliff.

"Josie, be careful, please," I say, but there's no way she's hearing me.

"And what a fun game it must be for you and Noah to play," she's shouting, "to just mess with me for whatever sordid thing he needs, but then cast me off, so that perfect you and perfect Noah can be together forever." The pain in her voice is unbearable, and I need to fix this—to fix *her*—but I can't find the words. "Don't you see it?" she goes on. "It's like perfect little Emma, so unassuming, so sweet, no marks on her, no dark past."

"No marks on me?" I ask. "What are you talking about?"

"Don't you get it?" she shrieks again. "They all see it on me. My messed-up life, how no one's ever even wanted me to be theirs except Chris."

I want to go to her, to put my arms around her, but I feel so frozen. "That's not true," I say. "Your mom . . ." I start.

"I know what you did, Emma," she says, and the skin on her cheek starts to twitch. "I know you messed around with Chris. He admitted everything."

My stomach drops so far I feel like I'm going to be sick. I take a step back, but the ground seems to teeter beneath me, and I almost fall. I shut my eyes, but it just makes it worse. "I still can't believe it," Josie says, and I try to open my eyes to face her, but I can't. She screams at me, her words echoing through my skull:

"The only thing I ever asked of you was not to get with my brother, the one person I have in my life who's mine, the only person who's kept my secrets and tried to protect me from our father hurting me."

I open my eyes. She's barely ever told me anything about her dad except for her memory from the day he died, the day she sat at the bottom of the stairs with his dead body inside the circle of broken glass. When she told me that she hated him, and that she wasn't sad when he died, was I supposed to intuit something more about the ways he hurt her? "I didn't know your dad hurt you," I say, my voice shaking.

"Maybe you should have used your imagination," she says. "Do I really need to spell everything out for you?" Moonlight catches my silver bangle on her wrist—the one Brad got me that I let her borrow.

"Josie, come on," I say. I reach out to touch her, but she rips away her arm.

"Get away from me!" she screams, but I don't listen.

I move toward her, saying, "I'm really sorry if I didn't understand what you were trying to tell me." I try to put my arms around her, but she tucks her head, her eyes narrowed into slits.

"You've never understood what I've tried to tell you," she says, her voice full of deep, resonating notes. Her hands are balled into fists, and when she flings my arms away, it hurts so badly that I cry out, and then we're both losing our balance, and her hands find my body again, shoving me back until my feet give way and I stumble. She screams my name, her voice more desperate than I've ever heard it, her hands still pushing as I fall backward, over the edge of the cliff and into the dark night.

FIFTY-ONE

Haley

Dean was gone. An officer had taken him away for more questioning, and Rappaport sat across from Haley now, offering what she assumed were supposed to be soft words of condolence. He'd told her his working theory of what Josie did to Emma, and Haley was stuck somewhere between a dream and reality, the pieces slipping into place like a dark puzzle coming together in her mind's eye.

Icy black water . . .

Emma falling.

Josie, at the top of the cliff, her teeth bared like an animal's.

Haley couldn't erase the images—she couldn't even fight them—so she let them come one after the other. She wasn't sure they'd ever stop, or if she'd ever be able to think of anything else.

"Should I leave you here?" Rappaport asked her carefully. "Would you rather be alone?"

Haley shook her head.

Rappaport opened a briefcase and retrieved a manila envelope. He unfastened the top, carefully pulling out a stack of photographs. "I hope these won't upset you too much," he said, but Haley was already reaching for them. Rappaport went on, "We insisted everyone at the party send us any photographs or videos they took that night. Nothing turned out to be helpful until now. Here's a shot of Josie," he said, "and you can see her wearing the bracelet." Haley leaned closer, finding it hard to breathe as she took in a grainy shot of Josie standing near the keg and clutching a plastic cup. Josie wore a bright red winter jacket that left an inch of her wrist exposed. The bracelet glinted against her skin. "You're sure it's the same one?" Haley asked, her heart constricting. She let her eyes travel to Josie's face. Josie's blond hair fell over her shoulders the same way it did now, but her ten-years-ago features were slightly rounder.

"It's a very close match," Rappaport said. "And perhaps more important, we have photos of your sister, and we don't see a bracelet on either wrist. It could have been caught beneath her coat, certainly. But I feel confident the bracelet you see here on Josie's wrist is the one that was found in the gorge. It means Josie had to have a reason to descend into that gorge, and I believe it was to put your sister's body in the water."

"How long have you known this?" Haley asked, her words echoing through the tiny room.

"Since right after the bracelet was found two weeks ago," Rappaport said. "I went through the photos within the hour, and I called Josie in the next morning for preliminary questioning, but I didn't push hard on her until our second meeting last week when I showed her the photos."

Haley's mind raced to put the timing together. She must have met with Josie at the café after Josie had been interviewed the second time. "Did you outright accuse her of killing Emma?" Haley asked. No wonder Josie had gone into full attack mode, trying to pin Emma's murder on Brad with the pregnancy test.

"No, but like I said, I pressed very hard. She had to know she was the prime suspect based on what we found in the gorge."

"Why didn't you arrest her?"

Rappaport shifted in his chair. "Because I had to obtain a warrant, which I now have. Obviously I wish I had tried to hold her, but I didn't, and now she's been attacked. My mistake, and because of it, we have two crimes. Josie will still be arrested, likely today before she's released from the hospital, but with the attack and the circumstances surrounding it being related to your sister's death, there's a better chance she gets away with your sister's murder. All we have to go on is the bracelet and a hunch. And if the case ever made it to trial, any jury would be sympathetic to a woman who was subsequently almost murdered after being questioned about suspicious circumstances. Which means I need to figure out who stabbed Josie, so that I can build a stronger case against her with fewer unknowns. So let's work together, shall we?" Rappaport asked, sitting up taller. "Let's figure her out."

Haley froze, her body made electric by his wording. *Figure me out,* she heard her sister say, just like in all the dreams, *look a little closer.* Rappaport stared as Haley started tapping the table with rapid-fire fingertips. "You said you have pictures of my sister," she finally said, trying to gather herself.

"I do," Rappaport said. "Are you sure you can handle seeing them?"

Yes, of course she could handle seeing them—she could do anything for Emma. She nodded, and Rappaport retrieved a second envelope, much smaller, and passed it across the table. Haley removed the photos with shaking hands, and there she was: *Emma.* Her heart seized. Of course she'd looked at photos and videos of her sister during the past decade, but she'd never seen any from the night she died. All she'd wanted that night was to meet Emma in the woods, but she'd never gotten past her mom. If only.

"We just have these three photographs," Rappaport said quickly, "and you'll see nothing seems nefarious."

Haley set the photos in front of her in a row. In two of them Emma looked like an afterthought, just a bystander caught in the background of a shot featuring other kids posing with smiles. But the final photo was a close-up. Emma's chin was tilted down, her light eyes held the camera, and because of the way her arms were held up to protest the photo, you could see the two bare, jewelry-free wrists the detective was talking about.

"This one," Haley said, pointing at the photo. "Who took it?"

"Chris Paxton," Rappaport said. "Or at least, we got it off his phone. He was intoxicated that night, but the detectives working the case claimed he sounded reasonably reliable a few days later when he told us he'd taken it. We have him here now for questioning, and he's telling us the same story. He claims he talked to your sister at the party, but that he was never alone with her that night."

Haley looked closer at the photo. Emma wasn't smiling, and her eyes looked resigned to having a photo taken. Or maybe it was the fact that Chris was the one taking it that made her uneasy.

Rappaport had told Haley that there were no fingerprints on the knife used to stab Josie, and that because Noah and Chris had helped Josie set up the open house that morning and Brad, Haley, Dean, and Priya had entered into the crime scene, there were fingerprints from all of them in the kitchen. The only other fingerprints were from Chris on a shovel leaning against a shed outside, and the cleaning crew who'd scrubbed the kitchen beforehand, and some from the woman who lived there and was selling the house. The forensics team was still working to determine what they could from the stab wound, but as of now they knew Josie had been stabbed at close to ten forty-five. There were footprints in the kitchen from everyone, including Noah and Chris, but if whoever stabbed Josie had exited the house through the ajar kitchen window, the snow had wiped clean any evidence of their escape. "So what if Noah's hiding something about my sister—like the fact that he got her pregnant—and wanted to shut Josie up?" Haley ventured.

Rappaport sat back in his chair. His voice was harder when he said, "Or what if Noah knew your fiancé was secretly meeting with Josie, and his jealousy sent him into a rage? *Or,* what if Brad Aarons was so terrified that Josie would come forward with the pregnancy test and that it would implicate him in Emma's murder that he attacked Josie? Or maybe his wife did, maybe Priya wanted to protect herself and her son from a husband in prison . . ." Haley's heart pounded as Rappaport went on. "Chris Paxton has had a few scrapes with the law, so maybe it's him. Or, here's an idea: What if something happened between Josie and your fiancé, who were meeting privately, and *he* tried to attack her for any number of reasons? We have several suspects, Ms. McCullough, each with motive. So as much as I appreciate your theories, what I really want to know is: Do you know your fiancé well enough to know whether he's capable of violence? Has he ever been violent with *you?*"

"*No,*" Haley said, holding his stare. "*Never.*"

Rappaport shifted his weight and let a minute pass. When he seemed sure Haley wasn't going to say anything else, or change her story, he said, "He lied to you about the night your sister died."

"He did," Haley said. It was true, wasn't it? Dean had lied about Emma. Haley thought back to the night Dean had found her at that bar, which she now knew wasn't a happy accident, but which she also didn't believe was sinister, either. After that night, the way they'd fallen in love had been so slow and careful; it wasn't forced, and it didn't feel weighted by the past. She trusted that.

And she trusted that Dean hadn't hurt someone.

Haley shook her head slowly, marveling at the feeling. *Trust.* What a slippery thing. Emma had trusted Josie and shouldn't have; her mother had trusted her father, and he'd cheated; and now Haley was choosing to trust a man who had omitted a truth about the night she lost the person most important to her, based entirely on a *feeling*. But maybe that's what trust was, and maybe that was what love was.

"Dean didn't hurt Josie, I'm sure of it," Haley said.

"Ms. McCullough," Rappaport said, his voice hard again, "in your fiancé's phone, we found texts with Josie that arranged for him to come early to the open house, to meet her there so they could talk." A pit formed in Haley's stomach as Rappaport went on. "The texts are very vague, but it would be helpful if you could confirm your fiancé's where-abouts from ten until ten forty-five yesterday morning."

"I can," she said. "Well, I mean, I wasn't there with him, but he was at the grocery store stocking up on water and food for the storm."

"The entire time?"

"Yes," said Haley, "and surely there's credit card activity?"

"There isn't," Rappaport said. "Dean says he paid in cash." Haley's heart beat faster. She'd almost never seen Dean pay in cash for anything; he always paid with the credit card that got him miles.

"We'd gotten in an argument that morning. Maybe he was flustered and forgot his credit card."

"But had cash with him?" Rappaport asked. "Does he keep his credit card separate from his wallet?"

"No," Haley said. "He doesn't. But there should still be a record of his purchases."

"We're still going through receipts from that morning, but we've been by the store with his photo," Rappaport said, "and no one remembers ringing him up. There's been a delay in obtaining security camera footage, but we should have it shortly."

"I have the food and water at home, in our pantry. You can come by and see it," Haley said, keeping her voice steady.

"But even so," Rappaport fired back, "Dean would certainly have time to do both: meet Josie, possibly hurt her, and still pick up grocer-ies so he'd have an alibi. Dean was the one who initiated the meeting. He asked Josie if they could see each other and talk, alone, and she suggested meeting early at the open house, where they could speak privately. Dean maintains that he didn't actually end up going there early or alone, that Josie called him and called it off. But we don't see any evidence on his cell of her calling. There's a received call from an untraceable number from that morning, but that's it. Dean claims that must have been the one Josie used to call him, but you can imagine that none of this sits very well with any of us. Dean and Josie were seeing each other privately, without telling their respective fiancée and spouse, and he was trying to get her alone the very morning she was attacked."

Angry tears burned Haley's eyes, and she tried to swipe them away, not wanting to be this way, to be this vulnerable. "Dean didn't do it," she said. "I don't know how to prove it to you, but I will."

FIFTY-TWO

Priya

Priya stood in the attic of her home for the first time in years. She stared at the canvases tilted against the walls, some of her finished paintings, some half-finished, and some entirely blank.

It had been Josie who killed Emma. Not Brad. Josie.

Priya wasn't supposed to know, no one was. The plan was to arrest Josie as soon as she'd been cleared from the hospital, but Haley had come by to tell Priya and swear her to secrecy, as though she somehow understood the switch it would flip inside Priya to know the truth.

A morning glow hovered on the horizon. Elliot would wake soon, and Priya would hold him close and whisper into his ear the things she loved about him. But for now she had other ideas. She stepped carefully across the attic and lifted one of the blank canvases upright. She found a bundled, dusty tarp and set it free around the canvas. Burlap covered her paints, and she lifted the sheet and studied the cans. She removed the tops, and the familiar pine and oil smell swarmed her nostrils and took over the attic. Brushes were scattered everywhere, and she found the one that looked the most pliable and plunged it into the paint. She coated it in inky navy, and her lips curved into a smile at the familiar feel of the smooth wooden brush, the weight of it so completely perfect in her grasp. She turned it over, marveling at the way daylight caught the inconsistencies and imperfections in the paint, little lumps and tiny bubbles that came to the surface and released almost imperceptible exhalations. And then with one quick gasp she streaked it across the canvas, her hands shaking, her heart quickening. The paintbrush moved back and forth as the tiny muscles in her hand remembered what to do, intuitively knowing how to create something that wasn't there before. She painted for minutes that could have been hours, feeling herself unspool and unwind, making space as the parts of her that had been lost for so many years began to come together again. Bolts of color filled her canvas, her touch tentative at first but gaining confidence as she went. She began to cry, but she kept going, brush against canvas, until she felt something inside her finally release as the guilt and pain that had been bottled up ever since Emma came to the doorstep all those years ago slowly released its hold on her.

FIFTY-THREE

Haley

In anatomy class that morning Haley looked down at Susie, her hands trembling as she followed the dissection instructions given by a substitute teacher named Dr. Cotler. It was hard not to think of Brad being held at the police station, wilting beneath the weight of everything that had happened, everything he'd been accused of. The anatomy lab, just like Waverly, was abuzz with the news of Josie's attack, and Haley could tell by the way the students stared at her that details about who was at the open house had filtered through the community.

Haley swallowed. Maybe she wasn't ready to move here after all. Maybe, after they'd put all of this behind them, she and Dean could move back to the city, somewhere more anonymous, and somewhere they'd never have to see Josie again.

Or maybe Josie would be behind bars before then.

I'm sorry, Susie, Haley thought as she worked on her cadaver, her hands numb as she dissected, following Dr. Cotler's instructions and the slides she put up on the screen. *I'm sorry I'm so distracted, and I'm sorry for whatever terrible thing might have happened to you.* Haley made the next cut into Susie's heart, trying to focus only on Susie as she'd promised, but she couldn't stop thinking about Emma. She felt as if she was out of her own body as she stared down at Susie, her vision going fuzzy, making Susie's heart double in front of her, the valves and ventricles, muscle and arteries all becoming one pulpy blur. Haley wasn't sure what was wrong, and she thought she was going to be sick, or that maybe the stress of everything that happened had finally become too much. She felt out of her body as she reached down and traced the spot on Susie where Josie had been stabbed just above her right clavicle.

A shiver passed over Haley. She put down her scalpel and grabbed the steel table, trying to stay upright. Sweat gathered on her skin, and she tried to breathe, to be okay, but she wasn't. Her hands didn't feel like her own when she picked up her scalpel again and clutched it in her hand, when she raised it above Susie's body. She felt herself release a fast, hard breath, and then she wrapped her other hand around the scalpel and plunged it into the trapezius muscle above Susie's clavicle. The other students at nearby cadaver stations turned to stare, one of them barely muffling a gasp. Haley stared at her scalpel sticking straight out of Susie, barely believing what she'd just done. *Look closer,* said Emma somewhere in the back of Haley's mind, and an idea began to form, something so wrong, so strange and disjointed it could hardly be possible . . .

Unless it was.

Below the clavicle sat the subclavian artery, one of the main branches of the aorta, and plenty of other important stuff, but where Josie had been stabbed there wasn't much besides the trapezius muscle and nerves. Certainly someone could have tried to stab Josie in the heart and missed, or thought their attack would do enough damage that it didn't matter—that was the assumption the police seemed to be operating under. But as Haley stared down at the scalpel, she knew that person couldn't be Brad, not if he was actually intending to do real damage. No surgeon or anatomy teacher would have made that wound and thought it would be fatal. And why would it behoove Brad to stab Josie without actually killing her? Just to scare her? No way—it was too much of a risk that she'd be able to identify him to the police as soon as she recovered.

Haley felt the other students' eyes on her, but she didn't care. Her mind reeled as the substitute teacher droned on. Wasn't it possible that instead of intending to hurt Josie but messing it up, someone had purposely inflicted a nonfatal stab wound? And what if that person was *Josie*? What if Josie had been so desperate to frame Brad, or even Dean, that she stabbed herself in the kitchen that morning?

Haley blinked hard, taking in Susie's serene features. Figuring out how to stab yourself so that you wouldn't be fatally injured as long as someone found you in time was something you could figure out from research online. Certainly it would take the heat off Josie, and with the pregnancy test she'd been holding on to, she had to think framing Brad for Emma's death would be a slam dunk. Who would care about a silly bracelet if Brad were framed for both Josie's attack and Emma's murder? Maybe Dean was just an additional possibility, to muddle the scenario if Brad didn't work. What if that's why Josie had been contacting Dean for all those secret meetings? What if it was to secretly throw suspicion on him when the police inevitably searched his phone after Josie was found stabbed on the floor of an open house he attended? Was that why Josie said she couldn't remember anything about the attack and who did it, so that both men would be potential suspects?

Haley's heart pounded. *The open house.* Josie had arranged for all of them to be there to find her, and she'd been the one to turn off the heat: she could have googled it, figured out how much easier it would be to keep herself from going into shock in colder temperatures.

How had Haley never thought of this before?

Dr. Cotler was showing a slide up on the screen, teaching on the superior vena cava, but Haley could barely breathe. She needed to get to the police station, to explain in no uncertain terms the possibility of Josie purposely stabbing herself in that exact spot, where no major veins and arteries could be hit. Haley was right—she knew it.

When Dr. Cotler finally called the end of class, Haley didn't move at first. She stood close to Susie, her hand resting on her shoulder as if she were comforting her, but maybe it was the other way around. Haley sent up a silent prayer of thanks to Susie, wherever she was, for helping her, and then she thought of her sister, feeling her closer than ever before. Maybe Emma had always been there; maybe she'd just been waiting for Haley to catch up with her, just like when they were younger, to see and know the truth of everything that had happened. Maybe Haley would spend the rest of her life trying hard never to forget that, to remember her sister for everything she was and everything she never would be, to honor her in the only ways she knew how.

Haley pulled the sheet back over Susie's body. She gathered her things and raced to the station.

FIFTY-FOUR

Haley

After a few hours at the police station, where Haley described to Rappaport her theory on what Josie had done to herself at the open house, Haley was back at the hospital and waiting outside Josie's room.

Rappaport had arrived at the hospital before her and was still inside, and Josie had already been informed of what they knew, and that she would be arrested for Emma's death upon her imminent release from the hospital. Rappaport had promised Haley time with Josie, and she planned to take it. Haley had to face her parents this afternoon, and she needed to bring them *something* from Josie: an apology, maybe, or at least an admission of guilt.

When Rappaport opened the door, Haley braced herself. "I probably shouldn't be doing this," he said pointlessly, "but we've already taken Josie's confession on the record for both Emma's death and what happened at the open house, and if you think it'll help you to talk to her for some closure . . . if you're sure . . ."

"I'm sure," Haley said quickly, before he could change his mind.

Rappaport held the door open for her. "Then go ahead, Ms. McCullough," he said. "Good luck."

Josie looked far worse than when Haley had last seen her, with purple circles beneath bloodshot eyes. She looked up at Haley with a hollow glance and then blinked a few times as though it was taking her a beat to recognize Haley. When she did, tears filled her eyes.

"I don't understand," Haley said. She thought she'd say more, but at the crux of it, what she'd said was true: she *didn't understand what had happened.* Josie was Emma's best friend. Emma trusted her, and so had Haley.

Tears spilled over Josie's face. She was quiet, and Haley felt terrified she wasn't going to say anything. A minute passed that felt like an eternity, and when Josie finally spoke, the words came out embarrassedly. "I was just so blindingly jealous of her," Josie said, shaking her head slowly, carefully. Her movements felt measured, and Haley wasn't sure how much of what she said could be trusted. Josie took a raspy breath, and Haley stayed quiet, the air hot and swollen between them, full of sharp things. "I liked Noah," Josie finally said, "which I know sounds insubstantial because we were all so young and it was just a crush, I guess, but then he started falling in love with Emma and her with him, and it was just so obvious that he was choosing her over me. She was just so *good*, you know? And I tried to put my feelings for him aside, to give him up to her. But then she got together with my brother, and he's the one person . . . he's the only person who'd ever been my family up until that point. And it felt so cavalier, the way Emma was about it. She had everything going for her, with Noah falling for her, but she still carried on in secret with Brad, and then my brother, who clearly had feelings for her . . ."

Haley tried to digest this new piece of information. "So if family is so important," she started, swallowing over a hard lump in her throat, "and if it's true about Chris and Emma, you realize that Chris might have been the father of the baby, who you killed along with my sister."

Josie cried harder. "They didn't sleep together," she said. "He swore to me that they didn't, and he's never lied to me, ever. The baby was Noah's. Haley, I swear to God it was an accident," she said, trying to sit up but failing. "I meant to hurt her, I admit that. I was so angry, and I pushed her. But I never thought . . . It was so dark up there, I didn't realize how close we were to the edge," she said, crying harder now. "Please believe me, Haley, *please*. I loved your sister. I was so jealous of her and furious that she'd been with my brother when she promised she never would, I just, I couldn't take it. Noah told me we couldn't ever be anything more than friends now that Emma was pregnant and it was his. I thought he liked me, too, but he said he didn't, that he only wanted to be with her, but I didn't want to believe that, so I told him the truth: that Emma had been with Chris and Brad, too, and Noah was furious, and he called Emma disgusting and so many other terrible things."

"I don't want to hear what Noah thinks of my sister," Haley spat. "I couldn't care less. You're the one who married him. You killed your best friend and married her boyfriend, and that's the most vile thing I've ever heard."

The corner of Josie's mouth lifted into a sneer. "You're just like your sister," she said, her mood changing in a flash. "Judgmental. And why wouldn't you be? With your parents who love you, with your perfect childhood . . ."

"My perfect childhood?" Haley shrieked. "You're talking about Emma, maybe. Emma's perfect childhood right up until you killed her."

"Emma wasn't a child," Josie said. "She knew exactly what she was doing, taking Noah, messing around with Chris, the one person who's ever even belonged to me, when she didn't even like him."

"Most roommates don't kill each other over that."

Josie sniffed. "Haley," she said, her voice softer again, full of sadness that Haley wasn't sure she could trust. "I was in a rage that night on the cliff. Okay? Temporary insanity and all that."

"This isn't a courtroom," Haley said. "And I don't think you'll have any luck with that defense. You've been lying to everyone for a decade. And you're lying now, saying you loved Emma."

"I did!" Josie said, swiping away a lock of bloodstained hair. "She was like a sister to me."

"Then you don't understand sisters," Haley said. "And if you loved her so much, you could have admitted what you'd done. You could have said it was an accident; you could have said *anything*. You're a liar, Josie. You acted as though you were trying to protect Emma from what people might have thought about her sleeping with Brad, her being pregnant, whatever it was you acted so concerned about. But you let everyone in this town believe she'd killed herself, to avoid the truth coming out that *you* pushed her. Do you realize how wrong that is, how psychotic? And why should I even believe it was an accident? Why should I believe anything you say about my sister?"

Josie started crying so hard that Haley could barely understand her. "Because I'm telling you the truth now," she said, her words staggered between sobs.

"But even now," Haley said, "even after the bracelet was found, you could have come forward. You attacked yourself to pin it on Brad! What kind of person does that?"

"I was protecting myself!" Josie shrieked. "Can't you understand that? I was terrified! After all these years, them finding out what I'd done? Me going to jail?"

"You belong in jail!"

Josie's head fell into her hands. "I'm sorry, Haley," she said. "Believe me when I say it, please believe me. There are things you can't understand, things I need to protect, I mean, my marriage, you know I would do anything to stay with Noah, I can't be without him. I . . . I can't go back there, to that night in the woods, please . . ."

"You can't go back to that night?" Haley asked, incredulous. "That's funny, Josie. Because my parents and I have lived that night over and over again every day for the past ten years."

Josie's pale eyes were wide as Haley backed away from the hospital bed.

"Goodbye, Josie," she said.

FIFTY-FIVE

Emma

Ten years ago

I'm falling with nothing to break my body's trajectory, the air around me so cold and heavy. I fall until I hit something as hard as concrete, and then there's a sinking feeling like I'm being sucked into something muddy, something fluid, something that's trying to claim me as its own. I can't breathe right; I can't think straight. In my mind I see my sister's face, peering over me with such concern, such love. The mud is numbingly cold, and I can't stop shaking, and I try to call for Haley, but I can't. I hear a shrill voice cut through the wind—*"Emma!"*—and for a second I think it's Haley, but it's not.

It's Josie.

I feel her hands on my shoulders. "Oh, no, no, oh no," she says, and then she takes her hands off me, and I feel colder without her pressing against me. I hear the dull beeping sounds her phone makes as she tries to call someone. "Hello? Chris? Are you there?" But I know her phone won't work, not all the way down here. She puts her hands on my shoulders again and squeezes. "Wait here, Emma," she says, and then she swears beneath her breath. I hear her hands rifling through the dirt beside me. I open my eyes to see her pick something up, and I'm pretty sure it's the pregnancy test that must have fallen from my jacket. She pockets it, and I open my mouth to tell her that she should tell them, whomever she calls for help, that I'm pregnant, but I can't seem to speak. "Just wait for me, Emma," she says. "Just hang on, okay? I'm going to find my brother. Someone will have service up there; we're going to get you help."

I wait, I do. At least I try to. Minutes seem to pass, and sometimes I swear I'm with Haley in one of our bedrooms, curled up against the pillows and talking, but other times I know exactly where I am: at the bottom of the gorge with every bone in my body broken. Finally I hear Josie's voice, and I'm pretty sure it's real, because I hear her telling someone the truth: "I pushed her! She's down there! Help her!"

I hear a male voice calling my name, but I can't make it out well enough to know who. I try so hard to wait, but it's so cold, and I'm so tired. I hear the voice call out again, and I realize it's Noah.

Noah, Josie. My friends. Thank God. Noah's getting closer, I can hear him calling, "Emma!" and then he's finally beside me, his hands at my neck, trying to find a pulse. I use every ounce of strength to open my eyes, and when I do, I see his face hovering over mine, his features blurring. I can hear Josie crying, but she sounds so far away, and I can't see her.

"I'm alive," I manage to tell him, so grateful to be able to say the words, and for the truth of them.

"You're alive," he whispers to me, and I can't make out the expression on his face, but I think he's smiling. I can't keep my eyes open anymore—I'm too tired. I shut them, feeling a little warmer with him there beside me. Josie's crying gets louder; she must be coming closer. Noah uses his hands to roll me over, and I don't know why he would do that when it's too painful and there's no way he should be moving me right now. I try to let out a cry of protest but nothing comes.

"Is she okay?" Josie shrieks, sobbing.

Noah doesn't say anything at first, and Josie cries even harder. An animal calls out in the distance. I'm pretty sure I can hear strains of music from the party, and I just pray someone there has service and can call an ambulance. All I want is to go home.

"She's dead," Noah says.

His voice is as cold as ice, and it takes me a beat to process what he's just said. My head is throbbing against the ground, and I try to open my mouth to speak, but I can't. Tears start, burning my eyes. I make a small sound, but Josie's wailing so loud there's no way she can hear me.

"Josie," I whisper, but the word doesn't make it past the cold dirt near my lips.

"Go back to the party, Josie," Noah says. "Wait for me there. Tell no one; do you understand me?"

"What?" Josie says, still hysterically crying. "Shouldn't we . . ."

"Shouldn't we what? Call the cops? Do you want to spend the rest of your life in jail? *You killed her.*"

There's only silence now. I try to lift my hand, but Noah's knee is pressing against it. And then Noah shouts, "Go!" and I hear Josie's footsteps pound the ground, her sobs shrinking.

Noah turns me back around, his hands going beneath my arms. Now that my mouth isn't pressed against the ground, I try to speak. "I'm alive, Noah, I'm alive," I whisper.

"I know, Emma," he says, dragging me over the ground, toward the sounds of the rushing river. "But wouldn't it be so much easier if you weren't?"

FIFTY-SIX

Haley

Snow fell again that afternoon, and Haley waited for the feeling of fury as she followed her father through the woods toward the cliff where Emma had fallen. Her hands were clenched and ready to tap her thighs, but the snow was pristine, the sky was white, and the world seemed so peaceful and washed clean that she didn't feel the need to tap, not even when her father's shoulders started shaking. Her mother was crying, too, but Haley didn't turn around to look. She didn't want to intrude. It was enough to be here together.

Dean brought up the rear of their procession. All four of them walked single file along the trail, no one speaking. Her dad pushed away the spindly branches and held them aside so his family could pass. As their boots crunched the snow, Haley thought about the Yarrow student who'd found Emma's bracelet and set into motion the revelation of the truth about her death. Rappaport had told Haley his name, *Oscar Mendez*, and she'd looked him up, memorizing his face so if she saw him on campus, she could stop him and talk to him. But what could she even say? *Thank you* seemed too paltry for everything his discovery had done for her and her family.

Birds called overhead, and Haley looked up to see sparrows flitting from branch to branch. The trail grew even more winding and then opened up to a small clearing. It was one of the highest points above the gorge, and based on where the bracelet was found, it was the cops' best guess as to the place from where Emma had fallen. When Haley took in the small clearing and the ledge above the water, she felt sure they were right. Her dad stopped, but Haley took a few steps closer to the edge, and her mom followed. Dean hung back. Haley exhaled, peering down into the steep gorge and out to the dark river. Her mother let out a small cry.

Haley turned back to her dad, and his gaze held hers, seeing her. Then he bent down and began to dig into the snow. When he reached the dirt, he kept going until he had a sizable hole. He stood again and carefully removed a piece of paper from his jacket. He unfolded it with shaking hands, and Haley saw it was one of Emma's sketches, a pencil drawing she'd done of their family. In the sketch, her mom and dad stood like bookends around Haley and Emma. Each parent had a hand on one of their daughters' shoulders. All four weren't smiling exactly, but they looked contented, peaceful together.

Haley's dad knelt to the ground and carefully set the sketch against the cold earth. "We're right here with you, sweetheart," he said. "We always will be."

Tears fell over Haley's cheeks. "Goodbye, Emma," she said. She reached for her mom's and Dean's hands as her father buried the sketch, marking it with stones.

Snow fell quickly, covering the shallow grave.

They would come back in the spring.

EPILOGUE

Haley

Five years later

Haley glanced around Mosaic and took in the new paintings lining the coffee shop's walls. Bright blocks of color covered the canvases, and Haley's eyes settled on a particularly striking one with streaks of reds and navy blues. She took off her snow hat, trying to smooth her messy dark hair behind her ears, inhaling the smell of roasted coffee. A barista she recognized smiled. Haley smiled back as she got in line.

She checked her watch. 11:59. Dean would be here any minute. He still never ran late, even now that Grace was here. Naming the baby Grace had been Dean's idea, actually, and she was absolutely perfect, a cherub with blond curls and big cheeks below light brown eyes, smooth fingers that curled around Haley's. Since the first moment Haley held her, Grace felt so incredibly meant to be.

The shop's door opened with a ding. Haley turned, but it wasn't Dean and Grace, and she felt agitated with anticipation. *Tap, tap, tap* went her fingertips against her wool coat. "Can I add a muffin to my order?" she asked the man behind the counter, because maybe Grace could try one today. She was almost nine months. Dean was so careful with Grace, and Haley knew she'd have to run it by him first before just offering a crumbly piece. She was pleasantly surprised that Dean had turned out to be one of those parents who read all the articles about what foods to introduce first, the kind of parent who cared about all the little things that made up Grace's life. It was endearing.

Customers chattered around Haley. She waited for the barista to make her coffee, checking out the paintings again. They were Priya's, and they were beautiful. Haley couldn't wait to go to the official opening of the exhibit tonight, and she imagined Priya in one of the flowing dresses she often wore now, her cheeks blushing as she took in everyone's compliments about her paintings. Priya's long black hair had been chopped into a bob, and sometimes she still went to reach for it, to twist a piece, and then laughed when she remembered it was gone. Priya and Haley had become good friends over the past five years, at first rehashing what Josie had done to cover up Emma's death, and then marveling at the way Josie had scared and toyed with Priya over the years by calling their illicit meetings. But slowly Haley and Priya fostered a friendship based on something deeper, something real. Priya and Brad weren't living together anymore, but they still saw a therapist once a month to help them coparent Elliot. Priya was doing so much better—her panic attacks had stopped completely—and that made Haley happy.

"Dr. McCullough?" asked the barista behind the counter.

Haley stepped forward in line and thanked him. She paid for her coffee and muffin, her mind on Priya and Brad. Haley had been right, of course, about a purposefully nonfatal stab wound at the open house on Carrington Road five years ago. Rappaport suggested that Noah might have been the one to inflict the stab wound, complicit in Josie's plan to frame Brad, but Josie took credit for all of it: the scheming, the lying, and the stabbing. She said she would do anything to protect Noah, and Haley believed her. After all, Josie had carried the guilt of Emma's death all these years, believing it was Noah who protected her from the repercussions of what she'd done that night, and Noah who kept her safe: her new ally in the world. But it wasn't long before the police realized Josie would have needed help, too, and forensics concluded there was no way a petite woman like Josie could have dragged the deadweight of a 130-pound body across the uneven terrain and into the water. As the only people close to Josie at the party that night, Chris and Noah quickly became the obvious suspected accessories to Emma's wrongful death. The police pressed hard on Chris, and Haley imagined that Noah had probably thought he was in the clear. But what Noah likely underestimated was Josie's loyalty to her brother. As soon as Chris was implicated, Josie came clean and told the police that Chris had nothing to do with Emma's death, and that Noah had dragged Emma's body into the river. In her statement, Josie said that she pushed Emma to her death by accident, and that Noah had tried to help her cover up the murder. "She was alive at first," Josie told the cops, "but by the time I got Noah to come help her, it was too late."

Rappaport had let Haley watch the video of Josie's statement, so she'd been able to see firsthand the way color had drained from Josie's face when Rappaport asked her, "How sure are you that Emma was dead when you returned with Noah? Did you check her pulse?" Whether it was because she was only twenty-one, or because she trusted Noah, it seemed Josie had never questioned him when he told her Emma was dead. Josie had stammered on the video, trying to recover. "Noah would never kill Emma," she finally blurted.

"Even though she was pregnant with his baby?" Rappaport had asked, and then went on. "I'm not saying Noah would have shown up in your dorm room the next day and killed a perfectly healthy Emma. But in the state Emma was already in down in the gorge, wouldn't it have been easier to drag her body into the river, alive or not, and escape to the good life in Australia, the life he thought he deserved?"

Haley had watched that clip over and over again. Josie's mouth twitching, her eyes going wide as saucers as she realized the possibility of what might have happened that night. "It couldn't be," she'd murmured, but there was doubt all over her face, and then she started sobbing. Finally she managed to croak, "Are you saying there's a chance I didn't do this?"

The police department brought a case against both of them, and they fell apart in court, no longer trying to defend each other, their weaknesses laid bare.

After the weekend of the open house, Haley's dreams became filled with Josie and Noah in the gorge hurting Emma. But when both of them were sentenced, the dreams stopped altogether. Haley still saw Emma in her mind's eye, of course, but it was the Emma of happier times—her sister, her childhood best friend, her everything.

The barista passed Haley a receipt. "Enjoy," he said, pushing the coffee and muffin across the counter. Haley turned around numbly, taking a sharp breath to redirect her thinking.

It was 12:03. Where were Dean and Grace?

Haley clutched her hot coffee and made her way to the rectangular table by the window. She considered the highchairs stacked against the wall, but Grace wasn't quite sturdy enough to sit upright inside one. Soon. Haley sat and daydreamed about the future when she'd sit inside Mosaic with Dean and Grace, when Grace would be two, and then three, then four, chattering in the quirky way little kids talked.

Haley was still smiling thinking about it when Dean arrived, Grace snug in his arms. Haley stood from her seat, already moving toward them when she realized Sarah had come, too. Haley tried to keep her smile just as big and not let on that she was just a little disappointed to see Sarah. It wasn't because she disliked Dean's wife; it was just that when Sarah was here, Grace usually just wanted to be held by her mother, of course.

"Hi," Haley said, unable to peel her eyes from Grace. "How are you guys? Grace! You're getting so big!"

Dean glanced at Grace and beamed. "Hi, Haley," Sarah said, unwinding a cashmere scarf. Sarah had grown up in the Midwest, and she was one of those women who looked beautiful in the winter, with pale skin and shiny red locks that looked lovely even when she tore off her knit hat. She was kind and gracious, and Haley had liked her from the moment Dean introduced them a few years ago.

"How are *you* is the better question," Sarah asked. "We saw the article about the case you worked on in Bronxville. Unbelievable, Haley."

Haley felt her cheeks get hot. She loved working as a forensic pathologist, but she didn't always love talking about it. Even when she did her job right, there was still so much that had been lost that it was hard to celebrate anything. But she knew exactly what she was giving the victims' families by solving cases, and that was enough, the thing that kept her going, the thing that filled her with purpose.

"You don't need to tell us about it," Dean said quickly, still always very aware of how she felt. "We just want you to know we're proud of you," he said. Haley considered his deep brown eyes, wishing, as she sometimes did, things hadn't ended the way they had, but also knowing there had been no other way, not when he'd lied about Emma.

"Thank you," Haley said, and she meant it. When Grace squealed, Haley felt grateful for the distraction. "Hi, Grace," she cooed. She had never known she had a voice that cooed until she met Grace that first week Dean and Sarah brought her home from the hospital.

Sarah squeezed Dean's arm. "Let's sit," she said, "I'm starving. Let me run up and get some food; be right back?"

Haley smiled and so did Sarah, and then Sarah turned and went to the counter. When Dean said, "Do you want to hold her?" Haley reached out her arms.

"Can I hold you, sweetheart?" she asked Grace. Grace looked up at Haley with her blinking brown eyes, seeming happy to be transferred into her arms. "She's perfect," Haley breathed.

"She is," Dean said. He took off his coat and set it on the back of his chair. "How are you?" he asked, his eyes holding hers.

"I'm good," Haley said, and when he raised his eyebrows, she laughed. "Seriously, Dean," she said. "I'm really good."

"You like the new apartment?" Dean asked. He'd offered to go down to New York City to help her move in, but Haley hadn't wanted to take him away from his family on the weekend when he worked such long hours during the week.

"I do," Haley said. "It's tiny, but I love it down there. It's so quiet." She'd lived in New York City since graduating from medical school, and the West Village was the most peaceful neighborhood she'd found yet. She kissed Grace's forehead, debating on whether she should tell Dean what she was about to. "I'm seeing someone," she finally said.

"You are?" Dean asked, eyebrows up again.

"I am," Haley said, smiling. "Henry. He's nice. I think you'll like him."

"Haley and Henry," Dean said. "That's cute."

Haley laughed. "Oh stop," she said. But she felt a buzz when she thought of her sweet new boyfriend, his nerdy-but-cute glasses, and dark blue eyes.

"Has he met your parents yet?" Dean asked.

Haley shook her head. "Not yet," she said, but she had a feeling it would happen soon. Her parents were doing better with time. Both of them had broken all over again when they learned the truth of what happened to Emma, but each year they seemed stronger than the one before. Haley stayed with them on the one or two weekends per month when she returned to Waverly for a visit. The fresh air was good after a week spent at her lab in the city.

Sarah returned to the table with two teas, soup, and a packet of organic baby yogurt, and in that moment Haley decided she wouldn't say anything about the muffin she bought for Grace. She gave Grace's hand a gentle squeeze. "Should I try to feed her?" Haley asked carefully, and Sarah smiled, passing the yogurt and a spoon across the table. "Priya's paintings look gorgeous," Sarah said, lowering herself into her seat. "We're going to the exhibit tonight if the sitter doesn't cancel."

All four of them sat that way, chatting about ordinary things like sitters and jobs, Grace never once wanting to leave the comfort of Haley's arms. When it was time to leave for her parents' house, Haley kissed Grace's cheek and said goodbye to Sarah and Dean. As she crossed the coffee shop, she thought of Emma, her first and truest love, imagining what it would be like if she were still here. She turned back only once, waving to her friends before opening the door and making her way into the bright and safe future that awaited her.

ACKNOWLEDGMENTS

Thank you to Carmen Johnson and Dan Mandel, the editor and agent of every writer's dreams. Carmen, thank you for bringing each book to the next level, for setting high standards, and for believing I can meet them. Your guidance, instincts, and expertise have made our books together something I am proud of, and your friendship and our shared language of what makes characters tick have made writing these books so enjoyable. Dan, thank you for such tremendous support and encouragement over the past decade of agenting my books, for your friendship, and for the keen career guidance that is the entire reason I'm a published writer.

Thank you to everyone at Amazon Publishing and Little A. Your dedication to these books puts them in the hands of so many readers, connecting stories to real live people, and I couldn't be happier to be one of your authors. Thank you especially to Jeff Belle, Lucy Silag, Emma Reh, Merideth Mulroney, and thank you to Kimberly Glyder for another beautiful cover.

Thank you so very much to all the readers who bought this book and spent time in its pages, and to the ones who write me to tell me what they thought of characters and plotlines. Thank you to all the bloggers and Instagrammers who spread the word about *We Were Mothers*, and thank you in advance to the ones who will spend their time reviewing *Open House*. Thank you to the editors and agents who've taught me so much over the past decade, Alessandra Balzer, Brenda Bowen, Lanie Davis, Kelsey Murphy, Sara Sargent, and Jennifer Kasius. Thank you to all the teachers who inspired me to write in high school, especially Mrs. Orr, Mrs. Harrison, Mr. Bedell, Dr. Danaher, Mrs. Betro, and Mrs. Kuthy. And to my teachers at the University of Notre Dame, especially Mark Pilkinton and Shannon Doyne, and to my theater professor, Siiri Scott, who helped me navigate the years in college that weren't always easy.

Thank you to my friends and family who read first drafts and give such helpful feedback and cheerleading, especially my sister, Meghan Sise; my brother-in-law, Roby Bhattacharyya; my sister-in-law, Ali Watts; my dad, Jack Sise; my aunt Joan Miller; my uncle Bill Sise; my aunt Angela Sise; and my friends Chrissie Irwin, Sarah Mottl, Sarah Webb, Nina Levine, Ally Reuben, Molly Hirschel, Debbie Stanley, Antonia Davis, Wendy Levey, Alex White, Michelle Kenny, Pete Kenny, Davey Tejtel, Brinn Daniels, Janine O'Dowd, and Caroline Rodetis. Thank you, *thank you* to Stacey Armand, who offered such terrific feedback, and is the entire reason the epilogue exists as such.

To my partner-in-crime and carpooling, Jesse Randol: I treasure your friendship, and so does my entire family. Every day you and your family make us feel loved.

Thank you to the librarians and booksellers who make my family and me feel so welcome in your aisles. Thank you to the terrific teachers who inspire my sons' love of reading, Kristin Cacciapaglia, Nicole Meinel, Patti Osborne, Roisin McGuire, Kirsten Zarras, Lena Nurenberg, Elizabeth Fortune, Barbara Nasti, Patty Peterson, and Susan and Haley Ross.

There are all kinds of ways that my community and my friends help me write books, mostly by caring enough to ask, "How's your book coming?" Thank you to all my friends and family, especially Erika Grevelding, Caroline Moore, Jamie Greenberg, Claire Noble, Megan Mazza, Tricia DeFosse, Kim Hoggatt, Jessica Bailey, Liv Peters, Heather

Trotta, Linda Harrison, Bob Harrison, Katelyn Butch, and to authors Fran Hauser, Fiona Davis, Micol Ostow, Anna Carey, Kimberly Rae Miller, Jen Calonita, and Noelle Hancock.

Thank you to Investigator James Castiglione for answering my police procedural questions. All mistakes are mine. Thank you to Dr. Constantine Demetracopoulos at the Hospital for Special Surgery for answering my questions about anatomy and dissection, and for brainstorming with me the ins and outs of the crime at the open house. To discuss characters and circumstances as if they're real is one of my favorite parts about writing, and I appreciate your careful attention to what I was trying to accomplish.

Thank you to all my extended family, especially Carole and Ray Sweeney, and Tait, Christine, Walker, and Josey Hawes. Thank you to my parents, Jack and Mary Sise, for raising me in a home with love and books and for supporting me all the way. Thank you to my sister and best friend in the world, Meghan, who made it easy to write about two sisters who would do anything for each other. Thank you to my brother-in-law, Roby; my niece, Rose; and my nephew, Owen, whom I love so much. Thank you to my brother, Jack, for a lifetime of support and friendship, and to Ali, Jack, and Darcy for being such wonderful people to call family. Thank you so very much to Lorena, whom I love like family, and who makes our whole house peaceful and full of love and a whole lot of laughs. Thank you to my husband, Brian, for all his love and support, and for talking about characters and plot points with me, especially on long drives. I couldn't do this without you. My children, Luke, William, Isabel, and Eloise, are the absolute loves of my life, and I am so grateful to them for loving me each and every day.

ABOUT THE AUTHOR

Photo © 2018 Jennifer Mullowney

Katie Sise is a jewelry designer, a television host, and the author of *We Were Mothers*, which was included on best-of lists by the *New York Post*, POPSUGAR, and *Parade* magazine. She has also written several young adult novels, including *The Academy*, *The Pretty App*, and *The Boyfriend App*, as well as the career guide *Creative Girl*. She lives with her family outside New York City. You can visit her online at www.katiesise.com.